The Angel's Lamp

The Angel's Lamp

Ashby Jones

**TOP HAT
BOOKS**

Winchester, UK
Washington, USA

First published by Top Hat Books, 2016
Top Hat Books is an imprint of John Hunt Publishing Ltd., Laurel House, Station Approach,
Alresford, Hants, SO24 9JH, UK
office1@jhpbooks.net
www.johnhuntpublishing.com
www.tophat-books.com

For distributor details and how to order please visit the 'Ordering' section on our website.

Text copyright: Ashby Jones 2015

ISBN: 978 1 78535 223 2
Library of Congress Control Number: 2015950495

A CIP catalogue record for this book is available from the British Library.

Design: Stuart Davies

Printed in the USA by Edwards Brothers Malloy

We operate a distinctive and ethical publishing philosophy in all
areas of our business, from our global network of authors to
production and worldwide distribution.

To David Groff

Fictionalizing the lives of historical persons is herein done with utmost care and respect. Such an approach attempts to emphasize how their prevailing, recorded personalities, might have responded in situations, which while based on the past, are often imagined.

– the author

"A terrible beauty is born."

Easter 1916

– W. Butler Yeats

Part One

Dublin 1916

"We beseech thee, boy, come walk with us again."

– From the Confession of Saint Patrick

Chapter One

On this cold day in May, twenty-seven year old Johnny Flynn, conscripted British soldier and now acting sergeant-of-the-guards, stood in the ancient west tower of Dublin's Kilmainham Jail staring out the narrow archer's window. The unforgiving silence between executions had unsettled his nerves, forcing him to hold onto the sill to keep from falling. Reluctantly, he lowered his eyes, looking down into the old Stonebreaker's Yard where the last execution had taken place only hours ago. The blood-stains of the rebellion's leaders formed dark rivulets in the rock dust. A wavering haze, tinted with seared creosote and gelignite, created a cloud of ghostly images that caused Johnny to wonder if the priests had refused the rebels' last rites, thus tethering their souls to the earth forever.

A gust of wind shoved the stench of mildew and sewer gas deep into his nostrils sharpening the odor of death, a harsh reminder that his duty up in the loft was far from over. Kind and gentle Patrick Pearse, one of the seven signers of the Proclamation that had led to the Rising, would be shot within the hour. The others would follow in short order. They were waiting in their cells, all but Connolly, the crippled commandant of the Dublin Brigade whose leg had been blown to bits in the General Post Office. Hearsay had it that Connolly would be allowed to die on his own in the Royal Castle's makeshift hospital.

A splatter of gunshots, unmistakably those from a British lorry, pierced the air outside the prison walls. Johnny squeezed the sill as the noise echoed like a reluctant nightmare before fading into the background. Exhausted and cold he leaned against the stones and closed his eyes. He had not eaten in a day. His arms were as heavy as the night he dragged his father's dying body home from Braley's, the old man's favorite pub. As his hands began to shake, it came to him that maybe, after having gone through all this, he had done the wrong thing in coming back to Ireland. Hope – given that such a word still existed – pressed its way through the thought. If he could just hang on until the last of them, perhaps he could find some justification in it.

"Thank God there will soon be no need for this."

Johnny slapped a hand over his pistol, wheeled and almost slipped on the iron grate, but Father Donovan grabbed his arm. "Easy there, lad," he said, clutching a small wooden box to his chest. Johnny knew the contents well because he'd had to check it many times before allowing Donovan to take it into the cells. The holdings never varied: anointing oils and candles, laced cloths and room to store last-second memories in the form of notes or locks of hair or buttons or rings. He also knew the Church would not let a priest perform the last rites before someone was executed, only afterwards – in case the soul had not left the body. Johnny couldn't understand what difference it made. He understood it no more than he understood the Rising itself or Maxwell's insistence on executing the rebels or the rebels' suicidal determination to be executed. None of it made any sense. Was it strictly the belief of one side locked against the unswerving belief of the other? It ate at him relentlessly because he understood both without understanding either.

"Angelus Domini …" Donovan began but then broke off the prayer, staring past Johnny out into the Yard. "This horrible place – all of them brought here after sentencing, all but poor Connolly. It's been the last home for rebels since the beginning of time."

Johnny was trying to think of something to say when Donovan shook his head and sighed. "Only the names have changed. To think of it…must we die in order to be remembered? And if so, to what end?" He looked up the stairwell. "And today, this very day, we have the likes of Patrick Pearse…" His ascetic face turned into the shadows. "Dear Lord, please lead him carefully through the mire of forgiveness."

Johnny was staring at the glaze in Donovan's eyes when the angelus bell rang, its echo spiraling past them along the stone walls. "I'm sorry Father, but I must go now."

"May God be with you, Sergeant. Your duty is far more difficult than mine. Let us thank the Almighty that you've not been called upon to serve on a wretched squad. There are always things to be thankful for. I will see you after the rites."

As Donovan turned and headed for the Yard, Johnny made his way up the spiral staircase to the catwalk, occasionally halting to catch his breath. Corporal Stevens, a lad who looked much too young to be a soldier was posted at the loft's desk. An unfamiliar, older private whose face was all but hidden in a nicotine-stained beard stood just outside Pearse's door looking at the wall clock. He stepped aside as Johnny approached. "You only got a few minutes before we take him down for the binding, Sarge. Four guards will be at your side. He could turn nasty at the end."

"Your name?"

"Sorry, Sir. Belton, private Belton."

"You've experienced trouble with others, have you?"

Belton grinned. "I'm new to this up here, but I've been in the Yard when they crossed the goal line."

Johnny tensed. "The goal line, private? Does this seem like a sporting match to you?"

Belton glanced at Stevens and then looked down at the grate. "No, Sir. I just meant to say things could go wrong, is all."

Johnny had never seen a rebel turn nasty. How could they, sitting on an orange crate, legs tied and arms pinioned behind them. Besides, they wouldn't have made any effort to flee had they been free of the rope and shown the way out. Each one had gone to the Yard proudly, fulfilling what they deemed to be their duty for Ireland, hoping not to be saved by some last minute miracle but praying that their deaths would create a revulsion so vast that all of Ireland would rise up against the British.

But that was then and now was now, he thought, looking through the Judas hole into Pearse's cell. Pearse was sitting on the plank bed, lips moving silently as he kissed the brass and wooden crucifix Donovan had giving him. In the cell's dim light, the bronze image of Christ cast an amber glow into the rebel's eyes, reminding Johnny of a fading lamp. When he opened the door, Pearse struggled to his feet, grasping the crucifix as he lurched forward to fetch a piece of paper from the bed. He was unsteady, as was every prisoner after a fortnight of prison fever, the precursor of typhus. Dinners of moldy bread and black water gave no sustenance, not even when accompanied by cat droppings, served as dessert whenever the round pebbles could be found.

Pearse squinted at the writing on the paper. "Sergeant, this poem is a gift to my mother, who has had to endure my unquenchable thirst for pride. I understand that mementos may be passed along to loved ones."

"As long as they do not speak of treachery," Johnny said.

"Is it possible for love and treachery to abide in the same words, Sergeant? May I read it to you and let you be the judge?"

"We don't have much time."

"It will be but a brief delay on the road to redemption."

Johnny wanted to smile but felt awkward and spoke through the impulse. "Be quick about it," he said and listened as Pearse read the poem aloud. He found himself drawn into the soft, flowing meter. The words were captivating, the meaning forthright, saying that despite the tears and sadness Pearse had caused her, his love for Ireland had brought her something infinitely greater than suffering, something she could hold in pride forever: a wonderful memory of a life possible only because of her undiminished love for him. His death was her gift to Ireland.

"Does it pass the test of treachery?" he asked.

Johnny became aware that he was nodding to himself and

came out of it. "Yes," he said.

As they stepped through the cell door onto the catwalk, Pearse handed Johnny the poem.

"Certain things cannot be destroyed, and someday my reunion with her will attest to that."

His smile broadened and his gaunt cheeks rose like scaffolding under the caves of his eyes. The skin of his face had been soft and smooth when they brought him to Kilmainham. In just days it had become coarse and grainy by the freezing moisture that clung to the limestone walls, soiled the blankets, and rapidly crept into the inmates' lungs. Nonetheless, his flesh seemed to soften as he looked down at the crucifix.

"The same sacred carving that blessed me at birth now arrives to bring a beautiful end to my life," he rasped, each word revealing itself in the quiver of his Adam's apple, barely visible in his corded neck.

Johnny stood silently, bewildered and in awe, before handing the poem to Stevens. "Take his mother's name and address and send this to her by courier."

Pearse kissed the crucifix again and calmly provided the information.

"We can send the cross to her as well, if you like," Johnny said.

"I would prefer to have it with me, to keep my eyes focused on redemption."

Belton leaned in. "The priest will take it from you as you enter the Yard. It would be considered sacrilege to have it on you when the shots are fired."

"Best give it to me," Johnny said.

Pearse's jaw tightened. He stared at the cross for a long moment and then nodding as if Christ had given permission at last, he handed it to Johnny. "I would have never suspected that you would want a memento, Sergeant. Will not the memories of this place be more than enough?"

Johnny cut his eyes at Belton. "The prisoner will need your

support down the stairwell. I will conduct the pat-down and meet you and private Stevens there. Say no more about it."

As they headed off to the stairwell, he nudged Pearse. "Turn your back to them and open your tunic."

Confusion registered in Pearse's eyes. Turning, he stumbled but kept his balance as Johnny grabbed his lapels. When he steadied, Johnny unfastened the tunic and quickly slipped the crucifix between the buttons of Pearse's shirt, tilting the cross-piece so that Christ's arms lay outstretched over his heart.

"Button up," Johnny said, stepping back. Pretending to check for a hidden pair of scissors or a knife, he patted Pearse's pant legs and moved quickly up to his shoulders. At last he pressed gently against the tunic. "There, it doesn't show."

Johnny had never seen such a look of gratefulness. As Pearse attempted to whisper, his voice failed and the words, "Bless you," came out mimed on his sour breath. Johnny took him by a sleeve and guided him to the stairwell.

When they reached the ground floor, they were met by four guards waiting to shepherd Pearse into the Yard and stand him before the firing squad. Their flinching eyes darted back and forth from Johnny to Pearse and to all corners of the corridor. Their breath came fast, as if they were confused about what they were about but they had been ordered to say nothing in the presence of the prisoner.

Johnny excused Stevens and Belton and the warder handed him the blindfold. His hands were sweating as he fumbled with it. On the first try an end slipped through his fingers and Pearse's bloodshot eyes snapped open. He glanced over his shoulder at Johnny. "Steady there. It is my dream to die this way, for Ireland."

It must have relaxed Johnny slightly for he succeeded in tying the blindfold on the second try, snugging tight a quarter knot and doubling it. He stepped in front of Pearse and centered the blindfold. "Can you see?"

Pearse grinned and his voice returned. "By the angel's lamp alone, and I can tell you, Sergeant, its hem still allows us to see into the darkness."

"Give me your hands," Johnny said, taking him by the elbows and gently pulling his arms back.

"Do ye have to tie them, lad?"

"Aye," Johnny said, taking a length of leather from a soldier next to Pearse.

"Why not let a man confront his tormentors? After all, they get to face me. I would like them to look me in the eye so that I might thank them."

"You wouldn't want me to break any rules, now would you?"

Pearse chuckled. He raised his head as if he could see the frescoes on the ceiling. "They don't know us very well, do they, Johnny Flynn?"

It was the first time any of the prisoners had called Johnny by his name and the warmth he had been feeling towards Pearse soaked in. Johnny finished wrapping the leather around his wrists and knotted the ends. He knew he should have tightened the strap until the veins in Pearse's hands swelled because that's how he'd been instructed, but of all those sentenced to die, he was the least likely to panic. He viewed himself as a hero, much in the legendary lineage of Robert Emmet, his real life idol who had been hanged and beheaded decades before. He felt that he, like Emmet, would pass unscathed through the decades to help Ireland stand on its own.

Johnny stepped in front of him. "Be still," he whispered and with a straight pin attached a small piece of white cloth on the sodden tunic just over Pearse's heart where he felt the tip of the crucifix. Pearse had worn the same tunic when he surrendered to General Lowe. Maxwell ruled that it was best he die wearing the garb because after all it was black, the color of treachery. His duty was done and well it was because he could not have spoken another word if he'd wanted to.

In that instant Pearse's face reddened slightly, not with fear or embarrassment but with radiance. He raised his chin and his neck tightened. He appeared much as he had the day he surrendered his sword, as if he had known something no one else did, something that went far beyond the place he was immediately headed. With one of the young soldiers shoving him toward the doors, he winked at Johnny as if he, too, was now in on the secret. With his chin still aloft, he moved down the dark hallway toward the Stonebreaker's Yard.

Johnny followed them to the heavy doors where Donovan was waiting with the anointing box.

"Father?" Pearse said, stopping before the priest.

"Yes, my son?"

"I am very happy. I am dying for the glory of God and the honor of Ireland. To die in such a manner is atonement. It was the fate of Cuchulain and thus it is mine."

Hearing the allusion to the young, mythological hero who gave his life in battle so that Ireland could live for all eternity, Johnny remembered his father telling the fable over and over again while ironically praising and damning the fallen conqueror. He watched from the doorway as Pearse walked into the Yard almost joyfully, until the soldiers stopped him in front of the sandbags and turned him to sit on a crate facing the firing squad. Johnny was glad for the blindfold then. It spared Pearse from seeing the pools of blood on the ground and the lorry at the far end of the yard waiting for his body, and yet he wondered if he might relish those sights.

At the order "Places!" six of the squad's twelve knelt. Johnny couldn't watch any longer and quickly shut the doors, imagining the hand signal for the order, "Aim!" Cringing, he envisioned the officer's gloved hand flashing open for the men to fire. Instantly, a volley rang out and he froze, anticipating the *coup de grace*. In seconds it came, seeming louder than the volley itself and possessing a binding finality, as though all life had come to a standstill.

It lingered, delivering a stabbing hum that traveled through Johnny's skull in vibrato. Entangled images abstractly set like hieroglyphics coursed past his eyes and he was forced to sit down on a wooden bench just inside the doors. He had to wait for Donovan, as was the custom, for the priest administering the last rites was required to report to the Sergeant-at-arms when it was over, to describe the condition of the dead man's soul just before it left on its journey. What condition *could* a soul be in, Johnny wondered. Each time he'd asked a priest, he'd received the same answer: a soul's condition described its purity. Had it regained a sufficient amount to warrant God's forgiveness? Only a priest could know.

As the doors opened, the air recharged with the detestable fumes of sewer gas. Johnny coughed and then heard what he knew to be the drumming of Donovan's long fingers on the wooden box.

The priest's eyes were aloft and beaming. "His soul was as fit as Saint Paul's," he said, smoothing his hand over the box's finely carved lid. "I trust it brings them comfort just knowing they will be forgiven, if only after their passing."

Johnny drew back in astonishment. "Father, did you say, *forgiven*? Do you believe these men actually sinned against God?" Embarrassed at the silence, he attempted to rephrase his thoughts. "I ask you again, Father, were we, are we, serving God's purpose?"

The priest's mouth became a pout. "Well, my son, what the rebels did had terrible consequences, and those few who supported them, mainly close family members, aided their cause and gave them inspiration. Innocent people died as a result. The Irish did not want a rebellion. They had already reached a certain accommodation with the British."

"Accommodation?" Johnny said, feeling the blood rush to his face. He wanted to turn away but he couldn't help himself and jabbed a finger at the window. "Try telling that to a city that lets those on the dole die because they aren't Catholic." He stood wondering where he might go from there. His thoughts were barely formed, hardly considered at all, springing from fatigue and disgust, but he could not let go.

"So, then, the executions, Father? Are they sanctioned by God? And before you answer..." Johnny's voice caught in his throat. "What about the young boy I came upon in the streets, no more than an early teen, a bullet hole through his left eye and a British soldier standing over him. Then he puts the match out in the lad's ear and laughs. Was that God's will?" The words crested sharply, causing Johnny to wonder if he was losing his mind.

Donovan stared at the floor. His lips began to quiver. "I can't speak for the Almighty. He has His reasons and sometimes they are lost on us mortals."

Johnny's stomach was in knots. It was an answer from a priest who had no answer. He was about to leave when Corporal Rennick, known to all as the Raven for his deliveries of harsh messages from the officers' quarters, came bounding down the stairwell, skidding to a halt when he caught sight of them.

"Sergeant Flynn?"

Johnny's chest tightened as he looked up into the anxious face. "What is it, Corporal?"

"Sorry for the intrusion, and to you as well, Father. I didn't mean to interrupt, but Sergeant, Lieutenant Danes just ordered me to try and find you before you went back to the barracks. He wants to see you in his quarters."

"Tell him I've already left."

"'Twill do no good, Sarge. He'll send for you at the barracks straightaway. He was telling, not asking. You know how he is. Best you see him now." He hesitated. "Besides, if he ever found out I lied to him, well, it'd go hard on me."

Johnny's heart pounded against his ribs. He could not go through it again. "The executions, Corporal? Have you heard anymore?"

"Not so far. There's not been a priest or family called for, unless you know better, Father. No squad called upon neither. The rifle-room's shuttered for now."

Johnny relaxed a bit. "Did he say what he wants with me?"

Rennick shook his head. "I know nothing, Sarge. But you'd better get down there. He called a while ago. I thought you were on the catwalk so I ran up there first. Then I went to the larder. I couldn't find you anywhere."

Donovan placed his hand on Johnny's shoulder. "It will be all right, lad. As the saying goes, 'There are no boundaries between the living and the dead.'"

Chapter Two

As Johnny entered the officers' duty quarters, Lieutenant Danes glanced up from a desk littered with papers. Lamps glowed on either side of him but the light they cast was barely enough to make out the print on the papers. His eyes were almost closed. As Johnny waited at attention, it seemed the lieutenant had gone into a trance.

"Sergeant Flynn at your command, Sir," he repeated.

"I heard you the first time," Danes snapped as though rudely awakened. "At ease, Flynn."

"Thank you, Sir."

The lieutenant ran his fingers through his dark hair, glancing at the papers and then at Johnny. "By all counts you've done a commendable job under the most trying of circumstances. You've kept things...how should I say it...orderly. Yes, orderly, if not dignified."

"There really hasn't been that much to do, Sir."

Danes frowned. "Whatever the reason, Sergeant, you were in charge and you deserve the credit. I know it's been an enormous strain on you...on all of us." He leaned back in his chair so the light from the lanterns flickered on his tunic. "I've put you in for a commendation."

After a moment Johnny realized Danes wasn't joking and felt his face flush with embarrassment. "Lieutenant, please don't think I'm ungrateful, but there's really no need."

"What there's no need for is false modesty, Flynn. The honor's well deserved."

Johnny decided to let it be. He took a step back and saluted.

Danes looked up. "There's just one more thing."

Johnny braced, afraid the worst was finally at hand. "Sir?"

"I'm transferring you to the Royal Castle. You've earned a break. It's the rebel Connolly. He's a very sick man, wounded in the G.P.O. If it hadn't been for our boys he would have died there, and maybe that would have been just as well. His wound is so bad that if he's not shot, the gangrene will do him in. That's what Maxwell's hoping for at any rate. But either way they're expecting trouble in the streets. If he happens to die from his wounds, we're going to be blamed for not doing enough, improper medical treatment, that sort of thing. If he does face the squad, well, that speaks for itself. You're to report to the Castle tomorrow before dusk, when the shift changes. Connolly may not be left without supervision for a moment. As far as I'm concerned your duty here is finished."

"Sir..." Johnny began.

"Go on, now, take your leave and get a head start on tomorrow's eve." Danes dismissed him with a wave of his hand and his attention went back to the papers. At the door Johnny turned again.

"Sir, if I may?"

"Yes?"

"What's he like, this Connolly?"

Danes considered him for a minute, rubbed his face with his hands and pushed back from the desk. "Give Satan credit. More than any of the others, the man has won the heart of Ireland. He's the most loved of the lot but the most dangerous of them all. Single-handedly he organized the Brigade to protect workers from police attacks during the strikes a while back. My God, he even believes in the equality of women. His eldest daughter Nora, a grape ripe for plucking if ever there was one, believes she can think as well as a man because her blood is part his."

Johnny recalled the day he escorted Captain Rolf to Countess Markievicz's cell to tell her of her fate – the Countess was the only woman officer in the rebellion and the only woman in the uprising Maxwell had sentenced to death. The captain began by informing her that General Maxwell had sentenced her to death before a firing squad.

"My prayers are answered. I am grateful," she said. "Thank the dear cuss for me, and when he learns the meaning of the word freedom, please have him send me a card."

The officer kept reading, clearly uncomfortable. "But given the prisoner's gender..."

"Gender?" she interrupted. "Does he know the meaning of a two syllable word?"

The officer's jaw tightened. "He has commuted your sentence."

She poked Rolf in the chest. "That will not do! I will not back away from the doors of death. Let them close behind me. Men have no corner on that."

"Madam, kindly remove your finger. Were it mine to say, you would walk directly through those doors and I personally would close them behind you, but my say-so is the equal of yours and on that we both score nil. You're to be sent to Monteith Jail immediately."

Danes' voice sliced into Johnny's memory. "There's no room in Connolly's vocabulary for compromise, or in his daughter's either as I understand it. She and the old bugger even protested Queen Victoria's sixtieth anniversary. Infantile and profane I would call it. But back to the matter at hand, Sergeant. Connolly was raised poor in an Irish compound outside London. At an early age, like so many of you, he joined the British Army and was deployed to Ireland thirty years ago now. Married an Irish woman named Lillie. Ever since, he's been a thorn in our side."

"Is there any chance he'll be executed? Word has it..."

Danes slapped the folder on the desk and leaned back. "He's not well enough to even make the journey to the Yard, much less face the ordeal with dignity. I doubt there's a chance. But if he is, the Irish will turn his grave into a martyr's shrine. On the other hand, if they just let him die from his injuries, in time he will fade from memory. In either case, your job is to stand guard over him. If he is spared the firing squad, see that he passes quietly. The less that escapes the Castle walls the better. Be vigilant, Flynn, but unobtrusive. Listen and remember because you could well be called on to testify in history's courtroom." He paused to let it sink in. "Get some rest beforehand. The duty could well be protracted."

Outside, Johnny stopped in the gloom of the foyer. Sending him to the Castle made sense on one level and yet on another he wasn't sure, unless sending him there was really because he was thought to have become too close to the rebels in Kilmainham. Maybe that was true. Why else would he have felt so confusingly sad up on the catwalk and even more so now as he was preparing to leave the place, hellhole or not?

"Sergeant, the lorry's here for you," a guard called out from down the hall and ran to open the front door, letting in a piercing gust of cold air.

"Coming," Johnny said. At the door he looked up into the arched dome. The mural there was beautiful despite its setting, he thought, stepping out the door and hopping up under the canvas of the lorry.

Riding towards the barracks it seemed that the night was a thick curtain against the lights of the lorry. It felt like he was being pulled through the streets by an invisible leash. He wondered if such a thing was what Pearse had meant by the angel's lamp, a trust in the unseen. He pressed his face against a gap in the canvas and gazed into the empty streets. If only he could understand all the many things that eluded him, then maybe he could share that trust. But by the time he reached the barracks and had gone to the larder for bread and a shot of whiskey, a dull fear close to his heart but afar, like the fear of an approaching storm, gripped his chest.

Chapter Three

He had had the dream a thousand times. He was running down the streets of Birmingham with a deflated futbol under his cardigan. He was six years old, maybe seven. Mr. Runney, the storeowner, wasn't chasing him, at least not yet, but every instinct in his body shouted out that the moment was near. He had stolen the ball because he wanted to practice. Every lad on the junior team was better than he was. The others had very little money as well but enough to afford worn cleats and a second-hand ball, and he had neither. They practiced with their fathers but his dad could barely make it to the bars at night. His mates thrived on good food, but his mum had cancer and could barely stroll the marketplace.

So he stole the used ball from a basket of discards at Runney's Restore, a place where old hurling and soccer equipment was brought back to life. Gray-haired and lean Mr. Runney, looking as though he could still carry his weight on the pitch, was examining a broken hurley and paying no attention. Watching him out of the corner of his eye, Johnny reached into the heap of balls and felt through them for the least damaged. Runney never looked up. Johnny took it as a sign that maybe God had given him permission for what he was about to do. Slowly he slid a soft, crimped ball up under his jacket and held up another to ask the price.

"More than you or your family have," Runney chuckled. "Put it back."

Trying to hide his sarcasm, Johnny bit off a thank you and headed for the door. Just outside the shop he began to run.

It wasn't until he'd crossed the road into the hills that he relaxed for a spell, but when his shanty came into view he grew anxious again. As he drew closer the sight of his mother bending over the splintered porch railing almost caused him to panic.

Then she'd been young, maybe his age now, but she walked like an elder, stooped over, cradling her cancerous breasts to ease the pain. Although he hadn't known it that day, she would be dead in less than a year.

He stopped at the bottom step and waited as she lifted her head. She stared at the lump under his sweater and then into his eyes. "Have you had a lamb for lunch?" she asked. She cringed in pain but her dry lips lifted at the corners. "Come, let me have a look."

Ashamed and embarrassed Johnny slipped the ball from under the sweater. "I'm sorry, Ma. I'll take it back right away."

Her lips trembled into a widening smile. "You'll do no such thing," she said, coughing. "God understands. He forgives such a small sin because...it was wrapped in love." She stopped to swallow some blood and then fought to clear her throat. "You did not want to offend your father by asking for a shilling. God forgives you as we forgive your Da for his frailties."

He awoke from the dream deep in the afternoon, just after late mess for the overnight soldiers. His stomach growled him awake and lying there shivering, confused by the quick transition from childhood to now; he could barely focus in the faint light from the latrine's window. Though he realized he'd eaten nothing since early the night before, he wanted a whiskey and a pint even more than food, something to supply him courage for what lay ahead. He squinted at his watch. He had to be at the Castle before the sun went down. He didn't have time to stop at Emmet's, the soldier's favorite bar, named for yet another ancient hero.

For some strange reason, as though he were shirking his duty, he would have preferred his station at Kilmainham but there wasn't a thing he could do about it. *And even if he could, where would that leave him*, he wondered. *Short of nowhere*, he supposed. For now, it was necessary to fling away any such thoughts, thoughts that any other soldier might have thought insane, and batten his mind deep inside the folds of his uniform. Three rebels left to go. Granted, all three as yet untried, but without question the Brits would deliver to each his expected Fate, though God willing, the ailing Connolly would be allowed to die on his own.

He told himself that waiting for a man's natural death to descend upon him would be a sight easier than gazing through the Judas Hole into Pearse's cell, feeling much like Judas himself, liking, if not admiring the rebel and yet knowing that he would be the one to bind him and lead him to his death.

Chapter Four

When he reported for duty at the Castle, dusk was settling over the building and a faint mist had gathered in the chill. The air itself, combined with the fading sepia of the building, so characteristic of this time of day, seemed to give rise to a nagging feeling that what he had come to do was something more than stand guard over a sick and dying man. He wasn't sure what it was or why he even thought it, but the sensation bothered him, made him apprehensive, as if something more ominous was at hand. Yet there had been no clue in the newspapers that lined the kiosks outside the entrance or in the faces of the few people who were milling about. There had been no dirty looks or cruel words or rocks thrown at the sight of his uniform. In the barracks all the talk had been about the end of the executions and the possibility of returning home sooner rather than later. There had been nothing terrible he could put his finger on. Still, something in the disappearing face of the building, something that seemed to be leaking from the darkening sky, something vague and yet intimate, made him ill at ease.

As the sentry opened the gate to the Castle Yard, the royal clock struck six. Johnny looked up, disturbing the lightness in his head, and saw what was fast becoming the shadow of the Statue of Justice standing high over the gate.

"She's got her face to the Castle and her arse to Dublin," the sentry said, smiling at the age-old quip.

Johnny nodded, noting the manned machine gun emplacements along the driveway. "I'm Sergeant Flynn sent down from Kilmainham, reporting for guard duty to tend the rebel, James Connolly."

"Kilmainham?" The sentry had an Irish accent stronger than his own.

"Yes."

"This will be easy duty then," the sentry said. He pointed to the center door on the ground floor. "Through there and up the grand staircase to the third floor. You'll want to report to the Royal Army Medical Officer; the R.A.M.C. officer as he's known, in case you're unfamiliar. There'll be a nurse to direct you. They've just moved Connolly to the Throne Room of all places. Imagine, the leader of the rebellion on the King's bed. Nothing better to soil the linens, if you ask me. As long as Connolly's alive, this place is more a jail than a home to viceroys."

"Why did they bring him here anyway?" Johnny asked.

"They thought he might die on them, so they took him to the nearest hospital," the sentry said. "That's what the Castle became that week – for our boys, of course, all but Connolly. Ten armed guards came with him, as well as a flank of medical types. They wanted to make sure he lived long enough to shoot him. Letting him die in his sleep didn't seem right. There's no punishment in that, one of them said to me."

As Johnny approached the Castle steps, more confused than ever over Connolly's fate, his father's stories about the Castle surfaced. How it had been the center of social activity in Dublin, prompting a poor and tattered crowd to gather at the gates, waiting for hours to catch a glimpse of the debutantes stepping out of the carriages in silks and satins. A poor and tattered crowd – the image of scrofulous, sick kids came to mind as he reached for the door. It opened and a smartly dressed R.A.M.C. officer stepped in front of him.

"Your business, Sergeant?"

"I'm Flynn, Johnny Flynn, sent by Lieutenant Danes at Kilmainham to guard the prisoner Connolly."

"You have papers?"

"No, I don't have papers. They told me late yesterday."

"Let me see your Army identification."

Johnny pulled the card out of his wallet and waited as the officer inspected it and compared his face to the fuzzy likeness on the card. Johnny looked over his shoulders to the stairway steps. They were lined with soldiers, so still and stern they looked like they belonged in coffins.

"Are they all for just one prisoner?" he asked.

The officer glanced at the staircase and handed the card back, neglecting Johnny's question.

"Up those stairs, down the hall to your right past the state-rooms. You'll be seeing First Lieutenant Rhodes."

Johnny climbed the carpeted staircase. Passing each rigid soldier he felt he was a moving target for their eyes. They followed him like the pictures of the long dead ancestors his mother had put on the wall along the steps up to his room. Even in his teens he'd never grown accustomed to their haunting eyes, and until the day he left to join the Army he'd climbed the steps with his head down. Now, he looked at the thick red carpet and then up at the gilded ceiling lined with high chandeliers and Doric columns. He went down Saint Patrick's Hall, through the Picture Gallery, looking even as the eyes of the dead followed him, and on down the Royal Corridor past the staterooms where a few beds of the British soldiers wounded during the uprising still remained occupied. At the end of the hall, a Red Cross nurse was sitting at a desk making notes.

"May I help you?" she said, her large eyes carefully examining his face.

"My name is Flynn, Sergeant Flynn, reporting to Lieutenant Rhodes."

"And your business?"

"He's expecting me. I've been sent to stand guard over prisoner Connolly."

She sighed. "That poor creature hardly needs any guarding. He needs proper medical attention. I'm afraid he won't..." She stopped and looked away. "Wait here. I'll see if the lieutenant is available. Sergeant Flynn, you said?"

"Yes."

She disappeared through a tall archway and soon returned with a Royal Army officer who looked younger than Johnny. He was slender and had a moustache so thin it barely mattered. He reached out for Johnny's hand and spoke before the nurse had a chance to introduce them.

"Flynn, I'm Lieutenant Rhodes. Pleased to see you. Maybe I can get some rest now," he said, his breath thick with the smell of cigars. He turned to the nurse. "Would you excuse us for a minute, nurse?"

"I'll fetch some clean bandages," she said. "By the way, do you know when Dr. Tobin's supposed to return?"

"Tobin?" the lieutenant said.

"He went to London to try and find if there was a way to stop the gangrene."

"I really don't have any idea who this Tobin is, nurse, but I suppose he's still looking," he said, grinning. A look of irritation crossed her face as she turned to head down the hall. Rhodes faced Johnny. His grin had become a smile and was now deferential. "They say you acquitted yourself admirably at Kilmainham. It must have been difficult there, to say the least."

"It had its moments, Sir."

"Well, you'll have none of that here. You've seen the official announcement?"

"No, Sir."

"Straight from General Maxwell," he said, taking a piece of paper from inside his jacket and reading from it. "The trials by court-martial of those who took an actual part in the Rising in Dublin are practically finished. It remains that we maintain the splendid decorum shown thus far and expected of British soldiers under all circumstances." He looked up and slipped the paper inside his jacket. "It goes on a bit but when the reading is done, the General's telling us it's over. As for me I'd just as soon see them through. We can't be seen as turning soft. On the other hand it is possible the population was beginning to turn against us. Now, I suppose they'll applaud our mercy and that makes for a fitting end, don't you think?"

Johnny squeezed his eyes closed and gave a huge internal thanks to the darkness and opened them. "It's good the killings are all but over," he said.

A pained expression came over Rhodes. "Killings, Sergeant? That's an unfortunate choice of words. These were honorable military executions. Out of respect General Maxwell let them die as worthy enemy. I suggest you see it that way."

Johnny set his jaw. "Begging the lieutenant's pardon, but I'm afraid it's hard to see things that way anymore."

The officer stared at him. His eyelids flickered and Johnny knew he'd won a small victory. The lieutenant's voice was off-key and slightly forced when he spoke. "You are to stay with the prisoner until you are spelled and even that depends totally on the situation here in the room. Is that understood? Tell the nurse and she will see to it, but take no leave short of your replacement being in the room. When you are here, I don't want to find you've fallen asleep or even turned your back on Connolly. He is sick, yes, but tough and cunning and I wouldn't want him doing anything untoward."

"Untoward?"

"Connolly knows the others have been shot and that de Valera now appears free from our marksmen. *Appears*, mind you. I gather his family told him that's the direction the court is favoring. By God, if it had been up to me I would have banished them from Dublin, but I suppose that's neither here nor there now. At any rate, if his sentence is commuted it will not sit well with him. He'll be demanding the same fate as the others and will perhaps do it by his own hand, if he can find the means. So, be on the alert, especially if his wife and daughter visit. Be sure a nurse searches them thoroughly before they enter the bedchamber, particularly the daughter. She's not above hiding a dagger in the source of all mankind. Keep a close eye on her. Is that clear?"

"Yes, Sir."

"And another thing. There is to be no discussing the Rising or anything about Connolly's compatriots. You follow me, Sergeant?"

"I do, Sir."

"Good, now come with me."

Chapter Five

Rhodes led him into an alcove guarded by two soldiers with rifles and fixed bayonets. One of them grabbed the closest leaf of the tall double door and opened it. Across the room in a large bed, a middle-aged man lay propped up against a mound of pillows. Connolly's face was ghostly white, the folds of his sunken cheeks slipping under the ends of a gray moustache. His arms were flesh hanging off the bones. Set above a mouth that seemed fixed in pain, his eyes were dark bags, more deeply inset than Pearse's even. A wooden structure that looked like a bird cage kept the bedclothes off his gangrenous leg. The odor of disinfectant and decay filled the air, reminding Johnny of Pearse's cell, and he winced as he caught it. Nausea rose in his throat.

"Connolly!" Rhodes barked.

The rebel opened his eyes narrowly and tried to clear his throat. "Sorry," he managed. "I'd just fallen asleep."

"What could sleep possibly mean to you?"

"A gift," Connolly replied in a low voice devoid of insolence.

"At least you can sit up smartly in the presence of an officer," Rhodes said and pulled Connolly forward by his pajama top while he stacked more pillows behind him. In one motion he shoved Connolly and the pillows against the head of the bed. "This is Sergeant Flynn. He'll be watching over you."

Connolly's face was twisted in pain. "Sergeant."

Johnny didn't know what to say or if he should say anything at all and so he nodded. In an afterthought, he asked, "How are you?" The question tumbled into an awkward lull, but Connolly smiled faintly.

"Other than a shattered leg, a bit of gangrene, and the recent news that all of my brave friends have been executed by the British Army, I'm very well, Sergeant. How about you?"

"Sergeant Flynn isn't here to chat. He's your guard," Rhodes said.

Connolly made a small wave of his hand. "I meant no disrespect, Lieutenant."

"None taken," Johnny said after an awkward pause.

"That's enough, Sergeant," Rhodes said. "I'm getting some rest now. I'll relieve you at midnight. Meanwhile, see the nurse on duty and she'll arrange your breaks. Have you any questions?"

"No, Sir."

Rhodes glanced at Connolly. "Keep your distance, Sergeant."

He went out, closing the door, leaving the room in yet a deeper silence. Connolly looked at Johnny with cool amusement, causing him to go to the window and peer out over the courtyard. Nonetheless, Connolly's voice came again. "Under the slip of the Queen, you sound Irish, lad."

Johnny turned around but hesitated to speak in case Rhodes was just outside the door. He waited for a moment. "Born in Cork."

Connolly's face softened and he smiled broadly. "Let me see. Your family took you away to England because of some injustice as they saw it? Maybe they were Protestant?"

"My ma was but not my dad," Johnny said, heartened by the assurance in Connolly's voice.

"That's often all it takes. What does your dad do?"

"He was a printer, well, a printer's helper, really. He died a short while back."

"I'm sorry," Connolly said. "Printing's a fine trade, but as a Catholic he most likely couldn't find work here?"

Johnny didn't think he should go any further. Connolly nodded. "No shame in that, lad. It's an old, old story been handed down for generations. I was raised in England myself." He looked around the room. There was tenderness in his eyes. Leaning forward he carefully adjusted the cage, grimacing with pain as he did so. "This thing makes me think I've stepped in a bear trap."

"You need some help?"

"There, it's better, now." Connolly eased back against the pillows. The sweat above his brows began to crawl into the corners of his eyes.

Johnny wanted to help, then brushed his hand across his pistol as he remembered Rhodes' warning. But it quickly faded. He went over to the washstand where he poured some water on a cloth, took it to Connolly and wiped his forehead.

"Thank you," Connolly said as Johnny put the cloth on the basin rim.

"How did that happen?" Johnny said, staring at Connolly's leg.

"I was in the G.P.O. I'd gone to position some of the men and a bullet hit me above the ankle. It shattered both bones. Foolish me, I was away from everyone – a dumb place to be – and had to crawl until someone saw me. It cost me a lot of blood, and they couldn't staunch it properly." He stopped to chuckle to himself. "If my dear friend, Pawth, had made the boots I was wearing that day maybe I would have turned the whole fight around. An elderly cobbler now and every bit a father when I was looking for work as a lad, he took me under his wing and taught me the trade…"

Connolly started breathing heavily and at the same time waved with his hand, suggesting to Johnny he wasn't finished talking about his friend. His mouth closed and he lay still for a moment. Johnny was about to go to him when Connolly's lips parted to a rasp and gave relief in a long, soft moan.

"Pawth always said we were going about it wrong, facing the Brits head-on while being so outnumbered." By mid-sentence his voice had begun to strengthen. "The way to beat them was this idea of sneak attacks paring a few against the many. Pick off a few in the dead of night, then a few more the next day. Scatter them about on the battlefield and send their courage into tatters.

He once told me that's really what he had in mind when he came up with soft-sole boots, rubber from tires held in place by creosote from telephone poles. So simple, so brilliant. If I'd had a pair on in the G.P.O., I would have come through nimble as a fawn."

"It's a wonder any of you survived. The place was in flames for almost two days," Johnny said.

"Were you there, Sergeant?"

Johnny was silent.

"No, no. It's okay. I mean, you're a soldier and a soldier has to do his duty. Though if it was your bullet that struck me, you could be court-martialed for being such a lousy shot," Connolly's eyes appeared to sparkle. "Are you a good shot, lad?"

It caught Johnny off-guard and he almost laughed. "Well, are you?" Connolly asked again, his face intent this time.

"Not especially," Johnny said.

"That's because they don't really trust you Irish lads with bullets," Connolly said. It made Johnny smile. In the next moment, as he watched Connolly lean back and close his eyes, he was reminded of Pearse, his calm friendliness, the lightness of his comments and the almost total lack of enmity in his voice. He thought of his father and the bitterness that was so often in his, even in his eyes when he drank and remembered Ireland. *These men weren't like his old man*, he thought. Somehow they seemed above hatred. They were determined and bound to do what they had to do, but they had not lost their humanity.

Connolly's eyelids flickered again and opened. He stared at the ceiling.

"My wife and eldest daughter came to see me this afternoon. They were ecstatic about de Valera's likely commutation. I must admit it took my breath away. But I told them dying was worth it and that I wished to go with my comrades. The cause cannot wither now, for if it does there will be no Irishman left willing to fight a war against England." Breathing hard again, he glanced at Johnny. "Maybe not even you, lad – or the thousand like you with parents who so sadly took you off our soil."

The muted question lay in the air until Johnny felt compelled to tell Connolly that it was his father, not his mother, who forced them to leave Ireland. She was a Protestant married to a Catholic and as a result she could not get medical help in Dublin, not even a stipend for cannabis to dampen the pain in her breasts.

One day, standing behind her in the pension line, Johnny's father overheard two Irish bureaucrats talking about her, saying, "This one's here every week and she shows no gratitude or courtesy for our efforts." The one talking looked up at her, saying, "Get out of me sight, woman. Learn to give thanks." At that his father had jumped ahead of her and lunged across the table to grab one of the men by the throat. "She's dying for God's sake!" Before he could go any further the Constabulary had him off to jail for a night of black bread and water. A week later, despite her objections, his father put them aboard a ship for England. They never returned. Until now, many years later, through Johnny, their souls wrapped in a British uniform.

Connolly broached the silence. "Well, in time maybe lads like yourself will forgive us our mistakes and come home." He paused for a breath. "This is your country and you're sorely needed to make it well."

Johnny could feel the pressure mounting, as if a deeper darkness was about to enclose him. It reminded him of how his father used to mash him not only between his love and hatred of Ireland but between his feelings of love and loathing for Johnny's mother. She forgave the old man for his many affairs and in the worst trick irony could play, he'd hated her for it.

This time Johnny let the silence grow and into it came Connolly's deep, labored breathing. When he thought for sure the old man was going to drift off, he rallied, tugging at the cage.

"Is there something I can do?" Johnny asked.

"Help ease the leg a bit to the side, if you will."

Johnny slipped his hands under the cage. He felt a small piece of paper under Connolly's left leg but let it be and quickly backed away. The smell was just too much. As the bedclothes lifted he recoiled at the odor and turned his head, holding his breath.

"There," said Connolly, "much better."

A gasping noise escaped Johnny's throat. "Sorry."

"No need for apologies. The stench of death is disgusting. I haven't gotten used to it either."

"Could be that doctor will come back with a cure," Johnny said, wishing he could bring back the words. "As for, you know, the other matter, it seems over now. They say the intent to commute the sentences of those remaining has come straight from the Prime Minister."

Connolly smiled weakly. "Have you ever known an Englishman to keep his word, lad?"

Johnny smiled. How could he not?

A knock on the door startled him and he turned to find Nurse Meeks standing in the doorway. "Do you need anything, Mr. Connolly?"

"No, nurse. They've sent me a fine soldier for the vigil. Did you perchance meet my wife and daughter?"

"Aye. Beautiful women, both."

Connolly's eyes glistened. "That they are. Smart as whips, too. Lillie and I have been married twenty-six years now." He glanced at Johnny. "She was educated far beyond me. I would have never written anything that made sense had it not been for her help." His voice trailed off and Nurse Meeks started to approach the bed but stopped when his lips quivered..

"What I put her and the children through for the sake of Ireland," he said. "Me never being home, living abroad for months and she with the seven...six...children. We lost Mona, you see." His voice broke as his eyes closed briefly and then opened again.

Johnny was frozen by it all. It seemed like a confession and he wondered why Connolly had chosen to make it now.

"I'd been in America for almost a year raising money for the Irish Citizens Brigade when Lillie and the children came to join me, but they didn't show up on the day I expected them. Nor the day after, or the day after that. I waited on the docks every day and finally after a week they arrived – all but Mona. I thought maybe she was still on the boat and they'd forgotten her in all the confusion, but that wasn't it. On the day they were supposed to leave … on that very day …" Something caught in Connolly's throat and he paused. "Her dress caught fire by the hearth while she was helping her sister prepare dinner. She died the next day, awake and aware the whole time. I never forgave myself for not being with her during those hours."

Tears were streaming from the nurse's eyes now. At last Connolly forced a smile. "I will be joining Mona soon and will sorely miss the other children. She and Ireland are compensation enough, but I will miss the other children, especially Nora. She is the firebrand, the one to whom the torch shall pass. So, it is done."

The cage quivered as he sank into the pillows. Nurse Meeks was at his side soothing his forehead with a cold cloth.

"Mister Connolly, it's dinner time. May I bring you something?" she asked.

"No, thank you."

"At least a bowl of broth. You must keep your strength up," she said.

His eyes twinkled. "Must I?"

"Yes. Now, rest while I send down for it."

When Connolly closed his eyes, Johnny went to the window. He pressed his forehead against the pane and tried to calm his thoughts. Down below, gaslights glowed in the streets. He hadn't noticed the sun had fully set. Why had this man chosen to unburden himself? Why hadn't he kept quiet and left the rightful distance between them? And then, annoyed, Johnny caught himself; hadn't he, a soldier with orders to keep his distance, done the same thing?

Nurse Meeks seemed to read his thoughts. "These last few days I've learned he keeps nothing to himself, and it's fascinating, every word. I think it's the kind of man he is, honest and straightforward and bent on finding humor where most of us could never imagine it hidden. His wife and daughter are the same way. So much so I couldn't bear to search them. It was offensive, would have made an accomplice of me and I'll not be a party to any of it, I swear."

"Why are you telling me this?" Johnny asked, his tone irksome. First Connolly and now she. They were burdening him – burdening him with friendship. Briefly he wondered if he had borrowed such a sodden reaction to kindness from his father. He pushed the feeling away but her eyes were still searching his.

"Because I saw the way he affected you. I saw compassion written across your face."

He lowered his voice. "I was just doing my duty."

"Lieutenant Rhodes is just doing his, but he would not have stood for it. He would have demanded quiet and seen to it. You listened. Two men just doing their duty? Very different duties, I'd say. I'll go for his broth now. Shall I bring you dinner?"

Her words weighed on him. "I'll wait until I'm spelled, thank you."

"Suit yourself but don't wait too long or they'll close the kitchen and you'll not eat until morning."

Chapter Six

The streets were quiet and through the window the night clung to him. Nurse Meeks was right. He had been affected by Connolly, by all of them, Pearse, Markievicz, Plunkett, every damn one of them. He couldn't deny it. *Was it all laid down long ago*, he wondered. Somewhere between his mother's cries of pain, his father's infidelities and his damning of Ireland, not to mention the songs, the cursed yet blessed songs he sang at Braley's? And not just the songs themselves, but in the hungry sadness of his voice and the gloss of tears that came to his eyes like a stout to the brim, never quite spilling over.

Connolly's voice surfaced like a quiet wave. "I have a son – Rory. He looks a wee bit like you, the same strong set of jaw and chin, wavy brown hair – even a fellow mate would call him handsome."

Johnny felt the warmth creeping up his neck. He was hoping Connolly wasn't about to start up again. "Get your rest, now," he said. "I'll wake you when the nurse comes back."

"Rory fought beside me in the G.P.O.," he said. "I couldn't say no to him. It was what he had been raised to do and he reminded me of it when I tried to send him away. His mother would have never forgiven me if he'd got hurt." He paused. "Come to think of it, she wouldn't have blamed me. She understood his duty. Yesterday Lillie told me Rory was arrested along with several other young lads and then let go after giving a false name. I imagine he's hiding out now, somewhere safe, I hope. I suppose he'll carry on, though he's given no guarantee. But my Nora? No question about her. Much older than her twenty-three years. Talk about fearless! I should have named her Sarosa."

Johnny knew it to be the Gaelic word for freedom. "Don't you want the fighting to end?"

Connolly's unflinching eyes regarded him with a look that

made him feel very ordinary. The unspoken word was, "No," Johnny realized. Suddenly, Connolly hacked and started beating at his chest.

"Nurse!" Johnny yelled. He rushed to the washstand for water and brought the glass to Connolly's lips. The touch of the glass seemed to revive him and he sipped at it greedily.

"Good lad," he whispered, letting his head fall back against the pillow. "I wouldn't want to be cheated out of one minute of this life."

"Nurse!" Johnny called again. He started to go look for her when Connolly held up a hand.

"Come here, lad."

Reluctantly, Johnny leaned over the bed. "Be still, Mr. Connolly, please. The nurse will be here soon."

There was a rumble in Connolly's chest and he cleared it with a wet cough. "You've asked a good question. The answer is this: yes, yes, I want the fighting to end. A thousand times, yes!" His voice strengthened as he struggled to raise himself slightly off the pillows. "But at what price, lad? That is the question. Tell me, what price does one place on freedom? Is it worth a war? Yes! Worth my death and a thousand other brave and courageous men and women? Yes! Worth even my family's death? Yes," he said, lowering his voice. "Yes, down to the youngest child. Because only with freedom can this war end!" His eyes roamed across the ceiling. "There are those who will see to it!"

"Mister Connolly, that's quite enough!" Nurse Meeks said, bustling into the room with a tray.

Connolly ignored her. His grip on the bedding tightened and his eyes bored into Johnny. "Does that make sense to you, lad?" He sounded almost desperate.

Johnny pried his fingers loose, easing him down on the pillows.

Placing the tray on a table beside the bed, the nurse said, "Sergeant, there's a corporal in the alcove waiting to spell you for a bit, but I wouldn't take more than ten minutes. Lieutenant Rhodes is a bit particular about such things. Besides, I went ahead and brought you some broth as well. You cannot eat here in the room. It's out on my table in the hall." She sat down on the bed and brought a bowl of broth up under Connolly's chin and held a spoonful to his lips.

"I'm fine, nurse, I can stay through," Johnny said.

"It won't do," she said, keeping her back to him. "You must take breaks. Surely you took them in Kilmainham?"

Connolly's eyes flashed at Johnny. Nurse Meeks glanced back at him, too. "You must go now." She hesitated before turning toward the door. "On your way out please send in the corporal."

"Wait," Connolly said, pushing the broth away. "Wait, I have to talk to you, Sergeant."

As Johnny left the room he could hear her pleading with Connolly to be still. He wondered how he'd ever find the courage to return. Now Connolly would want to know every last detail – how each of his friends died, their last words, everything.

"Johnny, is that you?"

He looked up to see his good friend, Ryan Dahl, standing by the nurse's desk. He and Dahl had crossed the Irish Sea together on the Nord and had been assigned to separate barracks only to find each other in Emmet's a week or so after the Rising. They had gotten to know one another that night but it was not based so much on what they said as in how they said it, without a soldier's feral blather but with a quiet acceptance of what the other said. They even stood together and sang to the music and occasionally laughed at something off-color. What their eyes and expressions shared was more than a feeling of compatibility. They could trust one another and not fear for their lives.

"What are you doing here?" Johnny asked through a broad smile.

"Just this evening they announced we're closing Richmond Barracks, parsing us out hither and yarn before the shipping starts. Said there was work enough over here, so I got permission to stop by but the streets are calming down. The work load is falling a bit. I've got time on my hands, so send for me whenever you want. Hell, mate, get yourself to Emmet's, for God's sake. I'll cover for you with a wink and a nod."

"Thanks, Dahl, but what do you make of all this we're hearing about a possible end to the executions? There's even been talk about commuting de Valera."

"That's the core of it. I guess Prime Minister Asquith gave them hell in the House of Commons, especially where Maxwell was concerned. They say the P.M. is coming to Dublin to see for himself."

"You don't mean it? He sure wouldn't be coming over here to flame the fires."

"It's over, the whole bloody mess is over, Johnny. They need soldiers in France and none's left in Britain."

"Corporal?" the nurse called out. "Give the sergeant leave to eat his broth, why don't you?"

"She's right. I'll stand in for you, Johnny. Have no worries."

"Be back in a few minutes," Johnny said.

"Take as long as you like."

Sitting over his tray at the nurse's station, Johnny began to feel the fatigue returning to his legs and arms, as if they, too, realized that they couldn't truly take a respite. He squinted and rubbed his eyes as the huge chandeliers over the grand staircase began to blur. Nothing he had foreseen, nothing he had ever dreamed of could have begun to prepare him for the moment when it was all to be over.

Nurse Meeks came toward the staircase glancing at her watch. He stood apologetically, the strange nostalgia still coursing through him.

"Nine o'clock. Lieutenant Rhodes is usually here by now, so you might want to come in, just in case." She glanced at his tray. "You haven't touched your food. Maybe I can get the kitchen to warm it up for you."

"No, no. I'm just not as hungry as I should be."

"Forgive me, but you're skin and bones. You're quite sure, are you?"

"Yes."

She began to fidget with her watch. "Sergeant, I'm so sorry about mentioning Kilmainham. It just slipped out. May the good Lord forgive me."

"There's nothing to feel sorry for. Nothing at all. I'll go back in now. The corporal's not exactly an old hand at this sort of thing. I knew him from before all this. We came over from England together."

"Returning home for the celebration?"

"By the looks of things, it seems to have gotten a bit out of hand."

She chuckled. "You're on 'til midnight, you realize. Make sure Mister Connolly gets some sleep and you, yourself, on your breaks. I don't want to see you both pass away together."

"Sleep it is, then."

Dahl was standing at the foot of the bed when Johnny returned. He put a finger to his lips and whispered. "He just drifted off, Johnny." He stepped away from the bed and put the flap back over the pistol in his holster. "A sliver dramatic all this, isn't it?"

"More than a sliver," Johnny said.

"When they sent me up here you would have thought I was being sent to guard a mad dog," Dahl said. "But then I come in here and the old bugger spends ten minutes asking all about meself, not one word about himself or his troubles. Hell, he seems like nothing but a kind old grandfather, and I'm not even sure he's that old." Dahl put his hands on his hips and looked up at the ceiling. "He asked me if I still loved Ireland and would I ever consider coming back to settle down. I answered, yes, to both, Johnny, and I wasn't lying on his behalf. Well, I'll be off now, but if you need someone for checkers or twenty-five, or better yet, someone to stand you for a Guinness, you can find me at Emmet's, and if the old man can hobble, bring him along."

"There's enough gas in the streets as it is."

Dahl grinned and started for the door. Then, he stopped. "Oh, by the way, the old fellow did ask if it was true you were stationed at Kilmainham. He came back to it a couple of times, he did. I just told him I couldn't talk about the disposition of another soldier. 'Following orders,' I said, and he seemed to understand."

Chapter Seven

Johnny went back into the room, careful to stay on the thick carpet where his boots were silent. He went over to the dresser and glanced at the sleeping Connolly. His mouth was twisted in such a way it seemed like the pain from his leg was getting through even as he slept. Before he could get to the bed, Connolly's head came up off the pillow and his eyes opened. The expression was of terror, as if he were clutching at the edge of a nightmare and about to be pulled back in. It reminded Johnny of the terrified look in the Countess's eyes when she was told she had been spared the firing squad.

Johnny reached out and gently touched his shoulder. "Mister Connolly, it's all right. It's Johnny Flynn … Sergeant Flynn. You're having a bad dream, that's all it is."

Connolly shook his head slowly. "Nurse gave me some more morphine. It sends a man spinning. I dreamt I was signing the Proclamation just under God's signature."

"Under?"

Connolly laughed.

"You need the rest," Johnny said. "Go back to sleep now."

The old man's eyes sought Johnny's. "You were at Kilmainham, I remember the nurse saying."

Johnny started to deny it, then nodded. "Yes."

Connolly's breathing quickened and he pushed himself up to face Johnny squarely. "How did they die?"

Johnny answered with a slight catch in his voice. "I'm told they died bravely, every one of them."

"But you were there?"

"In their last minutes but not...not at the very end. Only the priests and officers to bear witness, and..."

"And the firing squad."

"Yes."

A hint of a smile played on Connolly's lips. "The best seats in the house," he said, easing himself down again so that he was staring at the ceiling. "Strange, in all I've written I don't think I ever once touched on the subject of death. Did any of the boys ever mention me, lad?" he asked.

Johnny could not recall anyone ever bringing up Connolly's name, perhaps to avoid implicating him. "I'm sure they did," he hedged, hoping it would satisfy him.

"I'm glad to be joining them whether by firing squad or gangrene. Though to stand or if I must, sit before the killing squad would be my choice," he said. "I don't regret leaving this world. I've given my all in the name of freedom but my time is done. The cause needs fresh blood, renewed inspiration, young minds to map unique paths through insurrection. Let them stand on our shoulders for a while, if they must, but seeking freedom requires original ideas, not borrowings from those who failed. Sooner or later they must take leave and go it alone."

Johnny realized Connolly wasn't asking for confirmation. He just seemed off in another world, possibly trying to sort out the certainty of his death with the meaning of his life, teasing the two apart so that he could fuse them into one. Johnny felt he was eavesdropping but he couldn't help it. It reminded him of listening to Pearse read the poem he had written to his mother.

Connolly's moustache quivered. He muttered Nora's name but when he began to snore in earnest Johnny sat down in a leather chair at the foot of the bed. In the heat of the room his eyes grew heavy. The urge to sleep finally overwhelmed him and he slumped over and did not wake until someone shouted, "The prisoner shall rise!"

Rhodes stood in the doorway. Nurse Meeks knelt shaking by the wall as if he'd just shoved her aside. He took out his swagger stick and started for the bed.

"Leave him be!" Johnny blurted out rushing to Connolly's side.

Rhodes halted, shoved the stick under his arm and snapped to attention. "James Connolly, are you aware of your surroundings?"

"Yes," he said, cautiously.

"Can you reason and understand my words?" Rhodes barked.

"Surely."

"The King's Court has this hour found you guilty of treason. You are to be shot at dawn."

The words registered with Johnny and then again they didn't. Like death itself they seemed to curve back through their own meaning, retracting their impact until the silence exposed them.

Smiling faintly, Connolly bent over to clutch his leg. "A firing squad will be better than this infernal pain." He glanced at Rhodes. "And it won't last as long. 'Tis a favor you'll be doing me, lad." The look on his face became intense. "I'd like to see my wife and daughter."

"They are being sent for and should be here shortly," Rhodes said. "Meanwhile, Sergeant Flynn will stay with you...until it is time. Have you any questions?"

Connolly laughed. "Questions? Are you an infant? What questions would you have, were you me, Lieutenant?"

Rhodes looked away, but his cheeks glowed with anger when he faced Connolly again. "You were found guilty for crimes against the Crown. I assume you knew what you were doing when you signed the Proclamation. Further, you knew the uprising was simply suicide. You didn't expect it to succeed, but in the face of that, you carried on, sending hundreds to their deaths, and you're to die for it."

Connolly nodded. "Well said, Lieutenant, but was it not offset by the British assigning young Irish boys to die in their stead?

"The defense of the Realm is no rag-tag uprising, even if you manage to lead five hundred of your own men to their deaths. You were in such a state of idiocy out on St. Stephen's Green you had to call in women to do your fighting. What is that, if not barbaric?"

"Winning a war," Connolly said, "and before Calvary it shall truly be noted."

"Calvary!" Rhodes said, ashen now. "You think God is on your side? I ought to save the firing squad the trouble."

"Stop it! Leave him alone!" Johnny exclaimed.

Rhodes glared at him. Nurse Meeks was standing in the doorway now and he cut his eyes at her, spun abruptly on his heel and left. His men braced and followed.

"I overheard, Mr. Connolly ... I don't know what to say," Nurse Meeks said from the doorway.

"Nor I," said Johnny. He could feel his heart thudding.

"It's not right. It's senseless," she said.

"Don't you fret over me," Connolly said, "neither one of you. Nurse, do you think you could find me a little more broth, or perhaps an Enfield with a hair-trigger?"

She grinned. "I'll send down right away, for the broth, that is," she said, taking the tray from the dresser and hurrying out.

Johnny wanted to wave his hand and set time back, if only into the moment just before Rhodes entered, when none of this was happening and hope had begun to reset. "I'm sorry," he said. "I thought it was over. Asquith was coming..." His voice tapered off and it took a second for him to realize the words had come from his mouth.

Connolly was shaking his head slowly. "The lieutenant was right in what he said about the Proclamation. I knew what I was doing and it was a lost cause. We accepted that, everyone but Pearse. What a romantic that one. To him life was a heroic dream to be played out on the battlefield, much like the poems he wrote. I suppose it is fair to say the curse of Cuchulain is alive and well in all of us. Do you know about that, lad, the epic we Irish have inherited?"

"My father told me the story many times," Johnny said, moving a hand up the bedpost.

"As well a good Irish father should, and I'm sure it will find its place in you."

Johnny didn't know why but with all that had happened in the last few minutes he felt a genuine calmness in Connolly's presence, similar to Pearse, a sense that there was something more to life than simply being alive. He was about to ask him about this when Connelly's wife and daughter rushed into the room. Painfully, Connolly tried to lift his head off the pillow. He took his wife's hand and she hugged him so hard he grimaced.

"Lillie, they've told you," he said in a low voice.

"No, James, it's not that. It's not that!"

"Yes, Lillie, I fell asleep and they awakened me just now to tell me I was to die at dawn."

Lillie put her head on the pillow next to him and started to sob. Connolly smoothed her hair. "Don't cry, Lillie, you'll unman me."

"But your beautiful life, James. Your beautiful life."

"Well, Lillie, it's been a full life and isn't this a good end?"

Her face was gray and her lips tight, etched in unforgettable sorrow. Her stricken eyes locked with her husband's. Johnny had never seen a woman look at a man that way. He wondered if only in the presence of impending death could two people feel such passion.

Nora moved out of the shadows, like a shadow herself, to the edge of the bed. She, too, was crying.

"Don't cry, my love. There's nothing to cry about," Connolly said.

She wiped her eyes. "I won't cry, papa."

"That's my brave girl," he said, sliding his free hand awkwardly under his hip.

She returned his smile and stood back, tilting her head into the light of the lamp. Johnny couldn't help watching her fight to keep her word. Gradually, her concentration became so complete he dared not move for fear of breaking it. She stood as still as silence, draped in a long black riding coat that seemed better suited for a man than a woman. When she finally moved, opening the coat to place her hands on her hips, he could see a black leather belt so tightly drawn he wondered how she could possibly breathe. A crucifix hung around her neck and the Irish tricolors were pinned to her breast. Her hair was tucked inside her coat collar and the gaslight seemed to draw her pale skin back to the bone giving her stunning face a haunting, almost transparent look.

Connolly glanced over her shoulder at the officer and slid his hand from under his hip to reach toward her. His trembling fingers touched her face. "Later," he said. She looked puzzled and leaned toward him as he framed her face with both hands and kissed her.

"Later?"

"It has been bequeathed," he said.

She brushed at her eyes and her lips moved. "I don't understand."

He looked at Johnny. "You will. God willing, you will."

"I love you, Da."

"And our love of Ireland treads just barely below that, does it not?" he said, releasing her.

"Yes, yes," she replied.

Sorrow and pride blended to fill her eyes with love. Johnny felt he had trespassed into some holy field that was denied him and would always be. She glanced his way and he tensed, afraid of the hatred that would follow but she stared without any acknowledgement of him. In fact he was convinced she really didn't see him at all but was looking through him before turning back to her father and taking his hand again.

Lillie took both of their hands in hers and kissed them. "I'll have her to remember you, James."

Connolly was gently pulling them closer when Rhodes appeared in the doorway. "Five minutes more."

Lillie began to breathe in gulps and Johnny called the nurse for water. Connolly again tried to take them both in his arms, but he could barely rise from the bed. Nurse Meeks came running with a glass of water and gave it to Lillie but no sooner had it touched her lips than Rhodes was back in the doorway.

"Your time is up," he said.

Silence filled the room. "Farewell," Connolly said at last, turning his head as if he couldn't bear to see them leave.

Nora held Lillie by the shoulders and tried to take her away. She resisted until the nurse went to her, took her by the arms and helped guide her to the door. Nora ran back to the bed and kissed her father.

"I'm so proud of you," he said and then broke down, sobbing as she left the room.

Rhodes motioned to Johnny. "Sergeant, you are to report to Captain Stanley. You'll find his post in the hospital section."

"I'd like to say good-bye to this man first."

"If he's still here after you've seen the captain, you may say whatever there is to say. Now, move on."

Johnny looked at Connolly. "I'll be back in a few minutes," he said and stepped sharply around Rhodes.

Chapter Eight

Threading between the stretchers of wounded soldiers in the Royal Hospital, Johnny found Stanley's office, a pantry in the midst of what seemed like a thousand rooms filled with wounded soldiers. He knocked on the door and a voice called, "Come in."

The room was barely lit by a single lamp shaded by thick green glass. In the dimness the figure of a soldier was silhouetted against the window.

"Captain Stanley?"

"At ease, Sergeant Flynn."

There was a long silence which Johnny broke at last. "You wanted to see me, Sir?"

Stanley must have been thirty or so but the creases in his unshaven cheeks were of a man much older. His eyes showed no reflection. "It is midnight," he said, staring at his watch. "Midnight," he repeated, "and we are on duty as if there were no such thing, as if there were no sunlight either, only one continuous darkness."

Johnny watched Stanley open a desk drawer, take out a deck of cards and fan them on the desk. "Excuse me, Sir. You sent for me?"

Stanley studied his face. "The war has provided us an invaluable lesson on chance, hasn't it? When I return to my job as a teacher I'm going to tell all I know about it. Pick a card, Sergeant."

Johnny wasn't sure if Stanley was joking with him or suffering from the strain of his duty. He reached out and teased a card from the deck. He let it remain face down and took his hand from the table.

"Black or red? Turn it over, Sergeant," Stanley said, leaning over the table.

Johnny flipped the card over.

"Three of spades – black," Stanley said. "Sergeant, you have drawn the color and thus have been chosen. It's as cruel and simple as that."

"Chosen?"

Stanley looked up. "For Connolly's firing squad," he said. "Because he's been housed here at the Castle and the others at Kilmainham, Major Howe thought half the squad should come from each place. Given the time you served there, you qualify on both counts, but just to keep things fair, so that you need not bear this on your conscience, I've chosen this little game. You must never feel guilty."

Johnny felt a burst of panic. "Sir, with all due respect, I could not bring myself to carry it out. I request to be excused."

"You sound like a child asking if he can take leave to pee."

"Sir, what should I say?"

Stanley shuffled the cards, tapping them into a neat stack. "There is nothing to say."

"What if I could arrange to trade off with someone?"

"Trade off? Why would anyone want to trade off? Besides, I gather from what I've been told you've never served on such a squad. It is your fate. 'Tis in the cards. The order stands."

"But Captain, I know this man and his family," Johnny pleaded.

Stanley looked at him hard. "Where do you know them from?"

"Connolly's family came to visit. I was upstairs the entire time with them. It's like I got to know them personally. I knew what they…"

"Is that it, the extent of it?" Stanley said. "It's not that you grew up with this family or knew them in any way before all this happened?"

"No."

"Sergeant, you are to report to Lieutenant Baxter in the

Stonebreaker's Yard no later than three a.m. There will be a lorry to take you and the others from the Castle. Baxter will brief you as to protocol. Father Donovan will be in attendance. If you're Catholic, you can talk to him when it's over. That will be all, Sergeant. Oh, there should be someone in the hall waiting to see me. Send him in on your way out."

As Johnny stepped out into the hall with his stomach churning once again, he almost forgot to send in the corporal waiting there. He motioned to the door and felt like he was sending the man in for a stabbing. His mind was racing wildly and he ached to lash out at something, kick a piece of the ancient furniture or break a goddamn vase. The tension tightened like a screwdriver in his chest. He was tempted to run out into the streets and start a whole other rising, only this time, without question, he would stand with the rebels against these heartless Brits. And then his impulses locked. He did not know what to do. He hated himself at that moment but kept on walking head down toward the Throne Room, drawn by something he could not identify, but drawn nevertheless in a current he could not see.

Nurse Meeks was standing at the end of the hall talking with Father Donovan. They turned as Johnny approached. Donovan nodded. The nurse had been crying. The three of them stood in silence for a moment. Meeks wiped her eyes. "There are officers inside, Sergeant, but I'm sure Mr. Connolly would like to see you. It will be all right." She glanced at the priest. "Sergeant Flynn kept the last watch. Mr. Connolly favored him, I believe."

"You have been blessed to know him," Donovan said. "Take your time. I left the sacraments at the door. I'll be back."

"Yes," Johnny said, quietly and effortlessly as if someone else was answering for him. As he entered the room he announced who he was and the officers standing by the window at the far side barely moved but one called out, "Be brief," and let it stay at that.

Connolly smiled weakly at Johnny and motioned him toward the bed. "I was thinking I'd seen you for the last time." He held out a closed, shaking hand and as it grazed Johnny's wrist and reached towards his chest, Johnny realized his real intent. With fingers as nimble as a magician's, Connolly slipped a small piece of paper into Johnny's jacket pocket and his hand trembled back to the bedside. "For Nora," his lips mimed and as Johnny watchfully bent closer, Connolly whispered, "I know the protocol for last offerings. The note might not have passed muster. Causing Nora and Lillie more pain was unthinkable."

Johnny stared at Connolly.

"What's the matter, lad?" Connolly looked toward the officers and lowered his voice. "I'm sorry. I wasn't thinking. I know the danger. Here, give it back. I'll leave it on my pillow where Providence might find it or the nurse when she changes these rotten sheets."

"It's not that," Johnny said.

Connolly seemed to consider the matter. "Is it that you've been through all this one too many times now, is that it?"

"Something akin to it," Johnny said, unable to look at the old man.

"Keep a close watch on your spirit, lad. Ireland is old but its people are forever young, bent on freedom. Nowhere in the world, except maybe in America, do folks share so readily in the spirit of the young. Nora speaks to that. Freedom shines in her eyes. Maybe you saw it yourself."

Johnny was about to ask where he could find her, when an officer came up behind him to tap him on the shoulder with his nightstick. "Hush!" he snapped. "Both of you, shut your mouths. There'll be no more between you."

Johnny could not speak in any case. Her eyes. Freedom. Is that what he had seen? He gritted his teeth and raised his head. For a brief time the moment vanished and was replaced by a glimpse of the future, a sense that his life was about to change forever.

Guilt flooded over him. Change? For the love of God, he was about to take part in this man's execution. He started to confess but caught himself. It would have been a court martial offense, no mistake about that. And yet, that wasn't the only reason, maybe not even a reason at all.

Johnny headed toward the door. He wanted to run back and hug the old man but instead kept moving forward on legs he thought would give way before he could make it out of the room. *"For God and Ireland, lad! Freedom!"* Freedom. The word was becoming a mantra in his senses. In the corridor he felt light-headed. More officers hurried past him by as he went along but he could not hear them. Barely, and only so, could he make out the image of Nurse Meeks sitting at her table.

"Are you all right?" She glanced at the soldiers across the room. Again, tears crested in her eyes. "Sergeant, are you all right?"

"Yes," he answered, just managing to keep himself together. "No," he said. "I'm not." Johnny asked if she had the time. She looked up at him quizzically, forcing him to lie that his watch was broken.

"Half past one," she whispered as if the two of them were in a conspiracy. "Are you going back to the barracks now?"

"Not straightaway, but soon."

A knowing look came to her eyes. "I realize it's hard, but if you'd not mind a bit of motherly advice?"

"No, no, not at all," he said loudly.

"Stay out of the pubs tonight. It's not fitting."

"Bless you, nurse," he said, not knowing what else to say.

At the top of the Grand Staircase he almost ran straight into Father Donovan who was rushing up carrying his brown box. They stared at each other for a moment like two actors who had forgotten their lines. It went through his mind to take the priest aside and ask for confession. Christ, he hadn't gone to confession since he was seven. Sitting in his father's lap in the darkness, the old man's sour breath reeking of stout, Johnny was prompted by a knuckle in the side to tell the shuttered priest about stealing the soccer ball. He had struggled to confess to his mother he'd been so embarrassed. But true to her promise, the local priest had forgiven him, though when his father heard the confession he'd been incensed.

"Sergeant," Father Donovan said, but Johnny was feeling the sting of his father's hand across his cheek when they left the confession booth.

"If ever you put me through that again and I'll give you a thrashing the Devil himself would be proud of!" his dad said, wagging his finger in Johnny's face. Before they'd crossed the street he'd grabbed Johnny off his feet and swooped him up in his arms and kissed him. "But I love you, you little bastard. I do." They careened down the street toward Braley's.

"Sergeant?"

"Father, there's something I…"

"I'm sorry, my son, but I have to hurry."

"Wait."

"Out with it then."

Johnny felt completely trapped. Finally, Donovan intervened. "You know he's to die, do you not?"

"Yes," Johnny said, now tempted more than ever to get it off his chest.

The priest shook his head. "That's why I've come, to hear his confession and give him Holy Communion. I never thought it would come to this. I was so certain he would be spared."

"My God," Johnny said. He looked up into Donovan's eyes. "They've put me on Connolly's firing squad. I wanted to tell him but just couldn't bring myself…"

Donovan drew in his breath and reached for Johnny's shoulder. His pink oval face shone in the light. "The hand of God is unseen but never absent. Only after time has passed do we know how it has moved and what it has touched. God has already forgiven you and I'm sure James Connolly forgives you as well."

"Father, I couldn't bring myself to tell him." Johnny said. "He doesn't know."

"But God does and He will see to it. He is with you, Johnny Flynn, as He has been all along. I must go now," he said, withdrawing his hand.

Chapter Nine

The bare comfort of the priest's words disappeared before Johnny got downstairs. He began to feel more alone and cowardly than ever. An ambulance pulled through the gates and stopped just in front of him on the circular drive. The driver, a yawning corporal, stepped out. An unlit cigarette hung from his lips. He patted down the pockets of his coat and pants and looked up at Johnny.

"Say there, Sarge, you got a light?"

"Sorry, no," Johnny said.

The soldier jerked the cigarette out of his mouth, looked at it and threw it to the ground. "Christ, they get us up in the middle of the night for this and you'd think they'd keep us supplied with fags and matches, not to mention whiskey for the chill. Would you be going to Kilmainham?"

Johnny nodded. "I would be."

"You and a few others?" the driver asked.

"I suppose. Yes."

The soldier pulled a flask out of his back pocket and offered it to him. "I'm here to take you. Then I come back for the prisoner."

Whiskey was the last thing Johnny wanted but he took the flask and sipped. More went down than he intended and he shook his head and coughed, handing it back to the corporal. "Thanks."

"That's what I mean. They should give you your own, each one of you, considering what they're making you do. It'll take away the chill and help steady your nerves, but on that don't worry, you can't miss a man at ten paces." He chuckled, took a swallow of whiskey and slipped the bottle back into his pocket. "You can jump in the back and wait for the others out of the cold, if you like."

Johnny opened the huge rear doors and climbed in. There was a cot along one side, but otherwise it was an empty shell that echoed the sound of his boots on the steel floor. He sat just behind the driver's seat. It was quiet and not too cold. With eyes closed he tried to focus on the emptiness but his mind left no space for anything except that which lay before him. He wondered if he should simply keep on drinking, but that wasn't an option, not now. What he really wanted was to get far away, by himself, away from soldiering and this idea of people exchanging their souls for life. The thought came to him that maybe what once had been normal could never be again. He thought of Nora Connolly, so unlike any woman he'd ever seen and so striking – how she stood as if fighting a strong wind at her back, the love in her eyes straining to connect with her father and the defiance on her face as she left the room.

The rear doors opened. The first soldier to climb in glanced at him suspiciously but said nothing. Four others filed in behind him, two smoking and seemingly oblivious as to where they were headed or why. The drinking corporal opened the cab door and got in, chuckling. "All the horsemen of the Apocalypse right here in my litter wagon."

The door closed on his laughter and the engine started. As they entered the streets of Dublin, smoke filled the vehicle but no one complained. The men sat in silence, staring ahead until one of them at the back spoke so sharply Johnny almost jumped.

"Any of you mates ever been on a firing squad?" the soldier asked.

Johnny thought all of them had answered, no, when a little runt of a soldier at the far end of the cot said, "Aye," softly adding, "I was posted at Kilmainham along with Sergeant Flynn down at the end there."

Leaning forward, Johnny could not see the man's face. "You would be?" he called out.

"Seamus Reye," the man said, making no effort to meet Johnny's stare. "I wasn't up there with you. I was down in the Main. It was like guarding a giant birdcage, only there won't no birds. Nobody there. So they tabbed you this time? I was wondering when they'd get around to it. They want as much Irish descent in it as possible. I'd say it gives them satisfaction and spreads the guilt. Washes the King's boots spanking clean."

The man next to Johnny glanced at Reye. "I never done nothing even comes close to this. What's it like?" His voice was almost a whisper.

"Don't think about it, mate," Reye said. "No sooner you're out there and it's over. It passes quickly, the briefing, the shooting and debriefing, all gone in a flash. It's not like you're actually killing anyone. That's why they pin a target on his chest, to make it like sport."

"As target practice?" another said.

"Aye," Reye replied, "something like that."

In the silence that returned, Johnny began to count the working gaslights they passed. Many had been shattered but even so the bluish-gold haloes seemed to spread, filling the gaps and casting an unending aura along the street. For a moment he was lost in the confusion of what he knew to be there but wasn't. There was no inside or out to the buildings, just passing holes and through them more emptiness and through that darkness. It was like being driven through a room of mirrors, drawn into the infinite sameness with the eerie sense that none of this was happening. But it was, and he was more than an observer.

The man next to him dropped his face into his hands and began to moan. The sound reverberated and grew louder until someone shouted at him to shut up. He raised his eyes to Johnny.

"How can you just sit there?"

Johnny swallowed and looked away from the window. "It isn't easy."

But the man seemed not to hear and turned toward the back of the vehicle. "Pretend he's just a target?" he shouted. "I ain't a bloody murderer!"

"No, mate, yer just obeying orders, is all," Reye said. "And you won't feel nothing when the time comes. Squeeze off a round and it's over. You'll be back in the barracks for breakfast."

Another chimed in. "Fuck your target practice. It's killing, pure and simple. I was on Mallin's squad, back at the beginning of it."

"Why didn't you say so?" Reye said.

"Because I ain't proud of it. It makes me feel filthy, like I was carrying this smell I can never wash off."

When the ambulance pulled into the lower yard at Kilmainham, terror had such a grip on Johnny that by the time the heavy doors swung open to let them crawl out, his recurrent stomach cramps had almost doubled him over in pain. The other men were inside and had formed up before he could stand straight. As he shuffled in to join the ranks he wondered when his bowels would unleash.

A lieutenant Johnny did not know came into the guardroom. "You there, Sergeant, get a move on! It's almost dawn."

Johnny glanced at his watch. It was almost three and he knew the sun would rise in about forty-five minutes. The lieutenant marched them into a windowless, dank room below Stonebreaker's Yard where those chosen from the jail were already waiting. Each of them was handed a Lee-Enfield rifle and asked if he knew how to fire it. Then they were called to attention and a lieutenant stepped out before them. He had a chin that spread like split rail and yet his mouth seemed crammed into the space between it and his nose.

"I am Lieutenant Baxter. Tonight, this duty marks the end of the Irish revolution. The rebels conceived it; you are bringing it to close. See *that* as your duty, not the men standing before you out there in the Yard. They were the two most responsible for an action that took the lives of over five hundred innocent citizens of Dublin. Their gall also led to the injury of more than two thousand more, many of whom will surely die. Women and children died and the cost to the Crown has risen to more than two million pounds. Now, the courts have spoken and the last link in this long chain of justice rests in your hands. Assume your responsibility proudly and without shame. You have the blessing of a nation. Stand at ease."

There was clicking as the men brought their rifles to rest. The lieutenant continued. "I realize some of you have served on squads before. Nonetheless, I have to go over the procedure with all of you." He stopped to clear his throat. "You have been assigned to execute the prisoner James Connolly. His will be the last execution tonight. Prisoner Sean McDermott of Kilmainham will be the first to die."

McDermott. Johnny had almost forgotten about him. A fine man, unassuming and cheerful. Somewhat like Dahl, always wanting to talk politely about the smallest matters. A guard trusted him with a penknife and well he should have because Sean then cut the buttons from his tunic and scratched his initials on them so that his family would have something to hold in his memory.

Baxter's raised voice cut sharply through Johnny's compassion.

"You will be marched into position after the area is cleared of his corpse. You six men," he said, pointing a finger at a group that included Johnny, "will assume a kneeling position and you other six will fall in standing behind them. A single live .303 caliber bullet will be placed into the breach of each rifle, save one. That lone rifle contains a blank. Thus, no man can ever be sure if he fired a fatal round. It is done to help clear your conscience should you be in need of such a thing."

He paused and one of the men who had been in the ambulance with Johnny, stepped forward. "Sir, what is the command?"

Baxter glared at him. "I will say aloud, 'Ready, Aim,' and at the drop of my hand you will fire. There is no verbal command to fire, only my hand, like this." He raised his hand, made a fist and then jerked it swiftly down to his shoulder, causing Johnny to shudder. "Any questions?" He looked at each of them. When no one said anything he glanced at his watch. "Very well, clear your weapons and then you six men on your knees, the rest of you behind them."

Johnny checked the chamber of his rifle to make sure it didn't contain a round and dropped to one knee. He hadn't noticed it until now but there was a black silhouette of a man on the opposite wall and over the place where his heart would be was a strip of white cloth. The lieutenant stepped out of the line of fire.

"Ready?"

"Aim!"

Baxter's arm pumped in the air. Rifle bolts clicked but not in unison. "That won't do," he said. "Again. Ready, aim!" He raised his fist and jerked it to his shoulder. This time there was one clean sound.

"Much better. Now once more. Ready!"

Johnny's finger tightened on the trigger and then a volley of rifle shots sounded outside. Baxter looked up, strain showing on his face. Breathing deeply to regain his composure, he said, "As you were. That will be enough. Quiet." His face was blank and then a single shot rang out.

Johnny gasped quietly, knowing it was the *coup de grace*. He wondered how he could bear to watch an officer stand over Connolly and put a bullet through his brain. The men were on their feet now, milling about and murmuring. The soldier next to him said, "Mary, Mary, Mother of God. Do they have to kill the poor bastard twice?"

"Atten … shun!" Baxter snapped, glancing at his watch, which caused Johnny to glance at his. It was 3:35. "Shoulder arms! Left face. Forward march!"

Single file they moved through the doors and up the narrow staircase. They were in a part of the prison where Johnny had never been before but it was like all the rest, damp and reeking of mildew, as if the stones themselves were rotting. Their boots clattered on the stairs. Johnny wondered if Connolly could hear them coming and fear ripped through his chest. The squad marched through the foyer and from there into the holding area where he had blindfolded Pearse. They halted for the lieutenant to open the doors to the Yard and for a moment Johnny felt that he, too, was about to be blindfolded and bound. Just then a soldier directly behind him said that he was going to be sick. Johnny called out, "Lieutenant, a man's sick back here."

"Which one?" Baxter barked.

"Me, Sir, I don't think I can…"

The lieutenant was at the man's side in an instant. "Listen here, soldier, there's only one thing worse than being on a firing squad and that's to be in front of one, so if you don't want a court martial for cowardice, which by God would certainly put you there, I'd suggest you keep your mouth shut and gut it out. You understand what I'm saying?"

"Aye," the soldier muttered.

Baxter hurried back to the head of the column. "Move out!" he called over his shoulder.

As they entered the Yard, the sun was still below the horizon but edging the sky with gold. As Johnny stepped into the cold, a chill crawled across his chest. He thought of the note in his shirt pocket, hiding above his heart much like the targets pinned on the rebels, and began to feel faint. Staring at the north wall, he bit his lip. There was a stack of sandbags splattered with McDermott's blood. Johnny couldn't help looking at the gravel below the sandbags for the crimson pool of blood he knew would be there. And it was, as dark and foreboding as the painting of a witch.

A group of officers and priests, with Father Donovan among them, were gathered at the huge south gate and as the lieutenant ordered them to split into two lines, three of the officers opened the gate and Johnny could see the lights of an ambulance waiting outside. As it rolled over the curb through the entrance, its headlights bounced eerily across the Yard until the vehicle stopped. One of the priests – Johnny thought it was Father Aloysius – moved to the rear of the ambulance and the doors opened. Just then an officer carrying a chair materialized out of nowhere. He placed a chair in front of the south wall and Johnny realized they were sparing Connolly the final indignity of having to be carried the length of the Yard. Lieutenant Baxter ordered column left and marched the lines directly in front of the chair ten paces away. Then he went to go join the party bringing out the stretcher. He took some papers from his tunic and handed them to a man with a shock of white hair.

"Doc Tobin," someone murmured.

"It is my duty to identify the prisoner and have my judgment independently verified," Baxter demanded.

Tobin glanced down at the stretcher. "I do swear this is James Connolly," he announced, then scribbled on the papers and handed them back to Fields.

The lieutenant turned to the firing squad. "Sergeant Flynn, over here. Double time!"

Johnny was so taken off guard he jumped reflexively. As he moved toward the lieutenant the huge wall seemed to encircle him. He stopped a few feet away from the stretcher. He couldn't look at Connolly.

"Come closer, Sergeant," Baxter demanded.

Johnny took two steps forward. Connolly's face was the color of slate and his eyes were closed. Johnny wondered if he had already died. "It's him," he said, stepping back.

"You're certain beyond question?" Lieutenant Baxter said.

"Aye," Johnny said, feeling the stone walls begin to move.

"That will be all, Sergeant. You may return to your rank."

Johnny went back slowly, faltering and keeping his eyes on the ground, telling himself Connolly had no idea what had just taken place. He took his position again.

"Christ," someone whispered. "You couldn't miss a sparrow from this range."

"Nor Connolly intentionally, if that's what you were thinking. They'd spot you in a minute," another countered.

Johnny had started to sweat profusely. His eyes stung. He wondered if his feet were really on the ground or if he had entered a dream from which he might wake in an instant and find himself at home. He thought of the blank bullet and prayed he had it, wondering, too, if the soldier was right. Would he be spotted if he inched his aim just above Connolly's shoulder? How would they know? To the left or right would be obvious, yes, but slightly up? There was no wire stretched across their vision at barrel level to prevent any movement, which he understood was the case in some executions. No, if he nudged the sight above Connolly no one would know.

Tobin watched over Connolly as they lifted him from the stretcher and placed him in the chair. Two of the bearers took care to set his leg on the ground.

"Holy Father, I can't believe what I'm seeing," someone in the back line said.

Another chimed in, "Would we be shootin' him if they'd cut off that leg?"

As they propped Connolly upright and roped him into the chair, Johnny saw that he was wearing fresh pajamas and thought briefly of Nurse Meeks; she had wanted Connolly to look as dignified as possible. It had to be her doing.

Connolly opened his eyes and Johnny raised a hand in front of his face to avoid being recognized. An officer stepped in behind Connolly and blindfolded him, but not before Johnny had seen Connolly smile. *At him*, he was sure.

Baxter motioned to the two remaining officers. They started with the rear line and worked around behind the front, taking each man's weapon and loading it behind his back. Johnny could hear the bullets lock in the chambers and he counted until the last man was done. Then Baxter gave the signal for the front line to kneel. When Johnny had settled on one knee, his leg began to tremble. He placed the butt of the rifle on the ground and held it with both hands, using it as a support.

As the priests moved behind the firing squad, Donovan placed his hand on Connolly's shoulder. "Will you pray for these men who are about to shoot you?" he asked in a carrying tone.

Connolly's chest rose. "I will say a prayer for all brave men who do their duty. Father, forgive them, for they know not what they do."

Yes, we do, Johnny thought and began to shake all over.

Connolly's lingering voice made it impossible for him to think beyond the brief realization. It was too much, too much, as if the poor fellow was talking directly to him. He tried to control himself, silently repeating that Connolly was bigger than all of them, that in the face of death the finale was his, no other's, and he wanted it to go off perfectly. It was his way of giving approval, his way of exonerating them all. Johnny did take some strength from that and breathed deep several times, clutching tight the Enfield and bracing himself.

Donovan walked slowly back to the group of priests. As Johnny watched, Father Aloysius met the young friar halfway and they spoke quietly. Donovan gave him a puzzled look and Aloysius presented his hands. Several of his fingers were covered with blood. Johnny knew it was McDermott's.

"Don't worry, Father," Donovan said in a voice that carried in the stillness, "I will do the anointing afterwards." The two priests moved to the rear of the firing squad and as Baxter stepped to one side, Johnny tightened his grip even more.

"Ready!" Baxter called and Johnny jerked the rifle to his shoulder. He could barely see Connolly for the tears that blurred his eyes. They pushed hard at his vision and began to stream down his face. His arm was shaking so hard he couldn't keep the rifle still. He could only hope that when he pulled the trigger the barrel was pointing far above Connolly.

"Sergeant!" the lieutenant shouted, but Johnny couldn't stop the trembling. The stock of the rifle was wet with his sweat and Connolly was a vague, pale image in the distance but he could see the old man struggling to sit straight in the chair.

"Shoot straight, Johnny Flynn!" Connolly shouted in a voice so strong it seemed to come from Baxter himself.

Johnny's aim steadied and the rifle settled on the target. Baxter shouted, "Aim!" and when his fist came down, Johnny was sure he'd fired before anyone else. Connolly snapped back in the chair and then slumped forward as blood gushed from his chest and ran down his legs onto the ground. Baxter took out his pistol, walked over to Connolly and pointed the barrel to his temple.

Johnny dropped the rifle, covered his ears and looked away. The gun fired and into the slowly descending silence came Donovan's voice: "Now it is truly up to God."

Chapter Ten

Five days of leave were granted all members of Connolly's firing squad. "To rest your consciences and if need be your souls in that this man was a cripple, though when your anguish settles you should be overjoyed," Baxter said after the benediction.

Johnny spent the free time a prisoner of his own nightmare, struggling with what he had done. He could not sleep for fear of bolting awake in a cold sweat, the image of Connolly's face looming before him like a death mask, shouting, "Shoot straight, Johnny Flynn!" He tried to make it go away by closing his eyes and summoning up every memory he could from childhood. He thought mainly of his mother, her smell and the way she walked, stooped over in pain, saying that all life was as God intended and thus there was no room for regret, only forgiveness and gratitude for what remained, but he could not bring back her face. It seemed to be hiding behind a veil or curtain of some sort. Yet, he could vividly recall his father's face, trembling that night as he lay dying in the fallen snow.

He tried to remember but the smell of cordite still heavy in the air soon masked his childhood and then too, Father Donovan came through clearly in his benediction, telling the executioners it would be best if they forgot they had ever served on a firing squad. "Never tell a soul, especially your families and friends. From what we know of history, few will forget ever what you did and no one but God will forgive you. As you live out this life, you must find a way to forgive yourself."

But Father Donovan's warning made forgetting impossible and forgiveness a word without meaning as Johnny could not avoid seeing and hearing every detail of the execution. They flashed before him constantly. Though it wasn't the sight of Connolly in his dreams that awoke Johnny. It was his loud voice. "Shoot straight, Johnny Flynn!" Over and over again until it became a refrain. Not a plea or a request but an order, stern and yet full of permission. Perhaps Connolly had known that he had needed help to go through with it.

He went to Emmet's to drown it out, but the forgetfulness found in a few pints only worked for a while, and then thoughts of the note in his jacket pocket would drench him in a cold sweat and soon have him shivering.

He was afraid to take the note out for fear that the temptation to open it would be too great. It was a piece of James Connolly's heart and meant only for his daughter, no one else. He had no idea where she lived or where she went to church or even if she was still in Dublin. And then at Emmet's early on the third evening of his leave, it came to him.

Visitors to Kilmainham had been required to sign a visitor's log when they entered. They could use an initial for their middle name but the rest had to be printed legibly and signed in full underneath. They had to give the time they entered and the time they left and they had to include their full address. For Connolly the Castle had by all counts been as much a prison as Kilmainham had been for Pearse. There may have been a log of some description.

Dahl reached across the table and clasped Johnny's wrist. "You're shaking, paddy."

"Something just crossed my mind."

"By the look on your face..."

Johnny could focus on nothing but getting to the Castle before the shifts changed at five. He kept looking at the huge Gaelic clock behind the bar and with only twenty minutes to spare he begged forgiveness and told Dahl he had to get back to the barracks.

"Would you be wanting me to accompany you?"

"No, no, it'll be fine. Stay and raise a few with the fellows when they get here. Tell them I wouldn't have been much fun, but between us I'm a pinch better now."

Out on the streets he hurried over the bridge to Bachelor's Walk, only to find himself back in the center of it all, surrounded by devastation on a scale so unsparing he couldn't have imagined a corner of hell so horrible. It all seemed designed to knock him off course. He slowed down and looked up river and felt sorry for the bombed-out houses. Their profiles seemed like a group of old rebels, waking stooped and stupefied in the shame of sunrise.

And then he saw the silhouette of the Statue of Justice standing high above the Castle Yard, the lamps beside her aglow placing an aura on her gown and past her the shadowed building with dozens of flickering lamps in the gothic windows, the dagger-like spires along the nave of the chapel piercing the darkening sky. His legs did not repent but pulled him forward toward the entrance where four privates were stationed. Hardly stationed, that is. Two were smoking and one against the stone sleeping, his shoulders hunched forward like a giant question mark, the other staring out at Johnny, but aloof, as if he was just another conscript who had helped win the war.

Johnny held out his identification. "I'll be but a minute. Once I guarded James Connelly and tonight there's a conclave of those who did."

"Think nothing of it, Sergeant. You're in the King's army. The Castle is yours," the private said.

Johnny grabbed onto the banister and took the steps two at a time. The paintings of long ago heroes had been removed from the Cathedral walls and chandeliers stripped from the celestial ceiling. He was aware of his boots skimming the rug, a hushing sound like a smoker releasing his breath in shame.

He reached the second floor landing and turned down the hall to make his way toward the Throne Room. As he approached the doorway the sound of planks being thrown upon one another startled him. Inside the room two laborers in gloves and coveralls, their faces covered with handkerchiefs, were dismantling Connolly's bed. A mattress stained with the old man's blood and waste rested upright against the chest-of-drawers. The bedsprings were propped by the window, the cage that had covered his leg next to them, upside-down like the skeleton of a giant insect. At the collapsed foot of the bed a wash barrel overflowed with soiled bed linen. The room reeked of death.

The workers noticed him. One stopped, put down his crowbar and leaned back on his heels. The other kept at it.

"Need help, Sergeant?"

"What are you fellows doing?"

"What does it look like we're doing? Orders from R.A.M.C., Sergeant. The old man had gangrene. Disease springs from it, they say. Mice and bedbugs were stopping by to feast on his leavings. Wouldn't suggest hanging around for any longer than you have to." The worker hesitated. "With all due respect, Sergeant, we shouldn't have shot a cripple, no matter who he was or what he did."

Johnny's eyes were starting to burn. "Did you happen to come across a visitor's log?"

"A what?"

"A book that visitors had to sign when they came to see him."

The men glanced at one another and shook their heads. "Best you see the nurse who was in charge. That'd be Nurse Meeks. She's got duty in the dispensary now. Down in the tunnels by the larder. But it's late. You might want to come back tomorrow."

Johnny rushed out of the room, trying to cough as he went down the stairs and through the tunnel into the annex. A dense glass door with a temporary sign strung across it that read *Dispensary* was lighted from behind. He opened it to the sight of an elderly woman with sparse red hair in a nurse's dress dusting the base of a footstool positioned at a counter. It looked more like a bar than a dispensary.

"Come for a need, soldier?"

"To see Nurse Meeks. Is she here?"

"Gone for the day," she said.

"What time does her shift start tomorrow?"

"Late morning. We aren't that busy now. Can I help you with something?"

He started to ask about the log when the door opened. "Sergeant? Sergeant Flynn?" Concern crossed Nurse Meeks' face. "Are you all right?"

"Yes, fine," he said.

She gave Johnny a hug. "I'm so sorry for all that happened. That poor fellow and his family."

"That's why I'm here," he said.

"What do you mean?"

Johnny glanced at the older woman and Nurse Meeks' eyes followed. "Hold on a minute, Sergeant Flynn, I forgot my shawl. Let me get it and then maybe you can lead me to the gate. We can take a moment there."

Johnny read her warning.

And there on the curb by the gate, out of earshot of the private who had gone to the alleyway to fetch a lorry for her, Johnny asked about the log without explaining why. When she didn't answer immediately, he thought that he would have to tell the full story. He began with the thought that Connolly had given him something personal but she interrupted before he could finish.

"I don't want to hear, Sergeant. It isn't mine to know. I thought the world of the old man and his women as well, and were I a man strong enough to hoist a rifle I believe I would have defended him to the end. But to your question, yes, there was a log, though General Maxwell sent his henchmen for it. It's probably either in the King's library or in his fireplace."

Johnny took a long breath.

"But I know how they signed, both his wife and daughter. They weren't trying to fool anyone, full names, plain as day.

What does it possibly matter now, unless someone thinks it wasn't them. Lord, I can't imagine even the Tommies being that stupid."

"Do you remember the daughter's address?"

There was a gleam in her eye, as if she understood at last, but the glimmer quickly faded. "'Twas the same for both women: 'Dublin'. That's all they gave," she said.

"Dublin? Nothing more? I thought they were required to..."

"It was my fault, Sergeant. I watched them sign-in and was well aware of the requirement, but I simply could not bring myself to ask for more, no more than I could bring myself to search them. Forgive me, if you will."

"There's nothing to forgive, Nurse Meeks. You should be proud of yourself for standing aside."

Once and for all he had to let go of any hope of ever seeing Nora and upon the realization, Connolly's voice hit him like a jolt of bad whiskey.

"May I offer you a ride, Sergeant?"

He barely heard. "No, no, thank you, Nurse."

When he stepped into the street his body seemed to chart a course of its own. Occasionally he bumped into a fence or wall and at one point almost stumbled over a group of men who were sleeping on the sidewalk, some steadied with their backs against a lamppost or a slab of broken concrete from the barricades. He stepped over and around them as if he were walking through a cemetery. The sound of boots scraping the cobblestones was broken by occasional shouts from the tenements cursing him or rats scurrying among the trashcans.

He came to a small gathering of destitute men and women kneeling outside St. Mary's. A priest stood amidst them crossing himself and saying a blessing. His voice spoke no definitive words, only a soft, muted flow, a song being sung to himself. A train blew its horn and the sound rolled into Johnny's ears like a volley from a distant cannon. He could only think that it was the tragedy of Cuchulain twice told raining down on him, the heroics over, the raven's beak deep in his shoulder draining hope away in a torrent.

Back at the barracks, he sponged off and fell into his bed. As sleep came he heard his father singing and watched as the two of them leaned against each other struggling through the streets of Dublin, his arm around his dad's shoulder. They wandered into a building and then into a huge room with a vaulted ceiling where his father told him to be quiet, that it was a hospital.

"But why are we here, Da?" Johnny heard himself ask.

"To pay our respects to that man," his father answered and pointed to a bed in the corner of the room. It was surrounded by a group of people dressed in black.

Even in sleep Johnny could feel his body strain to get a closer look at the man. Something in his head told him it would be James Connolly but it was his father, now vanished from under his arm and lying in the bed.

"What are you doing here with a rifle, son?" his father asked, alarmed.

"I came for a visit, to hear you sing."

"But I'm dying. I can't sing no more. I'm in too much pain."

"Then, I'll spare you that," Johnny heard himself say, bringing the rifle to his shoulder and firing.

The jarring of a boot kicking his ankle woke him.

"Flynn, wake up, you've got guard duty." Johnny recognized Staff Sergeant Egan's voice before his eyes came into focus. "What are you doing sleeping on the floor, Flynn? And for God's sake, cover yourself."

Johnny felt the hardness of the floor beneath his naked body and could not remember how he'd gotten there. "I dunno," he said aching as he scrambled to collect his uniform and jacket.

"Your leave is done, Flynn. You're being sent back to Kilmainham."

Johnny staggered to his knees and pulled himself onto the

bed. He buttoned his shirt and carefully slid his arms into the jacket, touching the pocket carefully, relieved that the note was still there. He sat with his face in his hands, wondering if he'd heard the sergeant right. "But there's no one left to guard," he said. "Don't tell me there're been more arrests?"

"Not that I know of. General Maxwell's overturned the rest of the sentences, the small ones, you know, for theft and such things we didn't quite have enough evidence for. Commuted over seventy-five of the bastards. But if he's changed his mind, I'd stand decidedly in favor of it. The people are stepping over one another to sympathize with the rebels now. I think it had to do with shooting the old coot in that chair."

A private in the shadows of the barracks chimed in: "Every rebel soldier, and I give them the benefit of the doubt, they now say was gunned down by us in cold blood. They say some of the letters the prisoners wrote are making it worse, not better like they once thought. Even the priests have turned against us."

Johnny remembered Donovan giving Connolly's benediction and lowered his head.

"Not that they were ever on our side, not so as I'd believe it," said Eagan.

"And the infernal, bloody requiem Masses for the souls of those who've been executed," the Tommy yelled back. "It's like witchcraft. I know you've been wandering out lately, but it changed practically overnight. Watch yourself out there. It ain't safe."

Eagan looked at Johnny as if he'd forgotten he was there. "Anyway, mate, you're to report to the jail at ten hundred hours."

"First Sergeant, where are the rebels buried?" Johnny asked.

The sergeant gave him a puzzled look. "Come again?"

"Where are they buried, the ones who were executed?"

Eagan glanced around the barracks, shrugged, and lowered his voice. "It's not exactly a secret, though they've told us to keep it to ourselves, so I don't suppose it won't do any harm to tell a fellow mate of rank. But listen, don't tell no one. It's the families, you see, they might want to dig 'em up and give them a respectful burial, seeing they're Catholics and all. The M.P.s took each and every one to Arbour Hill Barracks and threw them in a pit along the east wall. Threw them in without coffins, covered them with quicklime and filled the hole right away. No one will ever know their identities."

Johnny began putting on his uniform. Eagan started out of the room and then stopped, turning. "Not a word, Flynn, ya hear? You don't want to turn those graves into shrines, not now when the tide might be turning against us."

"Not a word, Sergeant," Johnny said, looking at his watch. It was nine-thirty.

He went around the barracks looking for Dahl and was told he'd just been posted to duty earlier in the night. The soldier couldn't say where. Johnny started to leave a note, explaining his assignment but thought better of it. He needed to hurry if he planned to go to Arbour Hill.

He expected to have to be on guard, given what Eagan had said and yet, although the streets were full of people, they were strangely quiet, mulling around as though his very own despair had descended on all of Dublin. They moved slowly, an occasional upturned face following him suspiciously. Many were simply loitering on a curb or in the middle of a street, gazing out over the ruins. They seemed to possess an innocence in the midst of all the destruction, looking as if they had been plundered through no fault of their own. He stepped up his pace, staying off the curbs as he passed by.

With each step bringing him closer to Arbour Hill, the melancholy began to lift slightly, as if something awaited him there, a key, a sign, something that would help clear his mind and set straight the day. For that, Kilmainham would have to wait.

Chapter Eleven

He put his head down and hurried on. He had almost made it to Usher's Island when he stopped in his tracks. Ahead of him four British soldiers were standing in the middle of a narrow street, rifles pointed at a woman being held against a brick wall by two more Tommies. It was a street execution.

He shouted and started running toward them. He heard one of the soldiers yell, "Fire!" But instead of a loud volley there was the muted click of the rifles and laughter as the soldiers let the woman go. She slumped back against the wall, struggling to scream. At last, just when Johnny thought she was going to pass out, she braced herself. "Bastards!" erupted from her mouth.

The word reverberated in Johnny's ears as he seized the man who had issued the order, turned him around and slammed a fist into his face. He had never hit anyone before. As his knuckles sank into the man's nose the soldier reeled back and with blood gushing out of his nostrils fell heavily onto the street. Johnny squared off with the rest of them, thinking he was in for the likes of a traitor's beating when they abruptly wheeled and fled. The soldier he'd hit struggled to his feet, slipped in his own blood, leaving his rifle, and ran after them.

Catching his breath, Johnny turned to help the woman and froze. Nora Connolly stood staring back at him with stricken marble eyes. He watched, holding his breath as she searched his face. His mind was deceiving him. The doors of reality had closed at last. Slowly, as if to test the ground beneath him, he stepped up onto the curb somewhere between alarm and fright, feeling like he was on a tightrope a hundred feet above ground.

"Stay away from me!" she said, her voice reminiscent of her father's.

Johnny took in her tautly pulled black hair and the green and gold ribbon pinned above her heart. "I'm not about to touch

74

you," he said. "Are you all right?"

"I know who you are," she said, inching along the wall as though slowly easing out from under his stare.

"I knew your father," he said and instantly the words sounded idiotic in his ears.

Her smile was bitter. "You knew nothing about him. None of you knew him. If you had he would still be alive, so don't tell me you knew my father."

Johnny held up his hands up in surrender. "I just meant I'd talked to him several times. I was with him the day he..."

"I know you were. Just say no more."

"You'll never know how sorry I am for what happened."

"Please be quiet."

They both fell silent. Her face softened slightly and despite his remorse, he couldn't help thinking how beautiful she was. There was a penetrating watchfulness in her eyes, as if she'd learned long ago never to be taken in. He didn't want her to leave.

"May I escort you somewhere?" he asked, cringing, the word "escort" sounding lord-like and British prissy. To avoid her look, he stooped to pick up the soldier's rifle and check the chamber. When he looked up her mouth was open in alarm.

"Here," he said, quickly setting the rifle on an angle between the curb and street. He brought his boot down sharply, shattering the stock. Leaving the pieces in the gutter, he looked at her. "I'm unarmed. I'll not be bothering you. I just thought, you know, in this part of town and all..."

She hesitated for a moment and her voice dropped to the same low register he'd heard at the Castle, a faint vulnerability flowing with determination. "I'm trying to find my father."

At first he thought that the horrors of what she'd been though had reset her sense of time, as well as his, and that she actually thought Connolly was still alive. But her eyes seemed to read what he was thinking and she added, "My mother and brother, we want somewhere to mourn him. It isn't right for the authorities to keep it from the families."

As soon as she said it he knew why he felt so compelled to go to Arbour Hill. He, too, was in need of a place to mourn.

"I know where he's buried."

She stared at him in disbelief, but there was a glimmer in her eyes, much like that of a child shown a magic trick. "Where?"

Johnny knew that to answer could mean a court martial or even possibly seed another rebellion but he no longer cared. "Arbour Hill Barracks, they say. There's a common grave for all who signed the Proclamation."

A brief, indefinable sound escaped her throat, and in a second she started down the street towards the quay. Johnny ran to catch up with her and grabbed her by the elbow. He realized it was a mistake as soon as he touched her. She jerked her arm away and turned on him, biting off the words, "Keep your goddamn British hands off me."

"But you can't go there. It's a military prison."

"I know what it is, and if what you say is right, you people have made it a morgue." She moved toward him slightly and he stepped back. "Before I'm finished all of Dublin will know, and there will be hell to pay."

"Don't. You'll just be making trouble. The Army will deny it and even if they're pressed, they'll simply move the bodies. Any chance of a final resting place where families can eventually go will be gone."

Her lips quivered and he watched, almost afraid to breathe, knowing she had to be hating him. Still, as her mouth took shape, he could not help feeling the same astonishment he'd experienced seeing her the first time. Her bottom lip slid out from under her teeth and she glanced at him. "My father thought you to be a decent man, even though he said you'd strayed. That was the way he put it, 'strayed.' For myself, I'd call it desertion."

He searched her eyes to see if there was any levity, any letting him off the hook, but there was none, and yet she'd continued the conversation. He didn't know where to take it, and in the chance she'd just given him he began to feel uneasy. After all, there really wasn't anywhere to go with her. Every moment beyond this was deception.

The note came to him. When he reached into his jacket pocket she stepped back. "Here," he said, feeling the crusty fold of paper for the first time. He handed it to her. "Your father asked me to give this to you. They forced you to leave the room before he had a chance to. I tried to find your address in the Castle log, but…this last week has been…"

"What has it been? Tell me," she snapped. "You are alive, no wounds that I can see and my father is dead." Her eyes returned to the note. She reached out and he placed it in her open palm, staring at it as if it were too precious to disturb. "What does it say?"

"I don't know. I haven't read it."

She cut her eyes at him. "You expect me to believe that?"

"It's the truth."

"It's a lie and you know it." But with that she clasped the note prayerfully between both hands, closed her eyes and kissed her fingers.

"It's stuck tight…" He stopped before telling her that most likely the residue from her father's wound had been responsible. "You might want to warm it somehow before you try."

She opened her eyes but held her vigil. "Perhaps sealed with candle wax after you read it?"

"I promise you, I haven't. I wish I could say more."

"If you could…if you could find it in your shallow British soul to say more, what would you call giving me this? Your so-called soldier's duty?"

Johnny thought of Connolly calling out moments before they shot him. *"I will say a prayer for all brave men who do their duty."*

"That's what your father would have called it," he said.

"And with all due respect to him, I would say that principle comes before duty," she said. "When the two meet, you're on hallowed ground. When they don't you're lying to your conscience, making deals with the enemy, as he used to say. Good day, Sergeant Flynn."

"I did not read it."

She went three paces and stopped, looking up at the sky as though she'd caught herself heading off in the wrong direction. She looked back toward him, but not at him. "When traitors appear to act with principle it is only a foil." Quickly turning she hurried off toward the city.

There was no calling her back for there was no rebuttal. He had acted more out of a need to see her again than any real sense of principle. He knew that. There would never be any way to breach the wall between them. He now knew that as well. It was as impenetrable as the one around Stonebreaker's Yard.

As he headed toward Arbour Hill, the despair returned, only it was much heavier now.

Chapter Twelve

It started to rain just as he struggled across the Liffey. Clinging to Nora's image like a drowning man to hope, his thoughts were pierced only by the occasional odor of the cobbles, a steely mix of grit and stone brought on by the eerie warmth of the rain. It smelled not unlike the cells at Kilmainham. Yet at the barbwire gates of Arbour Hill a wind was in play and the rain turned abruptly cold. A Tommy inside the guardhouse was lighting up but when he saw Johnny approach he quickly flicked the fag through a side window.

"Good evening, Sergeant. Can I help you?"

Johnny realized that he was in unfamiliar territory and despite his rank couldn't simply walk onto the grounds. He could see the soldier had twin chevrons. "Corporal, I don't have much time. I wonder if you'd let me pass. I was on duty here the other night and left a few belongings behind."

"In the prison or barracks?"

"The prison."

"That'll take some doing, Sergeant. They won't let you through straightaway even if you've been posted there, but you'd be knowing that I'm sure?"

"Actually, Corporal, I left my haversack, mess kit and all, outside, over at the East Wall, and I'm afraid it'll be ruined in this rain. A dumb thing to do, I admit."

The corporal glanced around and his eyes came to rest on Johnny. "The East Wall?"

"Aye."

"You came in with the ambulance?"

Johnny nodded. He knew exactly where the corporal's mind was headed. "Dreary morning, as were they all," he said. "The only thing cheerful was knowing the rebels were being laid to rest for good. My canteen is over there by the grave."

The corporal stroked his chin. "Christ, I heard you fellows digging. I heard more digging was needed as more was thrown under. Suppose you worked to the nubs. Wasn't deep enough, was it? Lord knows, Sarge, you done your duty and then some. Hold on a minute," he said. He bent down and Johnny heard a drawer shut. The corporal handed him a piece of paper. "Here. This will get you through – says you're here to pick up an order for quicklime. Show it to anybody who stops you, but don't tell them where you're going. I mean, we ain't supposed to tell a soul. This place has been vacated because of it. Quiet as a ghost in here. Far as I'm aware not one soul in Dublin knows." He laughed at the obvious. "Except those hovering over the grave, of course. But them I wouldn't be asking. Follow the road around to the back."

Johnny stepped inside as the corporal opened the gate and closed it behind him. The road in front of the wire was full of puddles and as he followed it, checking over his shoulder to see if the guard was back inside the guardhouse, he stumbled over a pile of rubbish that smelled like fresh horse manure. He tried to blow the odor out of his nose but it clung like smoke as he hurried around the corner of the building. There he stopped to get his bearings by sighting the smokestacks of the Guinness factory. Yes, he was heading east toward the wall. As he pushed ahead it began to rain harder and he thought of Nora wanting to come here. She would never see the inside of this place and probably never ever see her father's grave. As he came to the end of the building he stopped again.

He didn't know what to expect but this long rectangular depression of mud and water was not it. There was something brutally ugly and degrading about it, as if all the dead had been buried in a pigsty. He moved closer, knelt beside it and wiped the rain from his face. He reached out into water that covered his sleeve and brought up a handful of mud. As the water drained through his fingers, nuggets of lime were left in his hand. Rain much colder now was pounding on his shoulders but he barely noticed. He recalled Pearse's smiling face and Connolly's kind voice and as had been happening too frequently, tears welled up in his eyes, but again he could not cry. He thought about praying but couldn't find the words. What could he really say?

"Bless them, Lord and keep them safe? Watch over them and guide them? Let them enter the gates of Heaven?" It was all nonsense. In an impulse that came from nowhere, he brought his fists down into the water and whispered fiercely: "I'm sorry! I'm sorry for what I did!"

Repeating those words but mumbling now, he huddled over the water, arms tight around his knees. He watched the rain wash against the toes of his boots and closed his eyes, willing himself not to see or hear a thing. He began to shake and tightened his arms around his knees to keep from coming apart.

"Forgive me, forgive me, forgive me," he muttered and rolled forward onto his elbows.

He opened his eyes. From down this low the rain was hissing on the water and appeared as unending and turbulent as the sea. He thought of Kinsale Bay where his father had taken him as a boy and how once a storm had come up as they tried to go fishing in the channel. There were just the two of them in the small boat and his father had let go of the oars to hold him close to his chest as he shook his fist at the sky and screamed, "Don't you dare hurt my boy!" When the rain had stopped and they both were secure again in their own seats, his father turned so Johnny could not see his face and said in a broken voice, "We're even, Lord, you and me."

The rain was passing over the gravesite, and Johnny half expected some sense of relief to come over him. But it didn't. Instead, the water flattened into a shadow and slowly, as he sat back on his haunches, ashamed of himself, he looked down at the subdued surface. There was barely a reflection, only a dim shadow of his face. His heart sank.

Wet and covered with mud he began to walk down the path to the guardhouse.

"What in the world happened to you?" the guard asked.

"Couldn't find my sack and went digging for it. Thanks for letting me in," he said. The guard watched him curiously as he opened the gate and let Johnny pass.

"If it comes up, I'll call you. Where are you billeted?"

"Richmond," Johnny called as he stepped into the street.

He stopped at the Liffey and breathed deeply. In the distance the silhouette of Kilmainham looked forbiddingly dark. He wasn't going back there ever again. The puddles of rainwater between the cobbles reminded him of the streets in Birmingham the day he stole the ball. It seemed so long ago and yet so close. He wished he could go back, return it and tell Mr. Runney he was sorry. But what good would that do now? A wrong couldn't simply be wiped out with an apology.

He arrived at the barracks to find Dahl playing solitaire on the trunk at the foot of his bed. Dahl's hair was tossed from a toweling and his skin was steamed pink from a shower. He looked surprised to see Johnny.

"Christ, what happened to you? You been out all night rolling drunk in the rain?"

"No," Johnny said, coughing and realizing for the first time he was shivering. "I fell. 'Twas stupid, slipped trying a shortcut by the Green."

"You'd better get a shower. Nobody's around so the water's good and hot. Hey, come to think of it, what were you doing at the Green anyway? Your name's posted over on the wall as being on duty at Kilmainham."

Johnny glanced at a piece of paper hanging by the door. "Yeah, well...I'm here for now."

"You go take your shower and then come sit down and play a hand. I just got the rest of the day off. Was only at Boland's Mill for the morning. I dunno, they're running us all over the place maybe just to keep us busy."

The cards reminded Johnny of the lieutenant who had put him on the firing squad. "Give me a few minutes."

After a shower and shave he returned in a fresh uniform. It felt good to be warm and clean but he couldn't let go of Nora and Arbour Hill. As he sat down on Dahl's trunk he wondered what his friend would say if he told him what had happened.

As they picked up their cards, Dahl asked if he was feeling any better now.

"Some," Johnny replied. "I was colder than I realized. The shower felt good."

"I don't mean that, Johnny. I was referring to inside here," he said, tapping on Johnny's chest. "The melancholy you seemed to have the other night."

"It's better, I think," Johnny said. He fanned his cards and folded them, laying them on the trunk. "I'm not sure, though. Early this morning it was as heavy as I've known it and then seemed to lighten some on my way to Arbour Hill."

Dahl glanced up from his cards. "What the Devil were you doing at Arbour Hill? Peter Hughes – remember meeting him at Emmet's bar a while back? Well, every other night he stands guard over there and says it's empty now, except for an occasional ambulance."

"There's been an occasional ambulance all right," Johnny said. "But no patients. I can assure you of that."

"Well then, what were you going there for?"

Johnny stared out the window and tried to find the words to tell everything, but his mind was too jumbled.

"Do you have a cigarette?" he said.

"Johnny, I don't smoke and neither do you. What do you want with a cigarette?"

Johnny paused. He had to chance it. Dahl was his only hope. "Have you heard the rumors about Arbour Hill?"

Dahl shuffled the cards. "That it was for crazies until they were moved out to make room for the Sinn Feiners, the real crazies, who took our men down as they poured out of the Royal Barracks on Easter? That what you mean?"

"I don't mean the Prison."

"Johnny, forgive me, but you're talking in circles. Here…" he said and leaned back to reach under his pillow. He pulled out a pint of Jameson's Whiskey, took off the cap and offered the bottle to Johnny. "Let's get a head start on Emmet's."

"Not a bad idea," Johnny said, feeling grateful and taking a swallow. He handed it back and wiped his mouth on his sleeve. "I meant the graveyard."

"What are you talking about?"

The words came in a rush. "The rebels we executed, we buried them in a mass grave at Arbour Hill. Those were the ambulances Peter's been seeing. He either knew or didn't tell you or maybe they never told him. They don't want it known around Dublin."

"Damn, I'd just thought they kept them at Kilmainham."

"Buried them under quicklime so they could never be recognized."

"Jesus, defaming the dead."

"I don't know. I just thought it might do some good if I could see it. Maybe shut the door on all this. I talked myself in. The guard, he knew. It was raining, and I knelt in the mud, that's why I was such a mess." He reached out for the whiskey.

"Did it work? Did you feel anything?"

Johnny took a swig and gave the bottle to Dahl. "I don't know because there was something else that made it really strange."

He told Dahl about running into Nora and the mock execution the soldiers had put her through. He kept quiet about the note. Rather he found himself telling about the night he first saw her, how she stood in her father's dying presence with her eyes filled with so much pride and compassion. He had responded with as much love as anyone could possibly put into a voice, saying how proud he was of her and how she was now freedom's torchbearer.

Johnny went on, fast now, pausing only to find exactly the right words.

"I want to do something for her, Dahl. I want to take her to his grave."

"Jaysus, Johnny, you can't do that. You're the bloody enemy! She'd probably run a knife through you if she had half a chance. Get hold of yourself, mate."

"But I came to her rescue today. She knows I wouldn't hurt her. She'd chance it. I know she would."

Dahl leaned forward, chewing on a thumbnail. "Suppose you got caught. They'd put you up against the wall as fast as that," he said, snapping his fingers, "and it would be the real thing, Johnny. If they didn't shoot you then and there, it would be a certain court martial and the ruin of you! And they'd probably put her in jail for ten years."

"But if I don't help her, she'll try to go on her own. I'm sure of it. She's that way, her father's girl through and through. She'll have no chance going it alone."

"And for all that, what would you be getting out of it – the Pope's blessing? Come on, Johnny, you're not making sense. The war, Kilmainham, they've got to you and they're not letting go."

"It's true. They did for a while, until I woke up. They're still weighing on me, but this could be a way out."

Dahl took another swallow and set the bottle on the trunk between them. "It's a way in for certain, into trouble as big as you've ever had, Johnny."

Johnny picked up the bottle and sat there holding it between his legs. "I have to do something to help her."

"What do you propose? Are you prepared to knock on her front door and tell her you've come to accompany her to the old man's grave?"

"Aye, I am, but there's a slight problem."

Dahl took the pint out of Johnny's hand. "I'll say there is and it's more than slight!"

Johnny looked at him. "It's not that. It's that I don't know where she lives. I went to the Castle to ask Nurse Meeks as she oversaw the visitor's log. She told me the Connolly women had signed only Dublin as their home address and said that she, herself, had been in too much despair to require them give more. Nora was about the quays when I saw her, but she could have set out from who-knows-where. If I knew I'd gladly risk my life to take her to his grave."

"Your life? That's a bit dramatic, don't you think?"

"Look, Dahl, I shot her father. The very least I could do by way of the smallest pardon is take her there. If I could do this one thing, I might at least be able to live with myself."

"Do you mean by that, forgive yourself for something that you could do nothing about?"

Johnny reached out and put his hand on Dahl's shoulder. "But I did. I did have control, only I chose not to use it and there stands my fault, grievous to the end. I sanctioned Connolly's death and mine."

Dahl sat down on a trunk at the foot of his bed and wedged himself between his locked arms pressing stiffly down on the brimmed lid. Leaning forward slightly, he seemed to be turning something over in his mind. The window light was quivering on his face as his eyes returned to Johnny.

"She lied," he said, the words oddly soft.

"What? Who?"

Dahl glanced toward the roof. "Forgive me, Nurse Meeks, and God bless. Lying is a poor choice of words." He returned to Johnny. "The good Nurse Meeks was only doing what I have been trying to do since that day, to protect you from yourself. But as of what I'm about to tell you, now it's for you to do, and you alone. There is no more help to be given."

"What are you talking about, Dahl?"

"The Connolly's address was there in full, I saw it meself, Number 54, Pimlico. I remember thinking how strange they would live on a street with the same name as a London borough. Down from St. Stephen's, I believe it is. There, goddamnit, it's out of me system at last, and given the likelihood that you'll soon be on your way to your own final resting place, I'll be able to lift a tankard to your soul without feeling I'm any longer hiding something from you."

"I don't know how to thank you."

"Best you don't, given what you're in for."

He knew that he had to ask for one last favor, though it could well end their friendship forever. But without it, he had nothing to offer. He looked Dahl in the eyes, hesitating.

Dahl leaned forward even more. "Yes? Out with it Johnny."

"Can you persuade Peter Hughes to help me? He must have keys."

"Christ Almighty, Johnny, that would put quite a burden on him, to say nothing about the chance of placing you on death row alongside him – and by God, me too if they put the screws to him."

Dahl was right, no argument to be had, but there was a slight concession in the tone of his voice that suggested he had known this was coming.

"Would you try?" Johnny asked.

Dahl placed his hands on the trunk and straightened, staring at him. "I don't know why, Johnny Flynn. Maybe because I hate all this as much as you." He smiled again. "Who knows, but if it will help rid it from your mind short of being stood before a squad, I'll try. He's off duty tonight. No doubt he'll be at Emmet's."

* * *

When they met up with Peter, they stood talking away from the bar, broadly away from the reason they'd come, pulling the whole of the Rising and its aftermath this way and that. At first it was all banter and nothing more – Peter swearing he'd never again set foot on Irish soil and Dahl tamping down his real feelings to keep the mood as friendly as possible, saying only that he might like to return someday, "Maybe years from now when things are settled. I prefer the whiskey here." As Johnny listened, he began to realize that no matter the circumstance, he was leaning toward never leaving. It had come to that.

Two hours later and deep in their cups, Dahl finally brought up Connolly's execution and moments later turned to Johnny. Johnny took the cue and without hesitation he told the entire story, everything from the execution itself to his running into Nora, constantly watching Peter's eyes to gauge how the story was playing. When he finished he thought he'd failed to convince him and fell silent.

"Tell me again how you shot him," Peter said. His voice was low, and surprisingly controlled given the amount of beer he'd drunk. "You say he was tied in a chair and was dying anyway?" He shook his head in disbelief.

"Yes."

Peter shook his head again. "I just thought it was all talk, and here I sit with ye who done such a horrible thing."

Johnny stared down at his ale.

"How do you live with yourself, mate? Granted, I surely didn't like the bastard, none of the sods, but to tie a dying man into a chair and blow his heart apart ... there's something wrong with anyone who'd do that. Or am I missing something here?" He turned to Dahl. "Maybe there's something Johnny hasn't explained, something that would make it right, like maybe James Connolly set fire to a school full of children or maybe the bastard admitted he was the Devil Incarnate. Throw something like that in for good measure and maybe you can convince me it was all in a normal day's work."

Johnny thought of trying to explain that Connolly had actually blessed his own death and encouraged him to be an accomplice. But he knew Peter would never understand that. He brought the glass to his mouth, wondering whether he did himself. He set it down and interrupted Dahl who had launched a tirade in his defense.

"It's why I need your help, Peter. It's the least I can do for his family."

It was clear Peter was shaken by his outright admission of guilt and now this bizarre request. Johnny glanced at Dahl, but his friend did not look back. Rather he reached out and clasped Peter's forearm. "Open the gate for the old man's daughter. No one will ever know. You'll be doing the right thing, Peter."

"But how can you possibly find her again?" Peter asked.

Dahl glanced at Johnny.

"Connolly's address was in the Castle log at the nurse's station."

Peter's eyes bit into Johnny. "If anything happens I'll deny everything. Is that understood?"

"It is," Johnny said.

Chapter Thirteen

Johnny stood at the door of Nora's apartment, holding a rucksack. He set it down to knock on the door and after a wait, knocked again. Faintly, behind the lace curtains, she came creeping down the dim stairway. Her pale arms and a silver heart hanging between her breasts seemed to float against the darkness of her black skirt and blouse. She looked through the peephole and quickly shut it. The door cracked open just enough for her to stare out at him. "What do you want?"

"It's urgent." It was all he could think to say.

When she opened the door a bit farther, her face was cast in shadows and she seemed more mystifying than ever. She did not look at him but past him out into the street.

"You can't be seen here," she said, glancing at the rucksack and edging the door to a slight crack. "Say whatever you came to say and go."

Johnny was tempted to leave. Maybe when all was said and done he was not bringing relief but more anguish, anguish heaped on top of anguish as Nurse Meeks had said. But it was not his to decide, so he held on, whispering. "I came to take you to your father's grave."

"What?" she gasped, pressing her fingers to the heart-shaped pendant. The door drifted wider.

"You'll have to put these on," Johnny whispered, offering her the bag.

She drew back as if he'd handed her a snake.

"It's a uniform, the smallest I could find. I've arranged to get us in, but if anyone saw you – or a woman of any description – there'd be hell to pay for both of us. It'll have to do."

"A British uniform? Have you lost your mind?"

"Do you want to go?"

"Not like this, not with you."

"Unless Maxwell has a change of heart toward the families, you will never have another chance."

Her eyes widened. "Not bloody likely, that," she said, looking directly at him for the first time. He felt the bag being lifted from his hand.

"Wait at the corner."

After half an hour watching bugs swarm into the broken gaslight, he heard footsteps behind him. He turned expecting to see a clownish figure in a baggy uniform, but she had carefully fitted the uniform so that she appeared every bit the soldier. Her hair was up under the cap and somehow she had folded the shoulders of the jacket so that they flowed to her elbows. The burdensome sleeves were neatly pinned back and she wore the heavy men's gloves. Only the corporal's chevrons appeared too large, but not clumsily so, wrapping around her arms too far, like brocade. Even the pants appeared to fit, turned under to break naturally on her riding boots.

"What are you staring at?" she said.

"Nothing," he said. "How did you get it to fit so well?"

"My mother helped me."

"You told her?"

"Yes and asked her to come but she simply could not bring herself. If that bothers you, too bad. So far, this has been on your terms." She stepped into the street, speaking to the cobbles. "Let's go," she said, stopping at the far curb where there was no light. When he approached she quickly slipped a hand into one of the huge jacket pockets and drew out a pistol, pointing it at him.

"I swear to God, if this is something other than what you've said, I'll kill you and the consequences be damned."

"You won't be needing that," he said, recognizing the Smith and Wesson .32 caliber, one of the three weapons Countess Markievicz had also carried, which he had put under lock and key before she was released from Kilmainham.

"Walk ahead of me," she said, motioning with the gun.

He headed down Pimlico listening between his footfalls for hers. They came, filling the silence with hisses. After a few blocks along the quays he wondered if she still had the pistol drawn and could not resist glancing back. She was closer than he'd thought, about five paces when they reached Bridgefoot Street. Although he could see the outline of the gun in the pocket, he wondered if she was imagining her father in the ruins of the G.P.O., his leg blown to pieces by a stray bullet – maybe his bullet or Dahl's or even Peter Hughes', but in pain anyway, crawling back to the post he'd deserted to save a young soldier.

Johnny wanted to go back to her, so he slowed down at the entrance to the Mellows Bridge hoping she would choose to catch up. When she got closer, her hand was in the jacket pocket. Stopping, she glanced at the water and then at him. He took a step up on the bridge to give her suspicions some distance, then moved another step away, waiting for her to speak. He felt like he should perhaps tip his hat and excuse himself – that she would prefer to go on alone but suddenly she yanked her hand out of the pocket and grabbed the footbridge railing, looking around in desperation.

"Miss Connolly?" Johnny said.

"I have trouble crossing bridges," she said, her voice faint. "I can't look down."

He stared at her in alarm. He didn't have a notion what to do. If he went closer she might draw the gun, yet, clearly, she was asking him for help.

"You'll be all right. Just follow me and keep your eyes on my back," he said, hoping some assurance would do but the worry on her face only seemed to intensify. "Come on, now. One step at a time."

She was still looking down at the water, her eyes fixed in terror as it sloshed against the river wall. As he searched for another suggestion, her voice lost its reluctance and slipped away, low and full of embarrassment. "Would you take my arm?"

As she searched his eyes for a reaction, he stiffened. Her eyes caught the glow of the bridge's gaslights and froze. He moved slowly toward her and took her arm, half expecting her to jerk away or pull out the gun but she did neither, taking a step alongside him as he lifted her. Their eyes met at the top of the stairs but only briefly. He thought he saw a concession, that finally he'd passed some test of faith she'd been putting him through. But as soon as they were off the bridge she yanked her arm away without a thank you, yet now she didn't ask him to walk in front of her. Instead she walked beside him and even set the pace, allowing no hesitation or any suggestion whatsoever that she was bound by anything but a burning sense of purpose.

There were times when Johnny found himself falling behind, even having to step quickly to catch up. As they crossed Manor Street, she slowed, breathing hard. Yet she was right beside him as they approached the main gate of Arbour Hill.

Peter was in the guardhouse as agreed, but he could not disguise a look of disbelief when Johnny said quietly, "We're here, Peter."

Peter's breath reeked of cigarettes as he ignored Nora and whispered to Johnny, "If someone comes, you're on your own. I'll deny I ever knew you."

"Understood."

"And another thing," he said, so they both could hear, "I'm only doing this because I'm a friend of Dahl's, not for any love of Ireland. Each of you understand that?"

"Aye," Johnny said.

"Not even a wee bit?" Nora said, sarcastically.

Peter glared at her. "Not even a goddamn wee bit," he snapped. He glanced up at the sky and then at Johnny. "The clouds are breaking. Come in and be quick about it. And remember, this is the first and last time."

Johnny looked up and down the street. "Okay," he whispered and Peter opened the gate. Johnny reached out to guide Nora around the concertina wire but she had already stepped inside.

"You know the way. Now, off with you," Peter said. As they moved down the road, he said in a low voice, "You're fools, the both of you."

They walked without speaking. By the time the grave appeared the moon had broken through, casting a sheen on the crests of mud that seemed to roll over the long shallow pit. Nora moved toward it with caution and Johnny dropped back, wondering if he should stay with her. It came to him that he was intruding in her private affair and that she had to be given the freedom to say, think, or do what she pleased. He was about to look for a place to go but still stay in sight when she took off the cap, dropped it on the ground, and shook her head violently, bringing her hair down over her shoulders. In the same motion she took out the gun and stepped to the edge of the grave, clasping it by the chamber and holding it as if she were displaying it to a crowd.

His first thought was that she was going to shoot herself and the word "No!" was already in his throat when she swore, "As God is my witness, I will carry on your fight in this world, on the path of my choosing, as you entrusted me. Freedom has no price too great. I am, as appointed, your Sarosa!" With that, she plucked the gun out of the moonlight and plunged it into her pocket.

Johnny waited, unable to take his eyes off her. With the moonlight gleaming on the surface of the grave, she seemed like a siren on the bank of a river, freshly raised from the water but still cast in a light from another world. The uniform appeared even more fitted than earlier and with her shoulders set straight she seemed every bit a soldier. Her hands now rested defiantly on her hips, reminding him of the way she'd stood at her father's bedside lost in his eyes. Steadying herself with a hand on the ground, she knelt by the grave's edge and began to sob. The lone woman soldier became a girl many years younger.

It surprised Johnny to see her so vulnerable. She began to cry so hard her head and shoulders pitched forward toward the grave. Her hair seemed to float on the mud. He thought of himself beside the pit and wondered if she was having the same thoughts but a moment later realized she had come here out of love, to mourn, whereas he had previously come out of guilt, to seek forgiveness.

The crying came to an end and she stood up, brushing her hair back and tucking it into the collar of the jacket, the way she'd worn it at the Castle. She picked up the cap and tucked it under her arm and came over to him.

"There was no one like him," she said. "When I was a little girl he trusted me with messages to the boys, no one else, not even my mother. Once, when I was sixteen, he sent me all the way to Drumcordia with a message for intelligence. I was stopped three times and strip-searched once. When I told him about it, he cried, the only time I ever saw him cry, and told me what a fool he'd been, asking me to take such a chance. When I begged him to nonetheless let me help the Cause, he finally gave in, saying he guessed he had raised the likeness of himself, God forbid."

It was her mention of delivering messages that forced the words out. "The note from your father, were you able to open it?"

"You mean you want to know what it said?"

"No, I just wanted…"

"The answer to both is none of your business."

She kept on, her voice hesitating in places as she recalled her father's speeches, her emotions becoming charged as she quoted his views on the merits of the labor movement and socialism. While she spoke Johnny thought he liked far better her vulnerability by the bridge and here by the gravesite. The politics confused him and played with his brain in a way that made him nervous and wanting to leave.

A half moon hung in the deep night and the air was turning chilly. As Nora continued, her voice began to careen faintly off the walls. When she paused, it threw him. He had not heard the last thing she'd said and wondered if she had asked him a question.

"You cannot understand because you are British," she said.

"I was born in Cork."

"That's even worse; it makes you a traitor."

He wanted to defend himself, wanted even more to grab her shoulders and shake her. "It's time to go," he said.

"I will never leave this place." Her eyes were intense in the moonlight. "It took too long for my father to get here. Besides, I am his messenger."

"Come on."

"They wanted to commit him to a lunatic asylum. They tried often enough. They declared him bankrupt and sentenced him for not being able to pay his debts. In the end they had to shoot him like a wounded animal."

Johnny's words came so fast they surprised even him. It seemed he couldn't say anything right and he went on nonetheless. "He wanted it that way. It served his purpose. Now, come on."

It stung her. He could see that, but even if it was a cruel thing to say he tried not to care. Silent now, she followed him to the gate. When Peter bade them goodnight she paused to say a muffled *"Thank you."*

Johnny walked her home in silence. About a block from her flat she stopped and glanced at him. "I'll be fine from here," she said and put her head down. "He did want it that way. That is one thing you were right about." Her head turned away and she spoke with difficulty. "I don't know whether to love or hate him for it. But I know this: it is the British who will pay." As if not wanting to end that way, she looked at him.

"You are an Irish man, not an Irishman."

"I'm not so sure your father would have agreed with you."

"That would take some explaining, Sergeant, and I'm sure neither of us has that much time." She hesitated but then went on. "You have done me a great kindness and though I never intend to return it, I want to say I am appreciative."

She held out her ungloved hand and he took it, letting it slip through his fingers before he had a chance to clasp it properly. The finality of her words hurt as he watched her walk away in a rush. He glanced at his palm and brought it to his nose but there was no fragrance, only a light freshness as if a feather had landed there. As she hurried across the street, he followed so he could see her profile against the nearest gas lamp, but there she halted, as if she'd forgotten something, and looked off toward Saint Patrick's. Something in her expression suggested to Johnny that she felt she had made a mistake in being so harsh, but offering no more evidence than that, she lowered her head and moved quickly into the shadows.

He started back to the barracks, telling himself it had been stupid to think he could find any sense of forgiveness in her eyes or in her voice by taking her to the grave. She had thanked him, but even that had been cold and formal. And yet she had touched his hand.

The wind began to blow and black clouds gathered, leaving a vast and dark sky to remind him of his own waning hope of putting things right for her. He felt empty and dissatisfied but most of all, foolish. But that was easy to remedy. He never had to see her again. And the guilt over her father's death? Maybe that would lessen over time.

He had just about convinced himself all this was true when he heard her voice some twenty feet behind him. She was panting and he was amazed he hadn't heard her boots on the cobblestones. "The uniform," she said. "I forgot the uniform. I don't know how that happened."

He realized he had overlooked it as well. "Me too," he said. "Might give you a bit of protection wearing it?" As soon as it was out of his mouth, he wanted to slap himself.

She glanced at him and the thought flashed in his mind she might tear the uniform off and throw it in the street, her exposed body be damned, but instead, she did something equally shocking: she smiled. It was only a flicker on her lips and it vanished right away, but even so, it lingered in her eyes. He found himself smiling back, cautiously. Then she lowered her eyes. "I'll change and meet you at the same corner," she said.

Johnny walked slowly to give her time and wondered what he could say that might make her want to stay longer when she returned. It came in a flash. Ireland! Of course, Ireland! He would ask her about Ireland. Struggling to keep the cadence several paces below his enthusiasm, he stumbled over a loose cobble and almost lost his footing. It reminded him to slow down and he forced himself to take several deep breaths before continuing. He did not see the rucksack at the corner until he was almost upon it and it was only after he drew closer that he saw the note pinned on it.

"We are grateful for what you have done, but please, never approach our doorstep again." She had signed with her initials.

He stared at the bag, feeling like a mule had kicked him in the stomach. He'd wanted to see her again. He picked up the bag and started to leave when he recognized her shadow in the upstairs window. The curtains moved almost imperceptibly, as if she'd been looking out and had just let them go, he thought, but then told himself he might be seeing things. It wasn't much but still it rushed in to help fill the disappointment as he crossed the street and walked away blindly, headed toward the barracks through the awakened rain.

His boots stuttered down Cathedral Street and briefly he thought of Pawth Durbin, wishing he had a pair of his soft-soled ones. He turned on Marlborough. A few people were out and as he approached their voices grew silent. Eyes turned away but when he passed he could feel them on his back. At the corner of Hawkins Street a rock sailed over his head and slammed into the door of an abandoned house. He almost wheeled but kept on toward the barracks, thinking that to fight back would be like fighting a bad wind.

The flames in the wrecked streetlamps sizzled as he passed and their glow dimmed as he went on, reminding him of how Pearse had described the dusty throw of the angel's lamp. A pack of ragged children saw him and ran for a cover in a barricade of overturned lorries and twisted steel. He watched them disappear into the pile of junk as though they had been swallowed up by some mythical, villainous forest.

Johnny set off again, moving rapidly toward the barracks. The rain became an odd comfort until he thought of Arbour Hill and Nora kneeling by the sea of mud, her pistol aloft and the pledge she'd made to her father.

Chapter Fourteen

For his failure to show up for duty at Kilmainham he was confined to the barracks until further notice. He had trouble dealing with the vague and uncertain length of his confinement. Playing cards and sitting in on a few conversations occupied him for a few days but then he began to keep his distance from others, often lying alone on his bunk, looking up at the ceiling and out the windows across the room to the gun rack where the Lee-Enfields were kept under no lock. He thought of so many dead and his trips to Connolly's grave; he thought of the execution and still heard Connolly shouting directly at him, but he thought mostly about Nora.

But as the weekend approached, her face had become a blurry abstraction, with only fleeting glimpses available, the strange curl of her upper lip and the peak of her hair, the tiny vein above her temple and the pitch black of her startling eyes. But the pieces never came together as a whole. It was as though she were an animal moving through thick brush along the edge of a road.

He told Dahl about their visit to the grave, couching it almost as a humane courtesy he had extended her. He wanted to say more, wanted to tell his friend about the excitement in his heart at being with her, but the realization that he would never see her again made it pointless. And there hung the ever present weight of her father's death, especially when Johnny drank alone, for it was then, sitting on his bed wrapped in a blanket, unable to visualize Nora, that the old man's voice cried out the loudest. When it came, he did everything in his power to put both of them out of his mind. He drank more whiskey, played cards through the night and even did push-ups to the point of exhaustion, but the more he reacted, the more it haunted him.

As the hours passed, it began to feel like Kilmainham. And like at the prison, he had to get outside into the air, soiled as it was, no matter the consequences. It was easier than he would have suspected because the barracks guard had been gone for hours and as far as he could tell they had appointed no one else to guard him. Most likely due to what Dahl had told him about everyone getting shuffled around from post to post, some even being sent to the outer provinces. So he put on his uniform and headed for Emmet's, saluting the guard at the gate who asked if he would bring him back a Guinness.

Inside, Emmet's was a labyrinth of pathways through tables, booths and counters. Tonight it was teaming with soldiers. Cradling pints of black Guinness and shots of whiskey, they reminded Johnny of a scene straight out of Braley's. Squinting into the haze of cigarette smoke, he played two long games of whist to the laughter and banter of soldiers he did not know and afterwards excused himself to take the last vacant bar stool and drink alone. Four stouts, two whiskeys and the singing of Ina O'Railly, the barman's daughter, relaxed him some.

As her surprisingly soft voice floated in the room, he began to sing. His voice was not as good as his father's but he could carry a tune, especially *The Fields of Athenry*, which he knew by heart. A dull light fell on the piano keys but Ina's head was back and her eyes closed. There was a deeply felt grace in her voice, as if she'd lived every word, and judging by the silence of the room it was clear that it touched everyone else as well. A warm and gentle sense of joy came over him as she went into the last refrain and he saw, or thought he saw, the words drifting like soft liquid through the rafters at Braley's.

"Johnny Flynn," a garbled voice said in his ear. Dahl slumped down beside him at the bar. "Whiskey," he called to the barman, "and make it a double." There was a bruise over his cheek and his right eye was swollen shut.

Ina's voice disappeared into alarm. "My God, now it's my turn, who hit you?" Johnny said, surprised that Dahl could talk.

"It ain't as bad as it looks," he said glancing into the mirror.

"Jaysus, who's that staring back at me?" He spoke no more until O'Railly placed the tankard in front of him. Before he took a swallow he tested his jaw, moving it back and forth, then swallowed the slush and downed the glass in gulps. "Another," he called out through a grimace that caused him to grab his jaw.

"Dahl?"

"Come a bit closer," he said, gently squeezing the corners of his mouth and whispering through pursed lips like a ventriloquist. "I got a bunch to tell you."

"That can wait, Dahl. Just have your whiskey. We can talk tomorrow."

"It can't wait, Johnny. Move closer."

Using his hips Johnny nudged the stool a couple of inches closer. Dahl glanced at the mirror. His eyes roamed the room. "Closer yet, mate."

Johnny stood up and slid the stool together. When he sat down their shoulders were touching. "What is it then?"

"The rebels are getting letters out to their families, telling how they've been treated," Dahl said, wincing and rubbing his jaw with both hands. "Aye, that's better." His voice was slightly stronger now. "Lots of them been beaten, had their ribs kicked in and the like. The food is rotten and the guards piss in the drinking water. I was sent over to Marlborough where a hunger strike is going on. One of them died today. He was an old man, but Johnny they just let him go. No effort to do a thing about it. That's how I got this hickey."

Dahl bent to the glass and sipped without raising it to his mouth. He straightened, grimacing. "I tried to sneak him some fresh water and a guard kicked at me, yelling I should let him die. The old fellow was just sitting there, barely able to move, cradling his boots in his arms like they was his children or something. Just sitting there, whispering, 'Jimmy, little Jimmy,' over and over again with his cheeks tucked between these boots that had soles made of something like goose feathers and straw."

Johnny grabbed Dahl's arm. "What was his name?"

Dahl's look of surprise forced his hand away. "Got no idea, Johnny, he was just one of many. They didn't have no name tags."

"Was it Durbin, Pawth Durbin? Does that sound right?"

Dahl drew back. "What are you talking about?"

"The old man's name?"

"Johnny, I told you. I got no idea. All I know is a lot like him are going to die. We've become a bunch of fucking animals, you think?"

It had to have been Connolly's mentor and friend, Johnny thought.

Dahl's eyes were glassy. For a second Johnny assumed it was the pain in his jaw and then realized it was far more than that. He answered Dahl's question. "Yes, we have. We're animals."

Dahl struggled to keep his voice low. "Sooner or later there's going to be another revolt. Rumor has it, it's already brewing in County Cork. The call for unity is everywhere, on walls – on the cobbles, even." There was pain in his voice but the words poured out. "The Brits have gone mad. They're getting ready to ship the worst of our soldiers, the felons and drunks, the cruelest they can find here and abroad, the fecking crazies and send them off to Cork in droves to kill and disable at their will. They're called the Black and Tans. Maxwell wants to overwhelm the Irish, put them to rest by the score. *'Like 'twas done here'* is how the paper quoted the bastard."

Johnny vaguely remembered what Connolly had gathered from Durbin, that in waging war when the numbers were indefensible a different form of warfare was needed. *Scatter their limbs in the streets*, is what he'd said. A shadow drifted into the mirror behind the bar.

"Did you hear me?" Dahl said. "They're using it to call for unity, Johnny, so they'll keep it up regardless and that after we lost over a hundred thousand at the Somme, I heard. Some victory!"

Johnny's hand was shaking so he could barely get the drink to his mouth. Some spilled as it touched his lips and he set it down. He looked around the room and his demons rose. He could not keep them tucked away anymore. His eyes stared into the swirling mirror. For a moment Connolly's image coalesced and stared back at him. For a moment Johnny went rigid and then jumped off his stool, clenched his fists and shouted: "Shoot straight, Johnny Flynn!" He flung his tankard at the mirror. Glass flew everywhere. People screamed and took cover, thinking it might be a sniper or a drunken soldier off his limb. Even Dahl ducked behind his stool.

Everyone in the place stared at Johnny as O'Railly yelled, "Get the hell out of here before I goddamn brain you!" He turned to Dahl. "You there, get this numskull out of me bar!"

Johnny heard something altogether different as Dahl took his arm and led him outside into the deafening silence where he recalled Connolly's order, but this time it came not as a sudden thunder from the Yard, but by choice, for now he realized that not only had the order been intended for him, but for all of Ireland as well.

Johnny looked at a plaque to the heroic Emmet nailed to the side of the building and read the inscription written by the ancient hero: "Let no man write my epitaph ... When my country takes her place among the nations of the earth, then and not till then let my epitaph be written."

"You all right to be walking, Johnny?"

"I need a minute," Johnny said, barely aware of what he was saying but knowing that the caretaker's hand had shifted from one to the other.

Johnny wrapped his arms tight across his chest, trying to keep himself together. Something in the air reminded him of that instant just before Connolly shouted out. He'd felt it before, a sense of bridging two moments in time, being in two places at once, that split second before one fell into the narrow space between life and death. Maybe they all had, all the rebels who had faced certain death, as well as countless others he had never known.

"Johnny, it'll pass. Whatever's got hold of you will pass."

"We'll turn them back, Dahl."

"Johnny, let me go with you."

"Connolly spoke to it. He knew all along. And it wasn't with a thousand troops."

"Johnny, we'll get each other back to the barracks."

Johnny knew Dahl was probably right, that each needed the other but at the same time, he had to be alone. "See you back at the barracks," he said and started to walk away. It was his burden, not Dahl's.

"Could I follow you?" Dahl called out. "I'll keep me distance, I swear."

"I have to be by myself," Johnny said, moving away. He listened for his friend's footsteps and hearing none, he felt relief and slowed his pace. Looking down the empty street, all that he had witnessed seemed to shift in meaning. He saw Dublin not as much a victim of merciless destruction but much as he'd seen his mother, a slumped figure of sadness and pain, sickness and suffering. It seemed to him that only in the midst of it all, in this cellar of human nature where aloneness ruled, might there exist some hidden truth that would help him understand what he was supposed to understand but did not and maybe never would.

A fast flowing stream of the dead crossed his vision, all in tones of sepia, like daguerreotypes, his mother and father, Pearse and Connolly, the young boy with a bullet through his eye, and others only imagined, like Mona and Pawth Durbin. As he approached the Green at Trinity College, the images came to an abrupt halt.

An open motor car rumbled past with two British officers sitting as straight as pelicans. At the entrance to the College the car skidded to a stop, brightened its lights and the one-armed driver jumped out with a rifle, leaned across the hood and took aim. Johnny spotted his target. Showcased in an open window on the top floor of the building, a frail, blonde woman was hanging from the sill dangling a long white banner that appeared to have been cut from a sheet. The bold green letters read: "Free Ireland!" He could not see her face nor she that of the Brit aiming at her.

"Don't!" Johnny screamed but his voice was deafened by the rifle shot. Before either sound had disappeared, the woman's arms seemed to reach out toward the banner as it fluttered toward the Green. She slumped over like a puppet whose strings had been snipped. As the driver stumbled back into the car, the officers cheered and patted his shoulders and amongst the celebration they sped away.

Johnny felt an abrupt separation from all that lay around him, a loneliness that seemed to set him apart from the human race and for a moment caused him to wonder if he could spell his name. He felt tears building behind his eyes, the same tears that had crept up on him when he looked through the Judas hole into Pearse's cell, the very same ones that pushed against his pupils when he had knelt in front of Connolly's grave or watched the Tommy put a match in the dead boy's ear – tears he had never once been able to shed.

He wanted to run to the woman but there was no point. She was dead and in all likelihood there would be someone hurrying to get revenge. He put his hand on his pistol but then let go. There was nothing he could do. He scanned the Green. It was empty and still. His eyes went to her again. Blood was streaming down the walls of the building, forking at a lower window like a river split by an island.

A few citizens were beginning to come out of their houses and mill about, staring at the woman and at Johnny. As he slowly backed away, he could feel their hatred and didn't blame them. Some lit cigarettes and stood smoking in place, keeping their eyes on him like they might a mad dog. Others pretended to stare into the distance, ashamed that they were too afraid to take revenge.

On their faces he could see the toll the Rising was having on everyone.

"There'll be no more killing!" he wanted to call out, even more than wanting to tell them that he had not shot the woman. But instead he pulled his cap down and moved cautiously to the far side of the street unsure of what they might decide to do. Despite his worry he could not make himself run and stepped up onto the curb unable to make sense of his feelings. He was afraid and yet he wasn't. Neither was he cocky because of his uniform nor was he banking on their fear to protect him. It was something else, perhaps at last some grain of truth in the suffering, a whisper inside his head that said he was not alone, neither in his fear or his innocence. It was neither a commutation or a condemnation. In truth he did not know what it was.

He turned the corner for the barracks but did not pick up his pace. Within the space of two blocks he stood before the entrance. Four soldiers sat playing whist, boasting, smoking and drinking from tankards set on a bloodstained Irish flag draped over a large flat stone. A sergeant waved Johnny over with his pint. "Here, mate, for all you do!"

Johnny rushed past them into the barracks, stopping only to flash his card at the guard. Clutching his stomach to staunch the agony, he hurried to his room. If he could only be in another place, a world where he could befriend the poor Irish souls taken from this one and not have it considered treachery.

Chapter Fifteen

Later that night Johnny packed a lifted rucksack with his skivvies, two wool shirts, a pair of printer's pants, a knife, a razor and some thread to sew together the rips that would surely follow. Since arriving in Dublin he had saved a good portion of his pay, for there was no place other than Emmet's to spend it, and he stuffed the handful of shillings into the sack as well.

The barrack was nearly empty and the few Tommies present were asleep or too drunk to notice. He was tempted to leave a note for Dahl explaining what he was about but he didn't want to put his friend into what could turn out to be a horrible position.

He left his pistol in its holster at the foot of the bed and his rifle in the gun rack. He walked out, telling the guards that he was on his way to Kilmainham for duty. When one asked about the whereabouts of his uniform, he said that they had taken the lorries off the streets for the safety of the horses and ordered all off-duty soldiers to dress as a local for the same reason. He held up the rucksack.

"It's in here."

A block later he put a match to his military card and disappeared quietly into the streets.

He went by Nora's apartment. The windows were shuttered. The gas lamp on the corner was now out, its hood smashed flat by hooligans, most likely. The heat of its extinguished flame rose into the darkness like a leak in the night. He stood looking at her door, wishing it would open. *This was it,* he thought. But there never was an *it*. *It* had only been in his mind. As for Nora, she'd probably never think once about him ever again, and maybe it was better that way.

After a few steps he looked back toward her apartment. It may have been the heat rising from the lamp or his desperate hope that she was watching or perhaps the unshakable look in her eyes

108

when they met with her father's. It resurfaced for an instant, as if to suggest that perhaps she was watching him, following him to the grave. He was tempted to knock on her door, but something nudged the night toward Kilmainham and away toward the hills.

As he stared he became lightheaded and the moment seemed to somersault beyond him into tomorrow. The realization came without any warning whatsoever, not unlike a dream or a streak of lightning on a cloudless night. It bore no sound, only a heart-wrenching conviction: without forgiveness there could be no freedom. And yet forgiveness had to be earned – earned by something beyond contrition and guilt, beyond asking or pleading, beyond the dispensation of the confession booth. Earned by giving up far more than had been gained from the transgression itself.

His father had not attempted to earn forgiveness in any way. He had been too weak, too in need of an excuse to continue his unfaithfulness rather than face his cowardice – and Johnny's mother had doled out the excuses, giving license to his treachery. He was not his father and would never be.

He continued to the highway. Avoiding the lights he hurried down into the ravine between the hedges and the road. He wasn't sure where it ultimately led but knew that it headed west, toward the rebels' new front in County Cork, where, he trusted, there lay a chance for redemption. If they would have him, he would give to them what he had learned; there was a way to overpower the enemy in an outnumbered, posthumous world.

Part Two

County Cork

"Many times man lives and dies
Between his two eternities
That of race and that of soul
And ancient Ireland knew it all."

– Under Ben Bulben, W.B. Yeats

Chapter Sixteen

In an eatery close to Maryborough, after a short conversation with the owner during which Johnny ordered a corn beef sandwich and asked for use of the facilities, the man put aside the loaf of bread he was carving and with a suspicious scowl came right out and asked which side he was spying for. When Johnny stood there mute, recognizing that any option he chose was but a flip of a three-sided coin, the owner of the bar jabbed a finger towards the door and told him to go piss in the wind and never come back, shouting as Johnny rushed out that a coward's silence could not be trusted.

Hiking westward from small town to small town, pub to pub, he made every effort to hide his accent, masking it so heavily with resurrected brogue and a rasp he had picked up from the winds that it reminded him of Pearse's struggling voice. He was aware of the stranger's constant danger, that of being branded a traitor regardless of whether he was Irish or British. There were spies on both sides and either pedigree was equally susceptible. If the lineage itself fell into question only subtly the elusiveness would be enough to warrant a beating at a minimum. If the doubt were great, one could easily be shot through the head and fed to the crows. And the doubt was intensifying on both sides as the Brits were sending spies into the hinterland.

But he pressed on, culling out what bits of information he could about where people stood, always afraid to show his hand as none showed theirs, suspicious as they were of a stranger. Mostly he tried to connect at night in the bars, carefully threading his way through furrowed brows and enquiring glances, all the while afraid to press his luck until he came upon that one individual about whom he felt doubly sure. The idea of never seeing Nora again kept percolating in his mind, as did her father's voice and together the three of them moved warily toward the heart of southern Ireland.

To save as many shillings as possible for the bars, he slept in the fields, in barns, in the shadows of burned-out British mansions, in the crumbling remains of long ago churches and graveyards of the forgotten, pushing onward as the trees turned their fall colors. He was vigilant to stay clear of any British troops and their surrogates, especially the ungodly Black and Tans – the drunks, the convicts, the worst of the so-called British soldiers, the thugs who were so poorly regarded they were not even allowed to serve on the Continent any longer. So many were rumored to be on their way to assist the Royal Irish Constabulary that there was not available a common uniform for all. So they were required to serve in their uniform of origin, mixing the tan dress of many with the black of others and thus the name. But foremost to be dealt with was the Constabulary, the feared Irish police force that in fact was an arm of the British troops. All three damnable uniforms, those of the Tans, the R.I.C. and the regular army were easily recognizable, even from a distance, but it was their sudden mixed appearance in a bar or on a street corner that worried Johnny most of all.

The constant danger wore on him. He felt as if were limping across a bridge that was narrowing at the far end and would soon squeeze him into oblivion. The confines became so real that he often found himself extending his arms to push against the bridge's taper, and yet, as his brogue washed away all but a hint of his accent, the sense of isolation strangely began to steel his purpose.

The moment came at last. It was late one night in early September at Buckles Pub in Tipperary, where perhaps two dozen men's belts were hanging loosely from the rafters by their buckles. They swayed when he opened the door, clattering softly as they slipped on the nails. Johnny closed the door behind him and the sound settled quickly, as though the belts just remembered that their purpose was to stay still so that they might more accurately size up a stranger when he entered.

The room was sparsely filled. Two men sat in the corner, playing twenty-five, and two more to their right, smoking fags and arguing. Johnny seated himself next to an older man whose labored breath rode on the smell of mildew, causing Johnny to wonder if he had just been let out of prison. Though the dim candlelight veiled the fellow's features, in the mirror his eyes shone bright green under a head of dark red and gray hair.

"Pardon me, Sir," Johnny said, watching the man's eyeballs move near the corners.

"What is it, lad?" His thin, purplish lips barely moved.

"My first time in the pub. Could I ask you about the belts above and how they played in naming the place Buckles?"

The man turned his head and studied Johnny for a moment. His eyes were buttery and veined like a map. "Where might you be from?"

"Cork, by birth, but Dublin since I was a toddler."

"Dublin, a good place to be from." The emphasis was on the last word. It seemed to turn the man's statement into a subtle question.

Johnny tried to smile a smile like a wink that would encourage the old man to keep talking, to perhaps move past the tacit question or maybe back through it to show his true leaning, but instead a silence rose between them. Johnny watched his neighbor's placid face in the mirror and when the man motioned to the bartender at last, he decided to stay on the same path.

"My da moved us there when I was four. He needed work." Johnny paused. "He passed a while back." The man's eyes drifted to his, meeting them in the mirror with a nudge. "I'm going home in search of what he left behind," Johnny added.

"And what exactly would that be, lad?"

Johnny's mind was racing. He was tempted to stop playing games and answer firmly, "Redemption, you fool," but he knew that if he did, his life could end up in the man's hands. "His past," he replied.

The fellow was quiet for a bit, as if he were trying to sort through Johnny's answer. "Dublin for twenty years or so? Maybe that explains the inflection. I'm told a bit of British accent stirs the Dublin air. It must settle on everyone in due course." His hand and his eyes went to the rafters. "In answer to your question, lad, they'd be the belts of the dead hanging there," he said. "The Irish dead, that is."

Though it sounded like it came from deep inside a wound, the word *Irish* carried a tone of both pride and shame, not unlike that of Johnny's father. Realizing that he might still be out on a ledge, he dug down and with an effort of deep will, took it upon himself to ask, "By 'the Irish dead' do you mean the rebels?"

The man slowly picked up his glass, finished it off and set it down, wiping his mouth with a sleeve. He looked up at the barman who was standing by the cash register, nodding as the dim light shifted on his bald head.

The man raised his empty glass to the barman. "A shot of your finest, Owen, and one for this Dublin lad as well." He faced Johnny squarely. "The answer you seek is in the glass to be poured."

The barman glanced around the room and keeping his eyes on the door, reached under the counter to fetch a dark purple bottle with no label. He poured two tumblers to the brim and returned the bottle to the shelf, then carefully slid a glass in front of each of them. Leaning back against the far counter, he rubbed an empty tankard with his apron and pretended not to look at them.

The man slowly lifted his glass to Johnny and then to the rafters. "To Buckles."

Johnny lifted his as well. "To Buckles."

"Have your whiskey, lad, and tell me what you think of it."

Johnny brought the glass to his lips warily, wondering if his buckle was the next to go on high. He placed his bet and let the whiskey touch his lips, closing his eyes and swallowing. Waiting for a gut-wrenching, telltale reaction or at least the familiar burn as it went down, he experienced neither. To his surprise he found himself circling his mouth with his tongue, over his gums and cheeks to savor the incredibly smooth aftertaste. He had never tasted whiskey so pure. He finished the glass in two swallows and set it down, stifling his breath as the taste played out.

"I've never had anything like it," he said, glancing at his bar mate whose eyes seemed to smile. Johnny held his glass out to the bartender. "Another for us both and I'll stand for it."

"Do you know what you're ordering, lad?" the old man asked as Owen refilled the glasses.

Johnny drew back, feeling his face go rigid. "A whiskey, I hope?"

The man leaned toward him and lowered his voice. "Better than that, it's poteen."

"Poteen? What the hell have you…"

The man quickly brought a finger to his lips. "Keep your voice down, lad, and put a lid on your worries. Poteen's home brew, known in America as mountain dew. It's the best Irish whiskey there is, maybe the best in the world, made from distilled potatoes and grain by county locals right in their back yards, well, if their yards are out of sight of the Constabulary, that is. It's been declared illegal by the British government. They've got a stake in our commercial makers, the big ones, like Guinness, even in the small ones, I hear. The Brits only want us drinking what they can take a share of." He smiled. "Like I said, the answer's in the glass."

Johnny lifted his head toward the rafters. "The buckles, they belonged to rebels."

"Aye, and we to them, for they died on our behalf, and yours, unless you've been lying to me."

"I haven't been lying."

"The truth is sealed in your tone, lad." The man's eyes went to the rafters, followed by his glass. "They died for all of us, for your ma and da as well."

Johnny raised his glass, drank from it and smacked his lips. "But the police...the Constabulary, why don't they..."

"Close the place?" Owen offered.

"Yes."

"Because they think we are on their side and stupid enough to believe I'm hanging the belts in honor of their killings, in celebration, if you will. They think it is a grim warning to all who might be thinking about taking up arms against them."

Johnny began to feel even more comfortable, as did his drinking partner, who finally gave his name as McCulahy in a manner that encouraged Johnny to give his. The poteen cleared McCulahy's bad breath and moving the conversation gradually, he began to speak more assertively of all things Irish, building in tone and content from the Troubles to the Famine to the British land grabbers as well as the locals who admired their riches and wanted to live next to them in a munificence blessed by the King.

And then, as if the evening was hitting a crescendo, McCulahy rapped sharply on the counter with his knuckles. With a careful look at the door, Owen took a candle from beside the cash register, lit it and sat it directly in front of Johnny. At the same time, McCulahy pulled a piece of paper from his jacket, unrolled it and handed it to Johnny below the bar.

"Read fast, lad, and then give it back. If a copper comes in and sees you with this, you'll be buggered with a riding crop and then shot between the eyes – if you're lucky."

Neither of the men said a word as Johnny carefully unrolled the document and began to read the Irish Proclamation:

"IRISHMEN AND IRISHWOMEN: Ireland, through us, having organized and trained her manhood through her secret revolutionary organization, the Irish Republican Brotherhood, and through her open military organizations, the Irish Volunteers and the Irish Citizen Army, having patiently perfected her discipline, having resolutely waited for the right moment to reveal itself, she now seizes the moment...in full confidence of victory."

It went on for another two hundred words but Johnny had barely gotten beyond the first paragraph before his heart was pounding. He finished and his eyes rested at the bottom of the page. There were seven signers. He had known all of them but none stood out so grippingly as those of Patrick Pearse and James Connolly. Cold chills ran the length of his spine as he read the treatise again and shuddered.

Now, for the first time in his life, he thought he understood the confusing sadness in his father's voice that called out on Ireland's behalf when in the same breath he cursed her, and it seemed to explain his mother's insistence that they not move to England, despite how she had been treated by the Irish who did the British bidding in denying her care. In a surge of excitement he thought he might even be beginning to understand what those who insisted on dying for Ireland all knew. It came to him without words. He had done the right thing in defecting and it mattered not what anyone thought or believed.

As he continued to stare at the paper, McCulahy reached over and slipped it out of his hands, quickly rolled it below the bar and tucked it into his shirt packet.

"From the beginning I sensed I could trust you, lad."

"And I, you." Johnny replied and hesitated, lowering his voice. "I want to join the Volunteers. That's why I'm here."

"Now who would these so-called Volunteers be, lad?" McCulahy asked through a half-smile.

"The ones called upon in the Proclamation," Johnny said. "They're forming. I've heard the rumors."

"There are rumors and then there are rumors. It all depends on what you want to believe, some of them are preposterous. The telling don't necessarily make it true – or does it?" McCulahy said. "Maybe over time myth becomes truth, like with Cuchulain? Surely you're familiar?"

"As any Irishman should be. That given, can you help me?"

"Do you believe in paying revenue to the King?"

"Of course not."

"Or to the manor house?"

"No."

"And why aren't you fighting the Hun?"

"Because I'm here to fight the English, by God."

McCulahy kept looking into his poteen. His voice dropped more and he drew up close to Johnny. "If you really want to be part of the cause, lad, find your way to County Cork. There, the battle has begun. That's where'll find the past you're looking for."

"Who do I see?"

McCulahy took a drink and then spoke just above a whisper, "Sean Buckley. He's in charge of the Bandon Brigade."

"Bandon? Why not Cork? It's closer."

"You ask a question and then you question the answer, lad. You do that in the presence of Sean Buckley and you'll be on your knees in a second. Bandon, because though it's in need of men, it's the best organized, the First Battalion it's called. The Third Cork's okay, but history has shown they're softer down there. When the children were dying of hunger back in '46 and '47 not one feckin' Englishman was killed for it, not one. Michael Collins is from there, so you wouldn't rule them out, but it's the lads in Bandon you can really count on." He looked at Johnny over the rim of his glasses. "You're thin, but you look fit. You gotta be fit, lad, or one look at you and they won't let you in."

"Can I say you sent me?"

McCulahy's eyes bore into Johnny. "Don't offer unless they ask you and even then make sure Buckley's present. Between here and there don't mention my name to a soul. If it gets back to me you have, I'll hunt you down and kill you myself. Names are like code and my job as a recruiter is to do the best I can to send along fellows who can be trusted to die for the Cause, if need be. But down there they do the real investigation. Do you hear what I'm telling you?" Before Johnny could respond McCulahy continued. "If there're the least bit wary of your story, they'll kneel you down and put a bullet in your brain. So, get me name straight, the first one too. That would be Eoin, Eoin McCulahy. Can you spell it?"

Johnny thought the better of trying to break McCulahy's stare and spelled out the name. McCulahy smiled. "Now, let me do the honors and stand you another before you go and stand for us all."

Chapter Seventeen

Half-sotted but aglow with inspiration, Johnny headed for County Cork and Bandon, about sixty miles away. He used the main road from Dublin as his guide but traveled on it only at night. Whenever lights approached he jumped off the road and hid. When the moon was out and there were no clouds to hide him, he traveled in the fields, sleeping in a bedroll he'd bought in Carlow and washing his one change of clothes in streams and lakes.

He made his way around the Galty and Knockmedown Mountains; down through Fermoy and Tallow, and smaller towns yet, whose names he had never heard before. And increasingly the low, local voices adopted a higher key, allying with that of Eoin McCulahy. More and more they spoke about a wave of turbulence swelling in the east, rising on stories of British cruelty being met with Irish determination to exact revenge. There were even stories having to do with the souls of the dead rebels – Pearse and Connolly being the most mentioned. It seemed to Johnny that they appeared wherever hope needed resurrection. And that included him as well, only he saw their images somewhat differently, floating above Nora, sheltering her with a ghostly cloud as she ran toward him at last.

Anger focused on the Royal Irish Constabulary and the Black and Tans. In the fertile valleys beyond Cork, as he drew nearer to Bandon, the talk became the most hostile, for as McCulahy had warned, there the British had a stranglehold on the land and their grip was tightening with the addition of the Essex Regiment, the crazies from the Continent who killed for fun and games. Not only were they garrisoned there more strongly than in any part of Ireland outside Dublin, but they had successfully aided in ridding the land of pure Irish power and recycling it into the hands of the Anglo-Irish. In time it had even crept into the backcountry.

One evening on a dirt road near Cork, he stopped at an abandoned shanty, a round, sod hut with a roof of torn thatch. With its windows off-kilter and the door open on one hinge, it looked like a badly beaten Irishman. In the small yard pieces of broken furniture lay amongst scattered stones and bundles of dry brush. An empty chicken coop with broken nesting shelves lay tucked into the corner of the yard. But in the middle of it all was what caught his attention: a small apple tree near the coop. A half dozen apples lay scattered on the ground. He had not eaten all day and could taste the apples as he made his way toward them. They were wrinkled and slightly mildewed but for the most part still contained their color. He was bending over to retrieve one when a man appeared from the shadows of the egg house.

He was gaunt, his back curved like a bow. His trembling lips were white and lay open as if a shout had begun but not yet emerged, but then words came riding on a croak that sounded like frogs at nightfall. He cradled a dark red Irish Terrier in his arms and hugged the animal tighter as they came to a halt. "Take all you want but leave us be."

"I'm sorry, Sir," Johnny said. "I didn't realize anyone lived here...I'm just passing through on my way to Cork."

"To meet your regiment?"

"Regiment? If you mean the R.I.C....no. I'm an Irishman." Johnny realized there was no retracting it.

The man turned to the dog and kissed its nose. "We're safe, Eveleen." The pup did not flinch or respond in any way. The hair on its tail shifted due to the light breeze. Only then did Johnny realize the pet was dead. "You can have every last one of them apples. I grew them for Eveleen here. She liked the skins. Only animal I ever saw who did." He jostled the pup and smiled. "I couldn't bring myself to bury her. She was all I had and I loved her like a child. Still do. We sleep inside. There ain't no bed anymore and they ripped up the blankets but they cover us. I bundle Eveleen in one and pray for her to wake up in the morning, but I know she won't – the Constabulary seen to that. Hope is a trick God plays on us all. Take all you want. We're going for a walk now."

"The Constabulary killed her?"

"Their murderers for hire, the Tans or the Essex. Three of them come here with a killer Dobermann. Said they use them to sniff out the I.R.A. According to them, the rebels got a certain smell like scallions in garlic is how they put it. They couldn't find none here, so they knocked down the chicken house, busted up our furniture and said they was prepared to make a deal. Put Eveleen in the coop against the Dobermann. If she gets out alive, they said she'll earn her freedom. I told them she didn't stand a chance. Couldn't they see Eveleen was a terrier and terriers were gentle, kind dogs. She wouldn't even know how to fight. And they said, well then, it must have been seen to by a higher power."

"Jesus Christ," Johnny said.

"Might have been Him. At any rate they said they'd shoot her, if I didn't go along with it. Just when I asked them to shoot me instead they grabbed Eveleen and threw her in the coop. Before she landed that Dobermann jumped over the chicken wire and had her in his jaws."

Johnny put his hands on his hips and stared at the ground. "Like the bastards were using her for bait."

The man petted Eveleen, smiled as best he could and sniffled. "But some good did come of it. What the vermin didn't know is that a terrier, while it ain't no match for a Dobermann, has a killer instinct buried under years of being kind and obedient. You could have ten of them and never see that side but it's there, down deep. Well, Eveleen spun out of his jaws and nipped an artery in his neck. Blood poured out like a sluice and that Dobie started fighting with himself, biting at his own tail and legs. Then all of a sudden he went stiff and was gone."

Johnny felt like cheering.

"And what did Eveleen do? She went over to him and nudged him to wake up and licked at his wound like she was nursing him. They shot her for it. This no-good bastard pulls out a pistol and shoots her in the heart." The man kissed her nose again. Tears were tumbling from his eyes.

"Would you want me to...may I...bury her for you?"

The fellow squinted through his tears. "Time will come and I'll manage when it does, but thank you for your kindness. There is something, though."

"Anything."

"If you ever see a Tan with his dog, kill the bastard and feed him to the animal." The man turned and began to walk away.

Johnny started to run after him. It did not seem finished, there was more he wanted to say, so much more, though he had no idea what it was, but he stopped when the man disappeared behind the henhouse. After staring at the ground for a while, he made his way toward the main road, passing a woman clad in ragged shawls. With long blonde hair she reminded him of the woman in the window at Trinity College. She glanced up and moved to the side of the path to let him pass. Johnny wanted to tell her she had as much right to the road as he did but knew it would be a meaningless gesture.

He had been on the road an hour when a group of British soldiers on bicycles came up behind him. He knew it was too late to jump into the hedges and held his breath as they passed to his right, two columns, in perfect formation. For a moment he recalled the precision with which he'd been made to march and perform close-order drill in basic training, the rifles in perfect "present arms" mode just before a concise slap and switch to the shoulder, held there for an officer's admiration. *The British seemed more regimented than even the Hun*, he thought.

A moment later he heard a lorry approaching. He forced himself to stay on course, but his heart kicked in. The sound grew louder and he wondered if the driver was trying to run him off the road for the fun of it. A voice shouted, "Stand where you are!"

Johnny kept walking but caught the glimmer of a pistol in the corner of his eye. The voice barked out again. "I said, stop, or you'll be stepping into the ethers!"

He heard the soldiers on the lorry laughing. The words played to their enjoyment when the driver shouted again. He thought the voice had progressed too far to be of any real threat, but then again, maybe they were laughing at the bastard, in which case a bullet through Johnny's brain would show them he meant business. Johnny stopped abruptly and turned to the driver, a sergeant in a black uniform, the likes of which Johnny had only seen once, on the driver of the lorry outside Trinity College. The man's face was vast and resembled a dry pumpkin. His sweaty chin hung to his chest, pulling his tiny mouth into a slit. He kept the gun on Johnny as he stepped out. Another Tan in the passenger's seat yelled for the men in the rear to stay put and then came running around the front of the lorry.

"You hard of hearing?" the driver yelled, poking a stubby fist at Johnny's chest. As Johnny staggered back the driver jumped at him and stuck the gun into his neck.

"Your identification?"

"I don't have any," Johnny replied. Before he could say anymore he felt the sharp sting of the driver's hand across his face. Again he stumbled back but was determined not to give the Tan the satisfaction of rubbing his cheek.

"Where you from?" the man demanded.

"A small farm a few miles back. My folks were sent out for not having the rent. I went to try and find a few things for them."

"Back there? The stick and stone hut with an old fuck who carries a dead dog?" The sergeant from the passenger's side said, smiling. "I'm told that terrier bitch killed one of our best Dobermanns." He turned to his men. "That little bitch got what she deserved, don't you think?" They nodded and laughed.

More than anything Johnny would have loved to have carried out the farmer's wish on the Tan, but he fought it, knowing he would be trading his life for an emotional pledge and little more.

The driver leaned toward him, coming within inches of Johnny's face. "Lugging a dead dog around...if you people weren't so goddamn stupid, things like that wouldn't have to happen. I ought to kill you for being so fucking dumb, but a pistol whipping will have to do for now."

Johnny tried to cover his face but the butt of the man's pistol struck his jaw. Unconscious he crashed into a hedge. When he awoke it was dark. Bells were striking the inside of his skull. His jaw hurt so badly he was afraid to move it. Instead, he tested his face with his fingers. Red bolts streaked across his brain. He tried to open his eyes and almost panicked when the moon showed through one but not the other. He wanted to reach up and touch his battered eye but was afraid he would find his eyeball missing. He heard a fox or a dog howling in the distance – he couldn't tell which – and knew he was deaf in one ear.

When he licked his salty fingers he knew he was licking blood. When he ran his fingers over his jaw the pain was fierce but the bone didn't seem broken. He traced the pain toward his ear and discovered what had happened. His jaw was unhinged and formed a ledge half-inch wide.

On the verge of tears he knew he would very likely go into shock if he didn't stop the pain. He had to do something and do it now.

With that he placed his hand against the left side of his face, chin in palm, and then pressed against the other side with his free hand, bracing his head. He tried to force his jaw to move back where it belonged but the pain was too great. He dragged the rucksack up onto his chest and bit into the canvas. In one motion he grabbed his jaw and snapped it into place as pain ripped through his head. He wasn't sure what transpired next. It was a confluence of things that made no sense: fireworks flashed on the backs of his eyelids or on some distant horizon – he couldn't tell which – and he heard his own cry dampen into a whimper. He told himself the soldiers would be back if he didn't shut up, but he couldn't stop sobbing. He was like a child bent over a log and whipped bare-arse with his father's belt. He sobbed in great gulps but strangely there were no tears. Sweat ran down his collar and as the wind came up he started shivering.

He lay that way until nightfall. The wet ground soaked through his clothes, warming him by bringing down his fever, or so it seemed. With his body virtually tucked into the ground, an image of Nora came to him, her dark, haunting eyes searching and scolding, as if she had just found him in the hedges and didn't know what to make of it. She bent over him and he could see she was holding a lantern. Its aura seemed to be hemmed in by the darkness. In one corner of his mind he was certain he was dreaming and wanted to rise up on his elbows to make sure but couldn't will his shoulders to move off the ground. The light began to fade and she came closer, rain pouring from her coat, her pistol in hand.

"You killed my father!"

Johnny tried to jump out of the way and discovered his hands were tied behind him. He tried to yell but nothing came out as she raised the gun.

"No!" he shouted at last and in a flash she was gone but the lantern was still there, moving back and forth, coaxing his eyes to follow. When a hand touched his forehead the glow came into sharp focus but nothing more. He raised his head and tried to look around but the hand gently forced him back onto the ground. A lean closely-shaven face that reminded him of Dahl came into view. Concern flowed in the man's eyes. He raised a finger to his lips.

"Stay down," he said, setting the lantern on the ground. He lowered his head to Johnny's chest, listening. "Your heart's strong. Can you speak?" Johnny could see the bolt-action rifle across the man's back and tried to clear his throat.

"Here," the fellow said, taking the cap off his canteen and barely touching it to Johnny's lips. "Not too much now," he said, letting the water trickle over them.

Johnny coughed and he took the canteen away. "Better," Johnny managed as he moved his jaw slightly. It hurt but he could tell it was associated with the dislocation, nothing new.

"Don't think anything's broken," the man said. "You want to try and sit up?"

Johnny tried to say yes, but had to settle for a slight nod.

The man put an arm around his shoulders and eased him upright. Johnny felt like his head weighed a hundred pounds. His eye was still out of focus, but he didn't want to go back down. "I'm okay," he whispered.

"Let's get you off this road." With that the man moved behind Johnny and lifted him under the arms to drag him into a ditch and prop him up against the side. He went back for the lantern and knelt holding it in front of him. "Looks like you got kicked by a horse."

Johnny felt his lips crack but his attempt to smile was turned back by the pain. "A Tan's horse, it was," he murmured.

"What happened?" the man asked, then stopped himself. "I'm Billy O'Neill," he said, catching Johnny's glance at his rifle. "For hunting. It's good in these parts. Let me see that cut." He brought the lantern so close Johnny had to close his eyes.

"You need a few stitches above that eye or else it's going to keep opening up. Close to Cork's a place that can help you. Friends of mine. Reckon you can walk?"

"Think so."

Billy helped him to his feet. Johnny shook off his arm and began to waver. The whole world was moving before him, slowly at first and then it gained steam. Treetops swirled and the gamey odor of algae from the bog and maybe even the smell of bad whiskey all mixed to take him to his knees.

Billy was at his side. "You don't have the strength and you've got a fever, too. I can feel it from here. I'll go for the others. Let me get you behind a hedge."

Johnny reached out for Billy's shoulder and clasped onto it. "I can make it. I swear."

The dark blue eyes bent toward him and narrowed. "Why not?" Billy said, lifting him. "Better to die on your feet with a friend than in the bush alone I always say."

When they came up over the ridge, the sky dissolved from evening blue to black and they seemed to disappear into their own shadows. They kept moving and somewhere on the ridge the air turned to chimney smoke and Johnny's nose began to twinge. Johnny kept jerking his boots from the mud wondering how much longer he could last. As they continued downhill the lantern flickered, spit and went out. They slogged from the bog into a meadow and for a moment he felt that he wasn't even on the ground.

He heard the wind sighing under eaves and the baying of dogs as they passed a big house with a huge chimney stack. Billy pulled him faster and when he almost fell, the grip on his collar tightened and Billy jerked him roughly. "It wouldn't do for me to leave you here," he said. "An Irishman torn apart by British hounds. It simply wouldn't do," he said in a mocking English accent.

"But I'm a red terrier," Johnny said, smiling inwardly, realizing Billy probably thought him insane.

How far and for how long they stumbled along, Johnny never knew. But soon Billy was rapping on a door and Johnny saw the faintest light on his boots and the floorboards of a building beneath them. There was a fire and the sound of feet scurrying about, followed by a deep woman's voice.

"Why did you bring him here, Billy? He could be a spy for all you know."

"A spy beaten within an inch of his life by Tans? I don't think it likely. He might not be one of us but he's no spy. If he is, by Christ there's easier work to find. He needs your help, Shannon. I'll take responsibility."

A man called from another room. "She's right. You're bringing trouble to the devil's den."

As the room filled with laughter, Johnny felt himself being lowered onto what he took for a table. "I'll need hot water and clean rags," the woman said.

It sent people scurrying again and their voices became a jumble of urgent noises. Johnny's eyes opened, or he thought they did, but it was like he was trying to look through a fog. As he tried to twist onto his side, a rag came down over his face and his body rebelled at the first whiff of chloroform.

He surfaced into chaos. Something poured across his forehead and dripped down into his eyes, burning as if they had been pierced by thorns. Someone tried to make him swallow a brew that smelled like whiskey but he refused to open his mouth and felt a heaviness he'd never known before. There was nothing left of him. He wanted only to sleep. To sleep for hours and days, perhaps forever, but instead he slept for a night and a day, slightly below consciousness with his brain picking up ghostlike images of someone hovering over him. At times he broke through the haze only to find he'd been moved into a room he didn't recognize. He wondered where he was and if he was actually being taken from house to house, though he couldn't muster the energy to care. And there was the pain in his head, so strong at times he thought he'd been beaten again. At other times he could smell the odor of iodine and metallic dust as there had been in the Stonebreaker's Yard.

As his fever reached its peak he could feel the sweat occasionally bubbling from his chest, soaking his clothes so that they felt like a wet blanket. For a moment he was on the street headed to Runney's Restore drenched in rain. His arms and legs shook so violently he could hear something below him clacking on the floor. His teeth rattled, shooting pain from his jaw into his ears. Sometimes he thought he heard the sound of his own blood rushing from his heart to his limbs.

In what seemed like the next instant it turned cold. Rain was falling on him, pounding and pelting his body. He was certain they'd taken him to a grave and thrown him in. At that moment his teeth clattered so hard he called out in pain. His soul seemed to hover over him. Life was abandoning him. He could see his body lying in the ground and he could feel it calling out, offering the possibility of return. He raised his face to the rain and in that moment the full impact of Dublin hit him, tumbling down like an avalanche. His past, not his father's or his mother's but his alone. He felt it, the terrible anguish of having been part of a massacre and even more, and because of it all he could not die. He *would not* die. No, he would return to avenge Ireland and earn his redemption, and he would see to it swiftly.

Swiftly up from the cold, wet ground where they had laid him, the rain now viciously slapping against his face and shoulders. His eyes opened and he tried to wipe away the water as three images in the blur moved like apparitions.

"Come on, now!" someone yelled as the hand of another touched his forehead.

"The fever's broke at last." He recognized the woman's voice and thought he saw her clearly now, a face so speckled with freckles she looked like a jigsaw puzzle, but she faded too fast to sort out any of the pieces. Two men swirled into his vision. The one with black wavy hair and thick eyebrows Johnny thought he recognized.

"I told you he'd make it. Now let's get him inside," the man said.

All of the faces blurred even more as they knelt over him. Hands slipped under him and at the command of "Heave!" they raised him and took him inside and laid him on a cot. The walls drifted in and out and he thought he heard one of them say that he was asking for his father and he'd been told his father wasn't there. The words raced by him and he wasn't able to respond because he forgot the words as soon he heard them.

He was aware of being stripped, bathed, and placed under thick blankets. The sweet smell of whiskey, so sweet that it brought the memory of poteen to mind and he flinched, wondering how it could possibly be passing under his nose again. His eyes opened long enough to gaze at the woman's round face and the man he thought he recognized but the walls and ceiling were unfamiliar to him and he wondered if he was still being moved from room to room and if so how many rooms could one home hold.

"Welcome back, Johnny Flynn. I'm Billy O'Neill, if you don't remember. Shannon here brought you back to life all on her own."

The woman came more into focus. She smiled gently between broad, lofty cheeks. "'Twas you who did the work, young man. I merely stood by."

"I found you up by the hedges," Billy said. "You'd been beaten by the Black and Tans who'd paid a visit to the farm a couple of days earlier."

Johnny vaguely remembered them in the path that led from the farmer's shanty to the road and then he saw the image of the farmer cradling his dog, but he couldn't recall the pup's name. He reached up to touch his head and the scene changed. There was a lorry and the glimpse of a pistol and then his attackers came into focus. He recovered his memory enough to pin it with unsteady words. "Tans, Black and Tans."

"Did they carry two guns?"

"I'm not sure."

"The Tans usually only carry one. They don't have provisions for two. 'Twas most likely the Constabulary. They're veteran Brits and carry two most of the time, but in battle it's still hard to know which is which."

"What?" Johnny said. The words were getting lost again. He touched his forehead. From his hairline to his eye his fingers traced what felt like a long rough scar ridge that traveled across his forehead.

Shannon gently removed his hand. "Careful, I don't want you tampering with me crochet work. There now. Are you seeing out of both eyes?" she asked.

"Yes," Johnny whispered, relieved at the sound of his own voice. "I think so. Where am I?"

Shannon started to say something but Billy caught her arm. "We can't tell you that just yet, but you're in good hands. Shannon here's in the Woman's Auxiliary, the Cumann na mBan. Are you familiar with the name?"

He knew the phrase but could not make sense of it. "No."

Billy glanced at Shannon. "You rest now. There'll be plenty of time to talk later."

"Was I out in the rain?" Johnny asked.

"You were," Billy said. "We couldn't bring the fever down. It was the only chance we had. Either you were going to die in here, for certain, or out there, near certain."

"You put me in a grave?"

Shannon laughed as she laid a cold towel on the wound. "You were on the kitchen table, love, by a hole that would have become your grave, I suppose. We had no idea who you were. You got no identification on you. Whoever clobbered you probably took it. That's enough now. We'll talk later." With that she laid another blanket over him and he closed his eyes.

They seemed to open and close for days, gradually staying open for longer periods of time until he was able to remain awake for an entire feeding. Brief, polite conversations followed, always, it seemed with Shannon, and minutes later he would sleep again. As the hours passed the days became short tinted interludes between nights carrying the same reddish tone of the ruined buildings in Dublin. His dreams, if they could be called dreams, were immobile stares from the dead, even from Connolly who shouted out his order no longer but simply stared, eyes frozen as Johnny knelt on the firing line. Nora stared too, though it was through him, absent him, into a world of her own, just as she had in the Castle.

In time his splitting headaches became less frequent and even though his bad eye remained clouded, images grew steadily clearer, the detail improving from the outside in. Shannon was an outline at first like the lines of a child's coloring book, but slowly her clothes and features came into focus. She was as he first saw her, plump, pink and full of freckles, reminding him of Ina, the piano player at Emmet's. Her eyes possessed an uncommon kindness, if not charity, much like his mother's, he thought, as though there was nothing in life she could possibly do but tend the needy and forgive those who had brought hardship upon themselves.

At last he was allowed to go out onto the porch, mostly at night. Shannon would give him a glass of chilled water to keep him warm and sit with him, humming quietly, waiting for him to speak. When he did it was often slowly, staring into the darkness as if he was looking for the words themselves, wondering if he was making sense.

"Where is Billy O'Neill?" he asked one evening.

"Away for a few days," she replied.

"There was an older man here when you brought me in?"

"You can remember that? Very good."

"Who was he?"

"Billy's friend. Patrick Murphy, an Irishman of the highest order."

"Meaning?"

"Meaning he lived through the Great Famine twenty years ago and a sea of bloodshed and never once turned his back on his country." Beyond that she would not elaborate.

Later she let Johnny take short walks in the garden and soon he found his way down an overgrown road to a stream that ran through a thicket of poplar trees. There, the cool fall air seemed purified and restorative. Breath by breath he could feel his body returning to life. He no longer became dizzy when he stood and when he walked up the steps to the front door his heart was steady. He started to breathe more easily, feeling that at last he was gaining some control of his senses. A feeling of relief coursed through him, yet it was brief and intermittent, for he knew that soon McCulahy's forewarning would come to pass. When he reached Bandon he would have to face Sean Buckley.

Chapter Eighteen

Two days later he went downstairs to find Billy sitting at the breakfast table. A man who looked like his twin, but older, sat beside him. The direct stare of his heavily lidded eyes was a warning that he was not to be messed with. The men had already eaten and were drinking large mugs of coffee. Billy looked up as Johnny came into the room.

"Johnny, this is Patrick Murphy," Billy said. "Patrick, this here's Johnny Flynn I was telling you about." Murphy sipped his coffee but said nothing as Billy glanced at Johnny. "Shannon tells me you're fine to go now."

She nodded from across the room. "It's so, Johnny. You just have to keep your wound clean and have the stitches snipped in a couple of weeks."

Murphy took out a cigarette and lit it. His craggy face glowed in the light and his eyes darkened when he blew it out.

"Johnny, there's a few things we need to ask you," Billy said. His tone was almost apologetic. "That's in part why Patrick's here, to bear witness, if you will."

"What are you talking about?" Johnny asked carefully, as Shannon set a plate of scrambled eggs, potatoes and bacon in front of him.

"We need to know who you are, Johnny," Billy said.

"But you know who I am."

Murphy leaned forward. "Not your name, lad, but where're you're from, how you came here, and why? There's a war on. There are sides in a war and repercussions if you cross the line."

Billy waded into the silence. "We're talking about spies, Johnny. They are our worst fear. They feed the British like bottom fish."

"I'm no spy. You can make a bet on that. I'm wanting to fight the British."

"That makes my questions all the more important," Murphy said. "Why do you want to fight the British?"

As Johnny looked into Murphy's fierce eyes, his hands began to shake. The smell of the bacon made him feel slightly sick to his stomach and he pushed the plate aside. The room felt cold. He struggled to get hold of his thoughts. Murphy and Billy were silent as they waited. There was no way he could simply tell the truth. He had to lie and the lies had to be believable.

He began on firm ground by telling them his family was originally from Cork and that his father had fought with the Sinn-Feiners for Parnell. As he spoke he watched their faces but they were expressionless. He told how his father had been denied a veteran's pension and how his mother had been refused a medical dole and died as a result. He went on about how his father had lost his printing job to a Protestant and how his family had just given up under the circumstances. He was feeling good about how it all sounded when Murphy took out a pencil and a crumpled envelope and began taking notes. It made Johnny more nervous and as he stammered Murphy stopped writing. His eyes followed Johnny like a bull about to charge. Murphy glanced at Billy.

"We've heard all that a million times, if we've heard it once," he said.

Johnny didn't know whether Murphy was giving him license to continue or calling him out on the story, so he waited and watched Murphy's eyes. He blew cigarette smoke across the table and then bared his teeth as he inhaled deeply. "A million times," he repeated, letting the smoke out. There was something in his tone or maybe in the way he stared at the cigarette that suggested that nonetheless he believed the story. To give him some extra time, Johnny said nothing but kept staring at the nub of cigarette between his fingers.

"Did it turn your parents against Ireland?" Billy asked.

Johnny was careful to hide his relief. "My father sang of

Ireland until the day he died. My mother had died long before me Da," he said, knowing he was playing it close but feeling some satisfaction that he had not yet actually lied.

"So, you came of age in an Irish home set down in England?" Billy said.

"Braley, that's outside Birmingham, was mostly Irish," Johnny said, and then he started to tell about their neighbors and the bloody soccer matches he and his friends played against the Brits in neighboring towns. Murphy coughed and crushed out the cigarette between his yellow fingers. Johnny cringed as he watched the smoke rise from the flesh.

"How did you get from there to here?" Murphy asked.

It flashed through Johnny's mind to tell them he'd joined the British army just for passage. Admitting that much would be powerful, he thought, and the words were almost out of his mouth when he decided that any link to the British army would raise a million questions. "Paid passage with what little money I'd saved," he said. Murphy wrote something on the envelope and Johnny's heart began to pound.

"The boat's name?" Murphy asked without looking up.

"*Zenith*," Johnny blurted out, recalling the name painted on the little boat he and his father had taken out into the Gulf of Kinsale. Murphy wrote and Johnny knew if ever he checked, he'd signed his death warrant. "I don't think that was its real name," he said.

Murphy glanced at him. "Well? What was it then?"

"That's the name they'd painted on her hull, but it was only to disguise her true one. They'd covered that before I got on board."

Murphy's puzzled look became one of genuine interest. "Now, maybe you could tell me why they'd do a thing like that? Were you stealing her?"

Johnny almost smiled but stopped himself. "I can't say what we were doing. I've said enough already. After all, I don't really know who you are."

With a look of surprise, Murphy glanced at Billy. "Did I hear the boy right, Billy?"

"I'm not quite sure," Billy said, the barest hint of a smile suggesting to Johnny he'd scored with his bravado.

Murphy glared at him. His voice, which had been almost toneless, reflected anger now. "You are the one being questioned here. We might have something you need. You probably have nothing we need."

Johnny knew he had to control his desire to push it, but at the same time he couldn't back off entirely. "You're half right," he said, pausing to see if it had any effect, but Murphy just waited for him to continue. "We both need something. You need good men; I need a chance to fight and Ireland needs to be free."

"Back to the *Zenith*," Murphy said, never wavering.

"What do I get from you?" Johnny pressed.

"Maybe you get to leave here alive."

"He's not messing with you, Johnny," Billy said.

In the brief silence Johnny sat perfectly still. Placing his elbows on the table, he edged forward. He felt like an actor following a script, his limbs moving as if every action was planned, mouthing words that had been written for him. He looked directly into Murphy's eyes. "That may be, but I need more."

Murphy jumped to his feet, shoving his chair back. "Dammit, lad, the Tans must have damaged your brain, after all! I'm giving you fair warning. If I find out you're lying to me, you'll rot under Irish sod. Is that clear?"

Johnny nodded, feeling a small sense of triumph.

"I'm a section leader in the West Cork division of the Volunteers. That's who I am. Now, by God, it's your turn. What were you doing on the *Zenith*?"

Johnny realized the bargaining was over. There was nothing to do but let the story play out and see if Murphy believed it. "Running guns," he said. "German guns to the boys in Dublin."

"What port?" Murphy shot back.

"Howth."

Another silence ended when Murphy leaned on his knuckles. "Where's your identification?"

"The Tans must have taken it or maybe it's back there in the sod," Johnny replied.

"Where were you headed?"

"Bandon."

"Bandon?"

"To find Sean Buckley."

Murphy appeared startled. "How do you know him?"

"I was told about him by a fellow in Tipperary. He said the Bandon Brigade was the finest in County Cork."

Murphy looked at Billy. A smile played on his lips. "That may be," he said. "Who was this fellow you speak of?"

Johnny remembered McCulahy had warned him never to mention his name to anyone but Sean Buckley himself, but he knew he had no choice but to give it now. "Eoin McCulahy."

"McCulahy," Murphy said in an even tone, "a good Irish name. What else did he tell you?"

"That the fighting was also the fiercest around Bandon."

"The fighting's what each section makes of it," Murphy said. He retrieved his chair and sat down wearily massaging his face. "No need to go to Bandon just now," he said. "Bandon has come to you. My section is the northernmost part of the West Cork Brigade, part of the First Battalion. He paused. "And you're right. We need every good man we can get, but the operative word is good. We're out-manned and outgunned. The Brits have three thousand strong."

Billy stepped into the conversation. "We're low on rifles, pistols and explosives. There is no money – Volunteers are unpaid. There are no barracks, no stores to supply us with food." His voice dropped. "Sadly, it must be said it is hard to find a West Cork man who has sunk a knife into the chest of a bloody Brit –

all of which is to say, we stand alone."

"But for the Cumann na mBan, you mean," Shannon said, coming back into the room.

"Aye. What would we do but for the women?" Billy said. "They are as brave as the men and maybe braver." He glanced over his shoulder at her. "Stick with us and we might even let you vote."

She swiped at him with a dishtowel. "It comes with Home Rule."

"There'll be no Home Rule," Murphy said sharply. "Ireland is for the Irish to rule. There's no compromising on that."

"Somebody had better mention that to Michael Collins, then," she said. "Rumor has it, he thinks Home Rule is a good first step."

"Maybe somebody will," Murphy said, his voice rising. "Irish lads aren't out here risking their lives for the hell of it. I wouldn't be leading them if I thought that. There's no such thing as being half free. You're either free or you're not. That's what drives them despite being ragtag and tattered, not knowing the first thing about how to drill and shine their boots, going without food and sleep, and still getting the best of a superior enemy. They are willing to sacrifice themselves for what they believe to be right. That's *absolute freedom!*"

The room was silent as Murphy tried to collect himself. When he spoke again, his voice was lower. "I didn't mean to shout, Shannon. I realize you know these things, but maybe Johnny Flynn here doesn't."

"There's something about him that says he does," Shannon said, "something that says he's seen more than he lets on. No one in this land has avoided The Troubles altogether. You of all people know that."

"Is that true, Johnny?" Billy asked.

Johnny knew that if he answered, yes, it would most likely be left alone, but he was tempted to say, *if you only knew*. He wanted to tell them about the night he blindfolded Pearse and the talk they'd had, how Nora and her father had looked into each other's hearts and what Connolly had shouted at him in Stonebreaker's. He wanted to tell them about the courage he'd seen on behalf of the rebels and the cruelty unleashed on them and of their overriding concern – their only concern it had seemed – that they might *not* be shot for Ireland because not to do so further removed the Irish people from their freedom. Yes, he'd seen more than he'd let on but he knew full well he'd have to carry it all to his grave in silence.

"I've seen my fill," he said, "and I want to right the wrongs."

Murphy pushed back from the table and wrapped his scarf around his neck. "Billy will take you into his Bandon section where we can keep an eye on you. He's the section leader. He's been here for a briefing."

"You won't have to keep an eye on me," Johnny vowed.

"You have our trust for now, but any suspicion that it has been misplaced and you won't be given a chance to defend yourself. It'll be that quick."

The words were sobering and for a moment Johnny stood still in the realization he could not turn back. He had committed himself. This was the real thing. Since he'd left Dublin it had almost felt like a game of playing soldiers, or trying to become one, but this was no game, nor had Dublin been. He had crossed the line at last.

"And one thing more, Flynn. You needn't go searching for Sean Buckley," Murphy said as he went out the door. "You're looking at him."

Chapter Nineteen

The next afternoon Johnny and Billy left on foot for Bandon, a journey of almost thirty miles through the richest meadows and most emerald valleys Johnny had ever seen. He didn't remember the countryside like this. All he remembered were the streets of Cork beneath his pram and how the salt air from the Bay made it hard to breathe. It had been nothing like this autumn brilliance set like a painting above the dark richness of the sod. Could he have possibly been born here?

"Don't be deceived by all this beauty. It's where the danger lies," Billy said, intuiting Johnny's fascination as they stood on a hillside overlooking a vast stretch of barley. "It's not the Tans or the Constabulary you worry about out here. It's the farmers. Unlike those in Cork and just north, they don't think of themselves as Irish and want to keep the status quo. They're indentured slaves and don't know it – or want to know it. Many of them are Catholic, so it's not Protestant suppression in the County. It's a determination to stay loyal and protect their narrow-minded way of life. If they see us they'll whip the gentlest horse to get to the R.I.C. or the Tans themselves. They're cowards all right but very dangerous cowards."

They moved slowly through the day and into the night. Johnny's backside was numb from the saddle and he was so fatigued there were times he almost fell off, but Billy kept talking, lecturing about everything from the *Dail Eireann* – a newly elected Irish parliament that supported the Volunteers as the official government – to the duties of an officer in the Volunteers. Like Dahl he said very little about himself or his family, other than the notion that he, like Johnny had fancied futbol and if ever he could turn back time, he would earn his redemption on the pitch. "To beat the Brits on the playing field would be tougher on the King than beating them at war," he said.

But that aside and unlike Dahl he talked nonstop about the need for swift and certain action against the British on the battle-field. He told of the newly formed flying column of which Johnny would become a part, a loosely constructed group of men trained to travel for days at a time and attack in small groups without warning, taking as many weapons as possible but with the original intent of releasing their prisoners in some out-of-the-way sink-hole or mossy stream or deep woods, leaving them unbound but with a strong warning: should they flee within the hour, they would be sniped by sharpshooters left within sight for just that purpose. And if they doubted the warning, they were highly encouraged to send out a chosen bog sucker to test the marksman's skills.

"But the even-handedness has started to change, and for good reason, not one we invented," Billy warned. "The handling of their prisoners began leniently, at least with us, even when the Constabulary and the Tans were beating the hell out of our boys. Even then we showed restraint, roughing them up only when they got belligerent or smart-mouthed or maybe when we knew for certain they had outright killed one of our lads. But now they've tightened the screws, Johnny. And that's what you have to accept – what all of us must accept, that if you're caught you keep your mouth shut. They're going to kill you no matter what. Nothing can save you short of becoming a spy for them and I'm proud to say we haven't had one reported case of that. Not a lad of mine would turn coat no matter what they put him through."

"In Dublin it was said they used torture," Johnny said.

"They use anything at their means, especially the Tans and those in the Essex Regiment; they make the R.I.C. look like saints. They're the ones the War has made mad, the ones whose brains were twisted by mustard gas or claustrophobia in the trenches or the sheer weight of hand-to-hand fighting, for one adds weight to the other. They're like animals that kill. Give them a taste of blood and they have to kill again, so if there's no one left to murder that day, they throw petrol on the dead and light them on fire. In Bandon, they captured two of our lads and took pliers and electric wires to their privates, neutered them, it's said. It might be you one day, lad. If you can't live with that, stop here where turning back is easy. No one but God and the soul of James Connolly would blame you."

"What did we do in return?" Johnny asked, trying to ignore the comment.

Billy gave him an intense stare.

"We had to do something," Johnny protested.

"There was this apprentice priest, shall we say, a Friar Dunning, recently appointed to assist Father Wells in Skibbereen. Our intelligence discovered that this so-called man of God was actually an undercover agent for the Tans, who regarded him with esteem, maybe in the same way one would regard a snake in a swamp. The good Friar spied on the parishioners, looking for those, who in his opinion and/or by way of rumor, had turned against the Crown. As a result of his determinations, the Tans conducted a number of brutal raids and arrests on our boys and civilians alike. As best we could tell, the orders to torture and take out the lads I mentioned came from Dunning. The piece of scum knew better than to ever stray outside the gates of his parish, but a few Sundays ago he must have mistaken the open doors of the church for the gates of Hell and went out to close them. As he reached for the portals, an angel straddling a nearby cloud and bearing an Enfield took aim and dropped him dead before God and all mankind. I have it from reliable sources that the parishioners spent Mass giving thanks. As you said, something had to be done."

"So, it's back and forth. First they strike, then us," Johnny said.

"Maybe it's that clean, maybe not. The lines have blurred, I'm afraid, but still we err on the side of clemency. The Brits do everything in their power to convince the people that they're the victims but if you express any doubt to them, you're looking at life's end. I'm proud of the restraint our boys have shown. No one wants to take a life unless forced to."

It made sense and yet it didn't, Johnny thought. *How could you win a war without retribution?* He recalled what Connolly had said about his friend Pawth and his belief that guerilla tactics should be harsh, limbs strewn on the battlefield as reminders of one's upcoming fate – the only way to put the Brits on the run. He almost said something but deferred. He was there to follow orders and hope for the best.

They continued on toward Bandon with Billy falling into great lulls and Johnny feeling the fatigue in his arms and legs as well as a dull throbbing ache behind his eye. His mind remained muddled, clearing at times only to close after a while like fog drifting through a forest. The hours passed begrudgingly. There were moments when images of the months past gathered in sharp clarity and those when time seemed to be slipping behind.

And in those lurid intervals he saw the faces of the condemned, some of whom he'd thought had blurred forever. He saw the blue veins of Dahl's temple and wondered what had happened to him, and followed time and time again Pearse's bounce to his doom. He saw the lieutenant raise his arm and give the command to fire and Connolly's body brace and in that horribly shredded moment in the Castle when she and Lillie learned of his fate, he saw Nora's anguished face promising her father she wouldn't cry. From there her image would stream across his vision in no particular order: her beautiful face under the dying streetlamp outside her apartment; the fear in her eyes when she came to the bridge; the sight of her pistol above the swampy burial ground at Arbour Hill. He saw it all, down to the last, his rucksack planted outside her door, sealed forever, her note to him so final in its brevity. And then the memories would vanish into the sound of a rustling leaf or the neigh of a hungry horse or Billy's voice going on about the war, nudging him along as surely as the Angel's Lamp had nudged Pearse.

At dawn they were within sight of Bandon. Billy called his attention to the British barracks and the town center that housed Angel's, the Essex's favorite pub where word had it they went nightly to celebrate the tallies of the dead. Then they veered off the path they had been following. A mile down the road they came to a weathered white house – the O'Brien's house, Billy explained – where his section of twenty Volunteers were billeted. It was to be Johnny's home, the place where he would sleep, eat and train for the next ten days. Buckley would join them the day after next and explain maneuvers to them at night.

It began the moment they walked through the front door. At once Johnny was told he would meet the other men but should forget their names straightaway and use only words like *paddy* and *lad* when talking to them. If he or any of the others were captured it might save the rest.

From sunup to sundown he staggered through an endless series of drills and field exercises with but a few minutes of rest scattered over the hours. His legs cramped at night. Constantly dreaming that he'd been shot, he would jump out of bed with his calves and ankles locked and burning. Soon sleep vanished altogether. The exercises and dreams fused into an endless stream of energy that sent him spiraling through the day, wanting to skip the mandatory night meetings altogether and continue with the games.

But in the early evening hours after they had reviewed the day, asked questions and swapped suggestions, he always looked forward to Buckley's comments which never failed to push beyond the day itself and focus on something that diluted the savagery and put things on higher ground. The leader's badgering but towering presence was a constant reminder of the column's primary purpose: "To stay on this earth, to survive, better yet, to exist, if you will." He would pause there, possibly to let the words sink in but often it seemed to Johnny that he was trying to decide if perhaps there was a better way of expressing what he intended. Invariably he would emerge from his soul-searching time-out to shout: "Yes! To *exist*, mind you! Even if we never fire a shot or take a prisoner, it doesn't matter as long as we exert continuous pressure on the lowlanders and in so doing, extend our existence into eternity!"

Another break and his voice would briefly fall an octave and by the end rise again. "Though bloodshed will often follow, killing is not what we are about. No, our mission is to strike fear into his heart and soul, if he possesses same, and into his mind if he doesn't, until he cannot sleep or eat or even write home without regretting his being. His disgrace will be Ireland's freedom!"

"But what if we're attacked?" a Volunteer in the back row asked.

"If there is no other way out, we will fight to the death!" Buckley replied vehemently.

To Johnny this said in perhaps cloaked terms that the main purpose of the People's Army, as well as his own, was to secure independence from Britain in the least painful way possible, or in a way that suggested that killing was not the only answer. While it had to play a role, the less the better, as long as the result led to freedom. Morally this gave them an edge, he wanted to believe, and made the executions at Kilmainham seem even more cruel and unnecessary than ever. He came away from each meeting more and more convinced he'd done the right thing by joining and threw himself headlong into the last of the exercises, mock field movements followed by time spent on a make-shift firing range.

As he watched the bottles and cans shatter, he felt himself completely prepared to serve a war whose purpose was freedom and a freedom whose purpose was peace. Combined, they spelled forgiveness, and if he had to die in its gain, he would.

Chapter Twenty

In the days that followed, the column broke up into smaller sections of fourteen or so members, constantly stopping to set ambushes from the woods and ditches that lined the roads. Failing any encounters, they took rest and food at small farmhouses where widowed women and children scratched out the barest existence. Johnny was always amazed at how friendly they were, how willing to put on a pair of old boots – often out-sized as they had formerly belonged to a brother or husband now dead – and set off to the neighboring farms to beg and borrow the fixings of a deeply nourishing breakfast for all in his section. Buckley would join them from time to time, to convey the latest intelligence and lecture on technique and discipline. But he often joked that the real reason he visited the section was for the breakfasts.

Three days later Billy took Johnny and two of the other men to visit Marm Dooley whose husband, Thomas, had been forced to run through their sparse garden while the Tans shot at his feet. He was hit in the ankles and fell. They forced her to watch and listen to his screams as they laughed and twisted his broken feet, demanding he admit that he was a spy for the Volunteers and reveal where they were gathered. He admitted nothing and when they took aim at last, he shouted only, "I love you, Marm!"

When Billy had said his condolences, he asked why they had sought out her husband as he knew for certain the man was not a spy.

"They said they had a writ from some judge who'd heard Thomas was a traitor," she said.

"What was his name, this judge?"

"They didn't say. The showed me a writ with Thomas's full name." She hesitated to squeeze some tears from her eyes. "He died as every Irishman should, true to his land, and I thank God for that."

Johnny marveled at the resolve in the poor woman's voice. It was akin to being in Connolly's presence, even if there was a huge difference. Both men had shown courage in the face of death, but if it had been the choice of the rebels to die, the same could not be said about Thomas. He had not *wanted* to die.

Later at camp Johnny began to ask Billy if he thought they were two different types of courage or was one false and the other real, or were they the same? But he was cut short when Billy pulled out a soiled map, thrust it at him and pointed to the town of Bantry. "This is where we'll find revenge for the poor woman. Right here in this gem of a town, Bantry," he said jabbing at a tiny dot on the map. "The judge who ordered the killing. Gaggins is his name, and that's where the fat bastard is."

"How do you know he was the one... ?"

Billy glanced at him, cutting the words. "Judges are scarce out here and he's the only one in this part of the county, a circuit judge the solicitors call it. Gaggins is the worst of the breed. He's a hanging judge and according to intelligence, a whoremonger to boot, with a wife back home in Dublin. He pays no heed to cases involving Volunteers. If you're suspected of being one, you're guilty, simple as that. A writ is nothing more than a checklist of the dead. He's had seven men executed already, all without a chance to plead before him, and I don't know how many others given years at hard labor just for breaking local curfews. 'Tis certain it was him and if it wasn't, throttling the bastard will make anybody else the King sends out think twice." He unfolded the piece of paper.

"Everything we need is right here. He's staying in the rear room at the Bantry Hotel for a fortnight. Intelligence has it that before retiring he goes to the window to pray. Most likely for more innocent locals to be brought before him." Billy looked around at the men and smiled genuinely. "I bet the billowing fuck will make quite a target. I'm taking three of you with me.

The rest'll go back to O'Brien's. You three," he said, pointing at Johnny and the two others who had gone to the Dooley's.

That night on the way to Bantry, Johnny told himself repeatedly they were doing the right thing and by the time they arrived on the outskirts of the tiny town he had almost convinced himself that killing the Judge could be justified. But still, something wouldn't let him off the hook. No matter the justification, it wasn't a battlefield shooting where randomness was often more the enemy than the enemy itself, draping a sense of eerie fairness over those who would survive and those who wouldn't. No, this was a planned execution.

As they began to move single file down the hill toward the town, he caught up with Billy.

"What is it?" Billy whispered. "We're almost there."

"Do you really want to do this?"

"What are you talking about?"

"It's not like we're in a fight, Billy. This man is a judge and for all his wrongdoing he's not a soldier. He's a civilian. We don't have a fight here."

Billy put up a hand and the column stopped. Staring at Johnny, he said, "What do you mean we don't have a fight here? This man is as much an enemy as any Brit with a gun. He kills our people so he can give thanks."

"So, take him prisoner."

Billy glared at Johnny. "Listen. I don't know what's got into you but we're doing this my way, so get back in line. I don't want to hear anymore." After Johnny had turned away, Billy called him back. "Hey, Flynn?"

"What?"

"We always tell our men they can leave the service any time they like. You're a Volunteer and that applies to any situation."

"I'm staying. I just think there might be a better way, that's all," he said, realizing that as soon as he said it, he had begun to question himself. It was a comment, a rejoinder, a way to end the conversation, nothing more.

On a set of raised railroad tracks behind the hotel Billy ordered the men to fold their sleeves over their elbows, double their pant legs over their knees and set their rifles in the crux of their elbows. "Our boots clatter and the noise'll carry in the night, so we can either crawl this way or take off our boots and carry them over our shoulders, but I'm ruling that out because if we're spotted, we won't have time to put them on. Even if we did, escaping barefoot would be hell on our soles." He paused briefly to smile at the bad play on words. "It won't be easy but once there the rails will be a good support for our aim."

As they crawled closer the muffled grimacing of the men was overcome by the noise from the hotel bar where it was obvious there was a fight and the Tans had taken sides, maybe even against the R.I.C. itself to prove which division was more disgusting. Sharp crashes followed one another, as if they were throwing chairs. Then came the sound of glass breaking, a loud cheer, clapping and laughter. The noise subsided and Johnny could picture the men picking up their bloodied comrades and carting them off to their room.

"Animals," Billy muttered.

The darkness seemed to quiver in the silence. Wedged sideways between the rails, their bodies tucked alongside one another in a long slice, the foursome was in a perfect position to fire a weapon. A lean back to a mate supported a shooting shoulder and the rails served as a stable rest for the hand that held the weapon.

"Maybe he's too drunk to get up the stairs," Johnny whispered in an effort to transition back to toughness.

"Or too fecking fat," a voice beside him added.

As if in defiance of their insults, lights in the Judge's room suddenly flared. The silhouette of a large man appeared at the window, blocking the room's light so that it could only color his shoulders and head.

"Ready," Billy whispered.

Johnny tucked the rifle into his shoulder and closed one eye. Thinking he could sense a layer of warmth between his finger and the hair trigger, he flushed as the past swarmed over him. For a moment he was returned to Stonebreaker's. He squinted, hoping he might miss Connolly but afraid to alter his aim, and then as a broad shape flooded the window, he heard Connolly's fading voice call out: "*Shoot straight, Johnny Flynn!*"

"*Aim,*" Billy ordered.

Johnny was shaking so hard the gun sight was twitching like an insect even though the stock was so snug against his shoulder it hurt. Like in the magic of a silent movie a woman appeared. At first she was naked to the waist but brought a pillow from nowhere and held it against her breasts. It was all so fast, so unexpected, Johnny could only wonder why no one had fired. It was as if they were frozen in shock watching the Judge put his arm around the woman and peer out into the darkness. She raised the pillow to his shoulder, folding it up and around his chin like a muffler, as if to tease him. He drew her closer. The next moment was a blur for Johnny. He couldn't tell whether he first heard the dull shot of a pistol and saw the man's head erupt in the flash or recognized Nora as the woman who had pulled the trigger. By then the blind had been pulled and a second later the light went out.

"Jesus Christ!" someone said. "Did you see that?"

Johnny's heart was beating so hard he could barely distinguish between the voice and the sound of the pistol reverberating in his head. He began to tremble, waiting for the hotel to come to life. Nothing stirred. He was about to tell Billy he knew the woman when a dark figure emerged from the back door of the hotel and ran for the woods.

"I almost shot her," Billy said, staring at his rifle.

Johnny pointed. "There," he said as Nora disappeared into the trees.

"Come on!" Billy said, stooping to run low over the ties. When they had gone about fifty yards he hurdled down the embankment and ran toward the woods. "We've got to find her before the Tans realize what's happened."

Johnny caught up with him as they reached the woods and they pressed on as twigs and branches struck them. There was no sign of her. He dropped into a shallow culvert and was momentarily split off from the rest. As he ran following the contours of the divide, his body seemed to take on a life of its own. His mind held onto the image of her face in the bluish streetlamps the night he walked her home. Strangely, he felt like he was rushing to meet her there. As he came out of the ravine he spotted the figure of a woman darting between the trees ahead. He could hear her footfalls in the brief silence between his. Running with a hand out to shield his face, he realized she'd heard him, too, for she moved faster. Then she vanished as if she'd been sucked into the earth itself.

Johnny ran hard and pulled up just in time on the high banks of a stream. There was a small bridge but Nora was up to her waist in the water, struggling to reach the other side. As he remembered her fear of bridges, he plunged in.

"Nora!" he called and for a moment thought his voice had been drowned in the noise of the stream, but she glanced back quickly and turned away, frantically grasping at the darkness.

Johnny's legs churned water, any fear of her gun now gone. He was gaining on her quickly. Diving forward he caught her by the waist and then falling, he dragged her back into the stream. He went under but held onto her as she struggled to get free. He could feel her clawing at his arms and trying to twist away but she only succeeded in pivoting toward him.

"Nora, it's me, Johnny Flynn."

Instantly the hatred in her eyes was replaced with fear and then astonishment as she recognized him. "You!"

"Quiet. The others will hear you," he said, elated that she

remembered him.

She slammed her fists against his chest and almost managed to break away, but he seized her wrists, squeezing until he realized she was in pain. He loosened his grip slightly. The moonlight gave her face an eerie pallor. As she threw her head back to toss a streak of wet hair from her eye, the pale light glittered in both. She stared at him.

"I saw what happened at the hotel," he said.

She was silent for a moment. "You know my true name, but that's all you'll ever know. Call your hounds. I'm ready for them."

"You don't understand," he said. "I'm on your side now. I'm a Volunteer."

"Liar," she said.

"Look at me! Do I look like I'm in the British Army?"

Hesitantly, she looked him up and down. "You're a spy, then."

He shook his head, smiling. "No, I'm a Volunteer, the Bandon Brigade."

This time he let go as she pulled away from him. Carefully, seeming to hold her breath, she moved back a pace with the current washing up against her. She did not take her eyes off him.

"So, I'm supposed to believe you were a spy for Ireland while you were in British uniform? Is that it?"

"No," he said, feeling the guilt as he shifted uneasily. Now he cast a shadow over her and her eyes were lost in the darkness. He wanted to see her face again but was afraid he might fall if he tried to move. "No," he repeated, his eyes searching the silhouette that had become her face.

"What then?" she said, her voice thick with distrust.

"You have to promise me you won't repeat anything I tell you."

"I don't have to promise you anything," she said. "Christ Almighty, I don't even know why I want to know."

"If you tell, I'll be killed," he said, wondering why he was insisting on going through with it. He looked hard at her. "The Volunteers don't know I was ever with the Brits."

"*The Brits!*" she almost called out in disbelief. "Where did you learn that?"

He felt as empty and foolish as he could ever remember. After an embarrassing moment he chanced it and moved so the moonlight lit her face again. Her eyes remained fixed on his and he told his story in a rush. He didn't mention her father or the rebels but told of his disillusionment with what the British had done to them. When he finished Nora's expression had softened slightly, but the steady stare of her eyes told him she was reserving judgment. Wordless now and hugging herself across the chest, perhaps from thought or cold, she moved back and forth in the water. "Unfairness to our own people...often downright cruelty," she said at last. "It was what my father always fought against."

She began to climb out of the stream and he followed. On the bank they heard the pounding of footsteps from the woods. Nora glanced at him and for the first time he saw a look of real terror in her eyes. "Don't dare tell them who I am," she whispered. "Please."

Johnny wanted to ask her why not. Her name would inspire everyone, if not raise her to some holy level, but boots pounding on the wood bridge told him that it was too late to ask. Billy wasted no time slashing through the water to confront her.

"You could have been killed, woman," he said, jerking his rifle within inches of her face. "These have hair triggers and I don't have an idea why they didn't go off when those blinds opened. We were there for the same purpose."

Nora shivered.

"She's freezing," Johnny said, noticing for the first time that she was dressed totally in black, as before, only now she wore riding pants under her long coat.

Billy turned to his men. "One of you give her your jacket."

The soldier next to him waited while Nora slipped off her coat and then threw his jacket over her shoulders. The other soldier started to hand his to Johnny but he put up a hand.

"I'm all right," he said.

Billy looked at Nora. "You'll have to go with us, you understand?"

"Yes," she said. "That's the way it should be."

"What's your name?"

The pause was less than a moment. "Sarosa. Sarosa O'Rourke," she said, making one word of it.

"Sarosa?" There was a glint in Billy's eye and the hint of a smile. "Doomed from birth to carry the name of freedom. Your parents must be proud."

She cut her eyes at Johnny. "Indeed."

"You're from the County?"

"I'm from Dublin."

Billy's forehead wrinkled. "Well, Sarosa O'Rourke, you're definitely far from home," he said and moved off the bridge past them, signaling for them to follow.

Johnny remembered her father saying he should have named her Sarosa, and so the name itself was not that surprising, but he still did not understand why she refused to trade on her birth name.

With that preying on him, he had trouble figuring out where they were going. When he asked Billy he was told, "You'll see," and nothing more. He knew they were headed west, that Cork was behind them to the north, but beyond that, the hills gave no indication. As they went on, no one spoke and all the while he wondered what Nora was thinking, if she was wondering if they were all British spies. He wondered, too, how this beautiful woman had managed to kill a man in cold blood and if the judge was the only one.

After an hour of walking they found their way to a lone,

ramshackle farmhouse in the middle of a bog on the outskirts of Cross Barry. The road to the house was hardly more than a path and Johnny couldn't imagine how Billy had known how to find it. They entered the dark storm cellar without a word. Billy lit a candle and tiny flames reflected in a hundred jars of preserved food on a shelf beside him. One of the men spotted a lantern, lit it, and the room came to life.

Billy waved at the jars. "Help yourselves," he said. "Berries, apples and God knows what all. Preen, you and Delvin take the first watch," he said, using the mates' names for the first time in Johnny's presence. "Flynn, I want you with me to question this woman. Better now while things are fresh than sleep on it. Lads, do your smoking under cover. We're miles from nowhere and the house hasn't been lived in for almost two years now, but I don't want to take any unnecessary chances."

"How do you know this place so well?" Johnny asked.

Billy glanced around. "It was my house once – before the war. The Brits threw out my parents and my wife and boy. They're all down in Kinsale now. When it's over they'll come back here. We'll come here together, all at one time to dance on the British graves. And before I'm done there'll be a mess of them out there in the bog."

Nora was staring at Billy and Johnny wondered how his story was affecting her and whether his own story had now become more credible.

They loaded up with jars of food and climbed a ladder to the ground floor. Preen and Delvin went outside and Nora, Billy, and Johnny sat at a small table in what had to have been the living room. They screwed off the tops of several jars and dug through the wax to eat the berries with their fingers. They barely spoke because their mouths were full and by the time they'd cleaned out three jars their hands and mouths were stained dark red. The stain brought a fullness to Nora's lips and he thought he'd never seen her so captivating. She caught him looking at her.

"What are you staring at? You look every bit the mess I do."

Johnny smiled to himself. "Nothing at all, Miss O'Rourke." He took a black bandana from his jacket. "Here."

"I don't want it," she said, wiping her mouth with the back of her hand.

"I'm afraid there aren't any dry clothes," Billy said, "and we can't make a fire, but when we're finished you can go upstairs and…"

"The walk did most of the drying. I'll not be needing any more clothes. Here, give the man back his coat," she said, taking off the jacket to reveal a dark wool sweater, tight about her, with a collar that rose up to her chin.

"Let's get started, then," Billy said. "We saw what happened at the hotel. Tell us about it."

"It's my business alone," she said, "just like I told this one before you arrived."

"That may be so in your way of thinking, but out here what you did goes way past just you because as sure as the winter's coming, we'll be blamed for it. No matter what you might think, what you did is truly our business. What I need to know is why you did it and how. Were you operating alone?"

"Yes."

"So, it was personal?"

"Of course it was," she said. "I don't normally go up to every man I see and put a bullet in his brain – though I'd probably be serving Providence if I did."

"So, it was between you and the judge, the something personal? You'd been before his Court? There was a verdict that wronged you?"

"Not me so much as others."

"Your family?"

Her eyes went from playful to serious and a sullen look came over her but she didn't say a thing. For a moment Johnny thought she was going to spill her heart out, but she blinked as if she'd just realized she had lost track of the conversation. "Yes," she said, "my father."

Johnny sat up. He wanted to help protect her secret but didn't know what to say. Any cover-up would be an admission he'd known her before and that would betray them both.

"He was a soldier and took part in the Rising," she said. "He was killed in the G.P.O. the day they surrendered."

Billy glanced at Johnny and back at her. "You're a veteran's daughter?"

"It would seem that way," she said, sarcastically.

Billy let it slide. "The Judge?"

"I learned about him in Dublin. He sent a young boy to his death in Waterford…the son of a friend of my family. I knew him…as a friend, more like a cousin, if you will."

Again, Billy glanced at Johnny and looked back at Nora. "Did you tell anyone or try to get word to us? Why would you take a thing on like this yourself? You're…well, you're a woman, and you hunted a man down and killed him."

She looked at him incredulously. "You're saying that's your job only? That I shouldn't bother myself? Why? So I can stay home and bake cakes for the boys on the line? So I can sit by my window and stare out at life while it goes by below me? What are you saying? That women don't have the same right to pursue what's right for Ireland?"

"No, I wasn't saying all that. We owe our lives to the Cumann na mBan. I was just trying to point out…"

Her voice was like a knife. "There's little you can point out to me! What you can do, I can do, farming, slaughtering, killing. Whatever the sacrifice, I can make it. I was raised to die for Ireland and that I can do, most likely better than either of you!"

"You can't fight the Crown alone or you will get killed," Johnny said. The words sounded so dramatic he wished he could retract them. He expected her to laugh or at least roll her eyes, but she just held her gaze. For a moment it was as though her stare had magically brought him to life.

Still considering him, Nora rubbed the table with her fingers, easing herself back into the straight-backed chair. "There are things worse than death."

Billy was shaking his head. "So, you just bought a gun, hopped a train, and came to Cork to kill a man."

"Not just any man," she said. "I've explained all that."

"How did you find him? The Judge's whereabouts are secret."

"The secret leaked out," she said.

Johnny noticed her hand was shaking. She saw that he noticed and took it off the table.

"Where's your gun?" Billy asked.

"Too dangerous to keep and much too heavy for running through the woods. I'll get another somehow."

"You want to stay here for the night?" Billy said.

"Yes," she said.

"And after that? Will you be going back to Dublin?"

"I'll be staying here."

"You can't stay here," Johnny said. "It's too close. If anyone saw you with the Judge or even around the hotel and all of a sudden you've vanished? That doesn't take much figuring out."

"It doesn't matter. I'll survive as long as I can."

Johnny looked at Billy. "How about the Cumann na mBan?"

She glared at them both. "I'm not a nurse and I don't want to deliver messages. I came here to fight."

Billy rubbed his face, waiting for her to say more but she just stared at them. Johnny could see the frustration in his eyes as Billy sat staring stubbornly at the table.

"You're not from here. You don't know the land, the people, who to trust, who to avoid. You wouldn't last a week," he said.

"Then it would be one hell of a week," she said.

"Suit yourself," Billy said, pushing away from the table. "You can stay tonight. Tomorrow we go our separate ways."

"Fine," she said, starting to get up. "Where'll I sleep?"

"Upstairs, small room at the top. Nobody'll bother you. There's a basin and water out back at the well."

For the first time since they had met at the stream Johnny saw weariness in her face. Until now it had all been held together by defiance, but it softened and as she stood she wavered slightly and sneezed. He stood to take off his jacket. At first he thought she was going to refuse it, for she turned her back to him. But then she did not move. Instead, she waited for him to drape it over her shoulders and when he had, she thanked him and without looking back she headed for the stairs.

Johnny and Billy went to another room and after they'd washed, they lay down on beds of straw. Lying there, staring at the ceiling, Johnny wondered what kind of woman could do what Nora had done. What was the mind of someone who stalked a man like an animal and then killed him? Maybe she was crazy, like one of the Tans, her mind twisted by the ordeal of the Rising and her father's death. But the same could be said of the rest by anyone, including himself, anyone who didn't understand their passion for Ireland and freedom. Even Billy's determination to kill the judge in revenge for the Dooleys' suffering might seem crazy to some, but in a manner of speaking there had been nothing crazy about it. The rules of right and wrong, of good and evil, of sane and insane, were clearly in suspense – did not apply to them, or to anyone in this fight, including Nora.

During the night it began to rain, and the thatched roof trembled as water spilled down onto the dry grass. Johnny wondered if she was asleep and if not, what she was thinking. Her mind was probably far away in some imaginary battle, or maybe she was in front of a large crowd, preaching about the atrocities of the British.

"Johnny?"

"What?" he sat up, quickly and then Billy shook him by the shoulder.

"Spell them at sentry," Billy said. "Those lads need some rest.

You can keep dry under the eaves all the way around the house."

"Okay," Johnny said, struggling to his feet and heading for the door.

"Take your rifle," Billy said, then grabbed it off the floor and handed it to him.

He followed Johnny outside, passing the lads as they came in shaking the water off. "What do you think about her?" he asked as he lit a cigarette.

Johnny watched the match light Billy's face and then flare out when he flicked it into the rain. "She cares about her country and is prepared to give her life for it," Johnny said. "In that way she's no different than you or me."

Billy stared out at the curtain of rain falling from the eaves. "Would you knowingly give your life for Ireland?"

That's why I'm here, Johnny thought, but the question had caught him off guard; for a brief moment he wondered if he was really that courageous. "Yes," he added, deciding he was.

"I don't know," Billy was saying. He put the cigarette to his lips and inhaled deeply, cupping a hand so the glow wouldn't be seen. He held it in for a long time and then blew it out, calmly, slowly, as if he could have held his breath forever. "How old do you think she is?"

"Mid-twenties, I'd say."

"Old enough to know what she wants and at the same time young enough to do something stupid to get it," Billy said.

"Well, you said she'd only make it a week on her own."

"I didn't feel good about saying that."

"Then take her with us," Johnny said, expecting an outburst. Instead there was silence.

"I'd have a lot of convincing to do. Can you imagine what Buckley would say?"

"You'll never know until you ask."

Billy chuckled. "And get my arse chewed out."

"Give her that chance."

"I'll think about it," Billy said, then dropped the stub of cigarette into the rut the rain was making as it sluiced off the thatch.

For a while Johnny walked the perimeter of the house, watching the horizon for lights. The rain came in waves, loud at times and then gentler as if there were the familiar but as yet unseen push and pull in the night. He used the house as a shelter, moving leeward when the rain came lashing in and moving to the far side as it softened. After an hour or so, it settled into a patter like the day he faced his mother after stealing the soccer ball. It wasn't the crime of stealing that got to him this time but the memory of her pained voice telling him all was forgiven.

"I heard what you told Billy," Nora said. She was right beside him.

"Jaysus!" Johnny gasped, clenching his rifle, annoyed with himself for having been so careless. "I might have shot you."

A brief smile fluttered and vanished. "You still can."

Wondering if she was mocking him, he turned away and stared at the rain, seeing nothing. A flash of lightning shuttered the night into a vivid landscape of distant hills, shadowing the horizon. Nora's shoulder touched his briefly and he wondered if she had flinched in fear or had accidentally moved too close. His eyes slanted toward her as the touch lingered for a second and then drifted away almost as if she'd not even noticed.

"I heard you ask him if I could stay," she said as the thunder rumbled into stillness and the sky went dark again.

"It wasn't yours to hear," Johnny said, trying to cover his awkwardness.

"'Twas hard not to, considering my door was wide open and you weren't exactly whispering."

"I don't think Billy'll allow it. There's too much he'd have to answer for."

"I understand," she said, "but I appreciate your effort."

"What'll you do, if he says no?"

"I'll find a way. My father's looking out for me." Something in the set of her face told him she was no longer present but in the Castle at her father's side. At that, reality came pouring back for Johnny, too. He tried to squelch it, telling himself it was deep in the past and best forgotten. She glanced at him – maybe feeling his stare, he thought, but when she did not turn away, he wondered if somehow she knew, and he began to feel guilty and nervous.

"Why did you ask him if I could stay?"

Relieved, he turned to her. "You belong here."

She smiled. At first he could only gaze in disbelief. It was a smile that revealed another part of her, he thought, maybe akin to the woman stepping up onto the bridge in Dublin. They stood like that for a moment and her smile faded, maybe because he hadn't answered with a smile. In his excitement the opportunity had passed. He'd felt it disappear like a dream he hadn't wanted to end, but it had and he knew it could not be recalled.

His voice faded to a whisper and he paused just long enough for a brief cough to annul the mention of her name. "Why did you take on another name?" he whispered. "If these people knew who you really were, it could inspire them to accomplish God knows what. I mean, even in battle, just knowing that your father was beside them in your presence…"

"Stop," she said and he was quiet.

Her fingers slipped deep inside her coat. He watched the impressions of her knuckles moving along the ridge of her left breast. She looked puzzled for a second and slowly pulled her hand out. A small piece of damp and wrinkled paper clung to her fingernails. Taking great care she peeled it off and tried to smooth it across her palm but it came apart along the fold. Johnny could see only the residue of printed words. Once in ink they were more like stains now. He could not make them out but knew that it was the note her father had entrusted to him. He wanted to lean closer so that he might try and make out what it said, but he waited.

She closed her eyes and read the indecipherable words aloud. "Sarosa, now it is for you alone – alone, as was I." She opened her eyes and blinked to clear the glaze. "Alone," she said. "Now do you understand?"

He might have argued or at least softly disagreed that her interpretation of the word had been too literal, but then again, to say such a thing with any authority would have suggested that he felt he knew her father better than she. He had been guilty of that before, outside her apartment, and it was no place he ever wanted to go again. As the edge of morning started to show over the hills, he felt his heart pounding and Connolly's voice came to him in a rush. *"Shoot straight, Johnny Flynn!"*

He flinched, ducking slightly, as if the bullet were meant for him and straightened. "You had better go inside," he said.

"Well, do you? Do you understand?" she persisted.

"Yes," he said. "You stand alone but for the shoulders of the unseen."

Her lips opened and she tried to say something but seemed completely taken aback at his turn of phrase.

For a moment he thought she felt he had contradicted her by suggesting she wasn't really alone nor would she ever be.

At last she managed to reply. "On his shoulders, that I do," she said, "and it is a vantage point like none other. Good night."

He heard her boots sloshing through the puddles. As she opened the door, he looked over his shoulder to catch her glancing back at him. He could not tell from her expression if he had intruded on some sacred ground or if she took his comment as it was meant, heartfelt and gird with understanding, but the softness in her voice had suggested the latter.

Chapter Twenty-one

The next morning Billy told him that he hadn't been able to make up his mind about the young woman but felt responsible for her safety, considering the service she'd performed for Ireland. With that they headed south to the camp in the Bandon back woods, zigzagging over the terrain and staying as close to the woods as they could.

It was eleven in the morning when they entered the small town of Kilmichael. The main street was empty, but above, a flock of ravens circled, swooped down close to the buildings at the far end. Then they saw something in the middle of the street that brought them to a halt. A body lay face to the sky, its arms and legs akimbo.

Billy split them up, he and the lads on one side of the street to comb for Tans and Johnny and Nora to approach the body. In the eerie silence, Johnny could smell the stench. He covered his mouth and a woman's voice called out.

"Get away from him! We don't want more trouble!"

Johnny looked but could see no one, so he turned back to the dead man whose flesh was caked in mud that had dried gray and cracked, making him seem to be a hundred years old. In the center of his forehead was a bullet hole, reminding Johnny anew of the frail boy in Dublin. Thankfully there did not appear to be any others. A piece of cardboard, warped by the rain, was tied around the man's neck. Billy reached over quickly and tore it off. He stepped back and read aloud for Nora.

"The body of this traitor to the Crown is to lie here undis-turbed until the King's mercy orders it buried. Any attempt by family members or others to do so before it is decreed will be met with swift and harsh punishment. Let this be a reminder that the eyes and ears of the Crown are among you everywhere. It is signed, the Essex Commander."

Billy handed Johnny the writ and as he tucked it into his trench coat, he saw that a few people had gathered in the road and were watching him. Most had rags over their mouths. "He should be cleaned and buried," Johnny said.

"It will just bring the Tans down on these people," Billy responded and asked the crowd, "Where is his family?"

A heavy, barefoot woman with the toes on her left foot missing and seemingly filed down to the nubs, stepped forward. "The Teagues. They left. Just up and went. They couldn't take knowing their only son was lying like this, food for them crows."

"What happened?" Billy said.

A man came out from the doorway of a candle shop. "Jimmy and two others from afar were following the British troop movement around Bandon. They were doing it on their own. They told the Volunteers what they seen."

Nora stepped beside Billy. "Would you get me some water and rags, please?"

"Mind your place, Miss," Billy ordered, but as they waited for the woman to fetch the water he had no choice but to leave her alone. "Christ, Flynn, do something," he said in a tone clearly confirming he wasn't sure how to deal with the situation.

Johnny almost laughed. "We'd better be on the lookout for the Tans. They'll be an easier match. Let her be."

The woman did not return and when Johnny asked if someone else would fetch water, no one volunteered. When several others drifted away in fear, he unfastened his canteen and handed it to her.

She poured some water on the edge of her tunic. A few gasped as she began to rub Jimmy's face but as she continued it grew quiet. After many turns the corrugated face became young Jimmy Teague again and weeping filled the silence. Then, she picked carefully at the edges of the bullet hole, bringing tiny bits of fractured bone up into the opening, to the point where it appeared to be a blemish, nothing more.

Soon the number of villagers increased and gathered around her. More wept; others gazed with a mixture of horror and fascination. Johnny and Billy tried to stay alert to any signs of the Tans but they were so held by Nora's ministrations they soon forgot about them.

A heavyset man with a full white beard marred with strands of chewing tobacco placed his hands on his knees and bent closer to Nora, nodding to himself. "Bless you, lass. Bless you. You are an angel of mercy."

And with that he knelt and touched Jimmy's cheek. "As Jimmy fought to stay on his feet, a raven did come to perch on his shoulder. It was the myth of Cuchulain sprouting into truth. I seen it with me own eyes, as did we all." His prayerful voice faded and he straightened, searching the faces for agreement, but no one spoke or moved until a lad, no more than eight or nine, stepped from behind the folds of a woman's mud-skirted dress. She reached out to draw him back but he pushed her hand away and inched closer to Nora.

The lad's eyes were beaming. "I saw what Mr. Farley saw, I did! The raven came to Jimmy's shoulder. That one there on the livery." He pointed to an aging stable on the far side of the street where a raven stood perched on the pitched roof. Everyone's eyes followed. The boy waved and as if it were a signal, the bird shrieked and shot skyward.

The boy's eyes settled on Nora. "He set off just like that from Jimmy's shoulders."

"Aye, little fairy," she said, "each of us finds a pair to fly from. That's why God made us the way He did."

The boy stood staring at her in awe. She glanced at Johnny who thought he saw a smile on her face, the same one he hoped he conveyed in return.

She handed the canteen to Johnny, then stood up to face Billy. "Your turn," she said.

There was no casket but a shallow grave had already been

dug in the small village cemetery. Given the Essex warning, four Volunteers did all the work. The villagers accompanied them to the site but several stayed buried in the woods peering out from behind trees while a few gathered at the grave. All were afraid to speak and seemed more anxious to leave than to attend so the ceremony only consisted of lowering Jimmy into the grave and hurriedly covering him with sod.

Back in the town everyone had disappeared. The section waited where they had dressed the body but no faces showed. For a moment Johnny worried that they'd all been rounded up by the Constabulary, or the Tans or worse, the Essex, but he knew they were probably more afraid now than when the section had come into town. But at least their boy was buried, magically restored. Near the fields of Bandon, Johnny was still thinking about this when Billy spoke out.

"Sarosa, while your words to the youngster were kind and well meant, in tending the young Volunteer you showed you are far too concerned about yourself and not nearly enough for others." Everyone stopped. "Winning this war isn't a matter of a few individuals acting on their own, doing what they think is right, but the effort of everyone working together as a unit, a team. You either accept that or go back to Dublin. You understand?"

Nora flushed and Johnny could see she was hurt but too proud to admit it, dressed down but too proud to cower. He wanted to come to her defense but Billy was right, what she had done had placed them in jeopardy, and yet something about it overrode the danger – something the lads and the citizens could take away that transcended their suffering. But as he held his tongue, her expression seemed to fight with itself. She was on the verge of tears, he thought, but nothing in her would let one tear find its way down her cheek. She'd have turned away first. Her lips quivered.

"That boy gave his life for Ireland, and I would have given

mine for his," she said.

"But his had already been given," Johnny said, pricked that she was so callous about any life, even her own. He thought of Eveleen and how he'd fought to keep control of himself when the Tans made fun of the killing. "To trade a living life for a dead one doesn't square the circle."

She stared at him. Tears rolled out on her lashes and eased down her cheeks, but she did not wipe them. She let them come and Johnny thought that even in her surprising tears she showed courage.

Taking the opportunity to wipe her eyes quickly with a sleeve, she glanced at Johnny. "You're right, it doesn't, but I would do it again."

Johnny couldn't think of anything to say that wouldn't make the situation worse, so they left the fields in silence. He was more exhausted than he'd realized and closed one eye to see if he could coax that side of his body asleep. With each step he was jolted awake. His head hurt from the incision. The constant joggling didn't help and as they all but stumbled down a slope he put his hand over the wound and pressed gently. The scar had held; he could feel its crusty ravine running to the bridge of his nose. The scab seemed to be widening as Shannon had said it would – how far, she hadn't known. He wondered when it would drop off, and if Nora found it objectionable. He looked back to find her five or so yards behind, lugging a rifle as if it weighed fifty pounds.

He slowed and waited for her to catch up. He reached out for the rifle, thinking she would not consider giving it to him, but she handed it off as casually as passing a stick. Without speaking they continued to move through the fields. Bandon was in sight now and so too the British barracks on the outskirts. Billy moved the section closer to the woods, keeping free of the road that eventually wound its way down a hill and split the town in half.

Johnny looked up and saw the overcast sky, waves of gray clouds crawling southward toward the sea. For a moment he felt almost overcome by the realization that all of this, the sky, the town, the spongy fields, the color of the leaves, even the British barracks were all part of the same world, bound together by none other than time and hatred.

He and Nora were a good ten paces behind the others when the words came out of his mouth. "Do you believe in me, now?" he asked. He'd expected her to remain silent but she turned her head and considered him.

Glancing ahead as if checking to make sure the others were out of earshot, she said, "I'm not sure what I believe, only that I am here and so are you and we appear to be on the same side." She motioned forward with a nod of her head. "I believe those good men, that they have accepted you as one of them, and knowing that makes me feel safer. But they don't know your past as I do, and out of their presence I wouldn't be caught dead in yours."

Her tone was so overly harsh Johnny thought she might be joking but her stern expression kept him at a distance. He looked out across the fields again and oddly found that he wanted to smile.

They walked in silence for several minutes. Then a shot rang out. It struck Billy in the knee and he screamed as he went down. Thirty paces ahead of them, rifles aimed, was a cache of enemy soldiers. From the distance Johnny couldn't tell if they were Tans or the Constabulary as they had no hats and their uniforms were lost in the shadows as they came out of the tree line.

"Down!" he yelled and they began to return fire. As the shots rang out he could hear Billy moaning on the ground.

"Mother of God!" Nora exclaimed.

Johnny looked back. She was kneeling over Billy's leg and trying to stop the blood with her hands.

"Get down!" he shouted. Shots whipped through the trees and he pressed his face close to the ground. When he looked again she was looking at him, panic stricken. Without thinking he jerked off his jacket and threw it to her. "Tie it above his knee, tight as you can."

The tunic hitting her in the chest seemed to jolt her into action. She was all movement, grabbing the tear in Billy's pant leg with both hands and in one motion laying open the wound. Using the arms of Johnny's jacket she twisted it into a knot around his thigh and tightened with all her might. As the gunfire kept coming Johnny rolled over to her and grabbed the sleeves and tugged, too. Billy grimaced in pain. He was sweating now and pale, but they had stopped the flow of blood.

"Here they come! Bayonets fixed!" a fellow named Hap called out ahead.

Johnny looked up. The soldiers were coming fast, bayonets thrust out in front of them like something from medieval times. "Stand and fire when I tell you!" he shouted. He waited until the figures had cleared all the trees and committed themselves to the open field where there was no protection. Clearly, they had no idea they were out-gunned. "Now!" he yelled, scrambling to his feet.

He sensed his comrades next to him and had he been able to turn around he would have seen Nora crouching over Billy, steadying his Colt with both hands, her arms shaking so violently she looked like she was about to come apart. But in the instant before anyone fired, everything went still. There was no motion or sound. And in a fraction of a second, everyone began to move as if they were under water.

The weapons sounded more like lorries on a distant road, coming at Johnny in slow and garbled waves. In the midst of it all, he recognized the double revolvers the enemy wore and the Mills bombs they carried and knew they were the Constabulary. In the same moment he realized his lads were in a fight for their lives. The R.I.C. would take no prisoners.

They drew from their holsters and traded shots like something from a story his father had read him about Billy the

Kid. The bullets flashed from the Brits' pistols in slow motion, emerging from patches of colorful light to pass his ears almost leisurely, as though trying to decide who should live and who should die. In a drawn out instant, it was decided. The enemy went down quickly but in succession, as if being checked off some ethereal list. The two left standing froze and for a moment Johnny thought surely they were about to surrender but he'd heard the many stories of fake surrenders when the liars would lay down their rifles and dip into their jackets for an acquiescent smoke only to pull out a gun.

"We surrender, me and my brother," one of the men pleaded. "Please, grace our mother with our lives."

"They're lying, Johnny. Kill them!" Billy shouted.

One of the soldiers turned to splinter off towards the woods while the other grabbed a Mills bomb from his belt and in one motion jerked the pin out and flung the grenade at them. It bounced to a stop at Johnny's feet.

"Throw it back!" Billy yelled.

Johnny grabbed the bomb and as quickly as the soldier had thrown it, hurled it as far as he could toward the fleeing Tans. It exploded in the air above them. Nora and Johnny were blown back onto their haunches by the concussion. A bloody arm of the Brit who had lied his way into the hereafter landed just a few feet away and his helmeted head was sent tumbling over the field. As the smoke cleared Johnny was shocked to see the other man hobbling towards the trees and stumbling around the bodies of his mates.

Pawth Durbin's demand that the Brit's body parts be scattered over the battlefield flooded his instincts and he sprang to his feet. No doubt Nora had had the same inclination, for she was ahead of him, pistol in hand with no signs of stopping.

Just as he was about to chase after her, he heard a single shot, brittle like the sudden snap of a branch. The Tan they were chasing fell to the ground just as Nora reached the litter of dead enemy. Johnny rushed to her side. She was staring at the blood soaking into the ground when a youthful Volunteer carrying an Enfield came out of the trees, smiling proudly. He bore an eerie resemblance to Jimmy Teague and as if brothers in triplet, to the boy on Sackville Street as well. He nodded to Nora.

"Ma'am," he said. "Name's Charlie. That's all I can give."

"Bless you, Charlie," she replied. "You saved us a round, or two."

The young man glanced at Johnny and looked down at the bodies. "We saw you from the road but these here seen you first," he said in a considered voice that had aged in battle, Johnny thought.

"The cowards broke away from the real fight," he said. "Left their buddies to fend for themselves. Look yonder, down the road to that drain short of the meadow. You see it? That's where we ambushed them. You lose anyone?"

Johnny saw a pile of dead Tans heaped on an approaching lorry. Seven or eight, he guessed, with blood trickling down their limbs and dripping onto the ground. "Nobody," he said. "But we got a man down. Section leader shot in the knee."

"I'll get some men to fetch him. He can ride on the other lorry. We're going to Cork. Will you be coming with us?"

"Bandon's where we're headed. We can take him there with a litter."

"It's still daylight and before long this'll be all over the countryside. I wouldn't want to be in Bandon but, hell, if you bring real harm to them there, them cowards would run for Kinsale to be on the next ship home."

"Give me a few minutes and we'll signal you. I want to talk with our Commander."

"Only a minute, mate. We can't hang around, and neither can you. As soon as we stack these here on the lorry, we're going to add petrol and set it afire as a reminder to the bastards."

"No need to kill them twice."

"Our days of kindness are over." His voice was brimmed with authority.

"As well they should be," Nora said. "We have to get back to Billy."

Everyone was waiting for them, and when they approached they all stood, all but Hap who was kneeling by Billy and trying to steady him. He was white as a sheet and shaking so hard that Johnny thought he could hear his bones cracking, but thankfully the bleeding had almost stopped.

"I'm sorry we left. I just..." Johnny began. Nora cut him off.

"And I, too, we wanted to kill the bastard for what they did to you, Billy."

"Good!" Hap said, steadying Billy's leg, which had begun to spasm.

"I know that feeling," Billy said, grimacing. "I had it...over the Dooley boys. It won't let you go 'til you see it through. You did right, both of you. And Johnny, the Mills bomb, that was..."

"Due to your quick thinking," Johnny said.

"Five seconds," Billy said. "That's all the time you got. The idiot threw it too soon. I was counting."

"You saved us," Nora said. "I only wish...the story will be told forever."

Billy looked at Johnny. "Johnny here saved us. Give him the credit."

Nora glanced at Johnny. He knew that to smile could have marked him as prideful, possessing bragging rights in the presence of someone else's misfortune, so he simply let Billy's comments linger in the silence between them, hoping that Nora had actually included him in hers.

He loosened the tourniquet and let the wound bleed some more before sliding a stick through the knot and tightening it again, telling them of the soldier's offer to take Billy to Cork. Billy's teeth began to chatter and he looked confused, as if he hadn't a clue what to say. He glanced up at Johnny as though he might have the answer. Then Billy grabbed at his knee, grimacing.

"If I stay with you none of us will make it to Bandon." His eyes hardened. "Tell them to come for me and you go on ahead with the fellows. I'm placing you in charge. Take them to the O'Brien's and fill Buckley in. God willing I'll heal and make it back to you."

Just as Billy passed the baton, the lorry carrying the dead Brits went up like a torch reminding Johnny of the urgency in the young Volunteer's voice. Time was precious. While moments ago it had barely lurched ahead, now it seemed to be moving much faster. In fact, it seemed that just in the last fifteen minutes he had been shoved into a whirlwind where all things were crying out to be taken care of at once.

After they'd put Billy on a litter and watched the Volunteers carry him off, Johnny's section started out. Occasionally he would catch someone looking around for his former leader and found himself again cursing the bastard who'd shot him. As they moved rapidly across the fields and into the far hills south of Bandon, his anger was heightened by the sound of armored cars revving their engines and shots coming from the center of town. As they got closer he could hear the bullets ricocheting off the cobblestones, shattering glass. News of the ambush had arrived. Revenge had already been set in motion.

As they climbed into the hills, moving carefully because the slope was covered with rocks, the wind began to blow from the west, chilling them to the bone.

"Bloody rocks!" Nora said, stumbling and lunging forward. One of the men grabbed an arm to keep her from falling, and for the briefest moment Johnny wished he had been the one who steadied her. She straightened and looked at him, her tired face set as hard and beautiful as a face could be. Her eyes were brief and puzzled, as if she was questioning the look on his face.

As the slope leveled out, Johnny halted the section. "Thank

God," he said, looking down at the O'Brien's farmhouse and hardly believing it was still there. The smell of the pine floors came to him and the tobacco the lads smoked, and within him the fatigue and anger was gradually replaced by the feeling he had done well fighting for Ireland. He clenched his fists and as an image of the lad who had spoken out for Jimmy Teague came to him, he shook them in celebration.

Chapter Twenty-two

Sean Buckley came to the farm to greet them that night. He had already heard the story of Billy's accident and that of this stranger, this crazy woman who obviously out of her mind had so wantonly shot a judge by passing herself off as a whore. Buckley had laughed at the thought of anyone needing to be insane to kill the murdering fuck.

"No more than one would have to be to seek absolution for killing a feral pig," he said. "And to think she tended Billy with no Cumann knowledge, only with the instinct of one who cares."

"It was this one here who knew what to do," she said nodding at Johnny.

It swayed Buckley's eyes toward him. "Billy made the right choice."

Buckley and Johnny talked later that night and he told Johnny that the Volunteers owed Nora anything she wished, safe passage back to Dublin or to America for that matter. After all, until the war was over she would be on every wanted list in the United Kingdom. "Beyond that, any president of Ireland worth his salt would give her the Order of the Land." He was open to suggestions, he said.

When Johnny told him she wanted to fight alongside the men, Buckley's face fell and his demeanor went from fanciful to serious. He lit a cigarette and leaned back, crossing his legs on the table. "I'll have to take that up with Michael Collins," he said, staring at the stove.

Johnny was asking what he thought Collins would say when Buckley interrupted. "No sense asking. I'll tell him later in the week. If this Sarosa O'Rourke can take the training, why not?" He smiled. "Sarosa? Can you imagine?"

Not allowed to see Nora for seven days as she trained, Johnny passed the hours in fitful anticipation of each day's end and the trainer's reports on her. Reading them, he felt a sense of pride to see that she was measuring up in every respect and that the men were accepting her well. In that Buckley had officially made him section commander, he further ordered that Johnny take it easy for a while to regain his strength.

He ate until he couldn't eat anymore and began to take long walks in the afternoon, venturing farther and farther away from the house. One day he went to a café on the edge of Bandon and ate fried eggs and chicken, sitting with his back to the wall, facing the window in case the Tans came in. He sipped at a mug of coffee and watched people come and go, wondering which ones in their lone and silent ways were secretly working for the Brits, who for the Volunteers? There was no way to tell, of course, for it was not in their eyes or gait, nor in the way their voices sounded, as perhaps it had been in his. They went along as if there were no war at all and nothing to be concerned about, but as he was leaving the café he saw a sign posted over the door that told of the atrocities being committed against the Essex Regiment by the Volunteers and warning that the penalty for collaboration with the Volunteers was death.

On Sunday Nora was sworn in as a soldier in the Volunteers and Johnny listened as she officially pledged her life for the cause of Ireland. The fifteen men in her training class cheered when she finished and there was hand shaking and back slapping all around. Then they all went behind the house to celebrate with food and whiskey. The sun went down behind the hill and the evening turned chilly as they joked and told stories about the week.

Buckley spoke, telling them the war had come to a critical stage, deadlier than any that had preceded it. The Brits were adding several divisions of a hundred men each, lauding them as a paramilitary arm of the Constabulary, the R.I.C. They were called Auxies and were equipped with newer, more powerful Mills bombs and were instructed to use them without discretion, be their victims women or children. Highly mobile, traveling in armored cars and Crossley tenders, they could strike without warning, like savages. They were murderers, pure and simple. All acknowledgement of the tenets of defensiveness and humaneness were gone. The enemy believed in extermination.

"If any of you brave soldiers want to turn in your weapons and make your way home or perhaps to another place that shares our values, like America, you'll not be faulted by me or Ireland. Saving yourself in the face of such odds should well be considered a blessing for your loved ones, not a mark of shame."

The gathering became somber. Everyone looked at each other. Leave the brigade? Surely Buckley was joking. If not, he was high on poteen or suffering from some long ago accident to his head. *We are waging a goddamn war!* The thoughts were transmitted in a startling flicker of eyes from person to person. There was soft murmuring, as if to allow time for Buckley to tell them it was indeed a joke. But as his unflinching eyes roamed their faces, they were still. "You can leave in the dead of night to void any shame that might arise," he said, adding, "The darkness will guide and protect you."

"Are ye having doubts yourself, commander?" It came from the back of the gathering.

"I am not."

"Sure sounds that way."

"I'll go to my grave fighting for Ireland."

Nora raised her hand and without any acknowledgement she stood, facing him. "We love her as much as you do, so why shouldn't we as well?"

"You shouldn't."

"But you just said…"

Johnny stood up and looked around at everyone, then turned to Buckley. "I believe there's been a misunderstanding. Forgive me if I'm wrong but what I heard Sean say was this: we have earned our right to leave and for that, should we decide to go, we are forgiven."

Buckley's eyes flashed appreciation to Johnny. "That's it, exactly, section leader," he said and asked for comments. There were none.

As the night wore on and the tankards began to run dry, exhaustion set in. Sated, the men sat around slumping against a tree or rock, voices low. A young soldier named Liam Crowley began to sing. His voice was crisp and high, almost touching a woman's range, and it flowed over them, soothing to a person. Johnny heard in the soldier's songs the voice of his father and had a sense of still sitting in Braley's as the old man took his fill and sang until the songs cast a canopy of warmth over him.

Absently his eyes rested on Nora, sitting against a rock across from him. She drifted in the wake of the whiskey he'd drunk, holding for a critical moment when he thought he was going to pass out and then coming back like a memory recalled. Her eyes were closed, her arms folded across her chest and her legs stretched out before her. She, too, had fallen asleep, he assumed as he struggled to keep her in his sight.

The singing ended and the rest of the men began to leave for the house but Johnny barely noticed, so intent was he on watching her. He should wake her, he thought, and crawled quietly over to her on his hands and knees. He was about to reach out and touch her shoulder when her startled eyes opened.

"I'm sorry," he said, his tongue thick. "I thought you were asleep. The others are gone."

She looked around in disbelief. "He was singing. Crowley was singing," she said.

"You were asleep then?"

She shook her head. "Remembering," she said. "I've heard those songs so many times before."

She was staring at him with an expression he could not understand.

"What is it?" he said.

She shrugged and smiled. "I don't know. We must be getting back."

He stood and reached out to help her up. To his surprise she took his hand. Hers was thin and small and he thought if he grasped it too hard he would crush every bone. Afraid to tighten his grip, she nonetheless tightened hers. Her hand was strong and he gripped back and raised her to her feet in one motion. The momentum took her forward and she stopped inches from him. The wind blew between them, rousing a curl of hair on her forehead. She lost her smile and looked at him curiously as he listed to the side and then steadied himself, still holding her hand. For a moment only, until she seemed to realize their hands had touched too long and then she pulled hers away. But otherwise she did not move.

Nor did he. He felt his heart beating and heard his own shallow breathing. *What would she do if he reached out for her,* he wondered. *Was she thinking the same thing?* And then he recognized that by her look she had no idea what he was secretly asking. He backed off, creating enough distance so that he was no longer tempted. "Time to go, I guess," he said, unable to find anything else to say.

"Past time," she said, causing him to wonder how stupid he'd been.

Chapter Twenty-three

The British began to burn down farmhouses, shoot horses and goats while executing locals simply because of their Irish birthright regardless of where their true sympathy lay. Bound to their lineage, it did a citizen no good to plead that he or she supported the British. The bastards would call him a liar and shoot him anyway, the preview for some having been Thomas Dooley, shot for sport by the Tans. But now the Tans had sunk to a deeper low. Now they were the Auxies. A new strategy, borne of ignorance and a severe deficit of conscience, was to burn down all houses, big or small, feeling that allegiance to their cause would spring from such behavior. They did not care whose side the dead were on before they were butchered or after.

By the end of the week Johnny and his section stood on a hill outside Bandon and watched helplessly as the Auxies set aflame a score of Irish homes. At dusk, they threw on more petrol and the flames leaped into the high darkness. At first Johnny's men were quiet, watching and listening as the enemy cheered. There was nothing to be said, for there was nothing that could be done. His section and its backup were severely outnumbered so he would not permit them to attack. Gradually, however, they closed ranks and began murmuring to themselves. Anger gathered in their voices.

"Load your rifles," he said, unable to contain himself any longer.

They crept down the hill toward the last farmhouse to be ignited. A band of twelve or so Tans stood silhouetted in the glow of the fire. When the roofline caved in, a huge ball of embers rushed into the sky and they cheered their loudest. Johnny did not have to give an order to charge and fire. The cheer did it for him. Everyone started to run and shoot at the same time.

He had lost control of the section but he didn't care. He was out of control himself and it felt good. The wind in his face, the anger pouring out of him, his legs barely touching the ground. He was alone and yet surrounded and he didn't care what the outcome was to be as long as he took some of them with him. Two of his men were faster and went into the lead. He didn't know where Nora was but he knew she was prepared to die. For a moment he had a vision of Connolly lying in his bed, insisting that he not be spared and confident that he would not be. In that instant Johnny knew he was going to die, too.

"Fire!" he shouted, although the men already were. He saw the Tans run toward their gun stacks for their weapons. Before they could retrieve them, two went down. Four freed their weapons and knelt to form a line of defense. Instantly they were met with gunfire from the section. When the remaining three broke away, Johnny carved Nora and Liam from the rest and cut off their route.

The startled men came to a dead stop and threw up their arms. There was silence away from them. Liam shouted over and Johnny knew the four who had banded together were dead, so now all were dead but those who faced him. Johnny stood with his rifle pointing at them but their eyes were focused on Nora. One ran his tongue over his lips and wagged it at her. Nora handed Johnny her rifle, drew her pistol, and moved straight toward the man. She jammed the gun under his chin. He stopped smiling and tried to twist away but she increased the pressure, forcing his head back.

"No!" Johnny shouted, jumping toward her as she drew back the hammer. Her thumb twitched and he thought he was too late. He slapped at the gun as it went off. The Tan screamed and fell to his knees, hands clasped over his ears. He kept screaming as Johnny jerked him to his feet. Liam had come up to cover him, holding aim on the other two while Nora stood with the pistol hanging at her side and her chest heaving.

Johnny pried the man's hands away from his ears and

shouted, "Shut up, goddammit!" When the man refused, Johnny slapped him across the face until he slowly crumbled to his knees in front of Nora.

"Put that away!" Johnny said as she slipped a round into the chamber of her pistol. He couldn't get it straight. Had he actually knocked the gun away or had she intentionally missed the Auxie?

She glanced at him and slowly holstered the gun. "Remember what they did to me that day in Dublin?" she said, glaring at the captive.

Thankfully, no one but Johnny seemed to notice the door she had unknowingly opened, but even if they had, he realized it could be easily closed by leaving him out of the real story.

Sweat was pouring down the Tan's face now and he looked at Nora with an expression that asked what she was talking about. "You're lucky," she said. "At the last second it came to me that a bullet through your head wouldn't hit anything."

The man's eyes twitched wildly. "You're her!" he said in astonishment. "The whore who killed the Judge! They said you'd joined…"

Before he could finish, Johnny had smashed the butt of his rifle into his jaw and the man collapsed, clawing at his face. A great globe of blood poured from his mouth and Johnny was surprised he was still conscious. He trained his rifle between the man's eyes.

"Kill him, Johnny," Liam said. "The bastard's earned it!"

Johnny grit his teeth and almost followed through but somehow reneged. "He's not worth killing. Stand up, you goddamn lowlander." When the man did not move Johnny motioned to his comrades. "Pick him up."

They knelt, draped the Auxie's arms across their shoulders and brought him to his feet. Blood was still pouring out of his mouth and his front teeth were missing. His head slumped over and he began to cough blood on his pants and boots.

"Blindfold all of them," Johnny said.

"You can't just execute us," one of them said trying to twist away as Liam started to tie a bandana around his head. One of the other men grabbed his comrade and held him steady as Liam finished the job.

"How would you know that's what we're about?" Johnny said, feeling the control he had mustered slipping away. "Could it be because this is the way the Auxies do it?" He shoved Liam aside and jerked the man to him by his jacket. "Answer me. Did you have the decency to blindfold young Jimmy Teague up in Kilmichael?" he shouted.

Unable to stop, he kept shaking the man and went on. "Did you make him look up at the barrel of the gun, so you could see the fear in his eyes? Did you make him stare at his poor wretched parents just before you shot him?" He was shaking the man so hard Liam seized his shoulders.

"He's too fucked up to answer, Johnny. Here, you've done your job," he said, carefully guiding Johnny away from the man. "Let us finish them."

Johnny became aware of how hard he was gritting his teeth and let the man go. "No," he managed. "They're going back to Buckley. Let him question them. They'll talk."

"You're sure?"

"That or die," Johnny said.

Chapter Twenty-four

That night he couldn't sleep. Visions of the Auxies in the field haunted him. He told himself they'd had it coming – and they damn well had. No telling how many innocent lives they'd taken and how many homes they'd burned, but still he couldn't stifle the guilt. Over and over again he envisioned their eyes, though he knew full well he'd been too occupied and too far away to see into all but the last of them. Nonetheless he recognized their fear and thought of how they must have felt overrun like a pack of animals, which they were. But still.

He'd turned the three survivors over to Buckley who was downstairs interrogating them. Johnny knew the questioning would be hard, but he also knew Buckley would be fair. He'd seen Sean send members of the regular British Army back to their barracks with messages, and somehow that always had seemed a more powerful and intimidating thing to do to the enemy than simply shooting them. But now they were dealing with the Auxies.

When Johnny heard the three shots it didn't occur to him the men had been executed. He ran downstairs thinking maybe the house was being attacked and stopped at the screen door. Buckley was standing over the three bodies, his pistol out. He nudged each with the toe of his boot. "Stone dead," he said, slipping the revolver into his belt and looking up at the men around him. "We don't have to waste any more bullets. Take them to the Bandon Barracks and leave 'em at the gate. Tag each one of them with a note that carries Jimmy's name and reads, 'An eye for an eye,' and be done with it."

Johnny was stunned and it showed, for Buckley called out, "What's wrong with you, section leader? I know you've seen the dead before."

"On the battlefield," Johnny said.

Buckley waved a hand at the night. "This here's not a battle-field, is it? What do you take it for, hallowed ground?"

"I thought you'd interrogate them and send them back. That's why I brought them here." As he spoke he heard someone running downstairs.

"What is it?"

Johnny stepped aside to let Nora out the door. She stopped as soon as she saw the men dragging the bodies away. She glanced at Johnny. "What's wrong?"

His head was swimming. "I didn't think he'd kill them," he said under his breath.

"It's going to get harder, Flynn," Buckley called to him. "I've done my best to warn you and the others. We're playing on a slippery field now where the grass has turned to bog. You make up the rules as you go and hope God forgives you the rest. Goodnight."

With that he left. Johnny and Nora stood without saying a thing, watching the bodies being dragged to the lorry beside the house. As they all disappeared around the corner, Johnny looked up at the sky. It was clear, the quarter moon stark against the darkness. He stepped forward absently and brushed Nora's shoulder. He mumbled an apology but she did not respond or even look at him. She, too, was staring toward the corner of the house.

"I'd like a whiskey," she said into a cool breeze.

He felt his voice crack through the tenseness. "Wait here," he said, heading back into the house. Within a minute he'd returned with a pint of Flanagan's and two empty fruit jars. He handed her a jar and poured, then poured for himself and slipped the pint into his breast pocket. They sipped and walked out to the low stonewall that surrounded the house. Nora set her jar on the wall and leaned her elbows on the stone, looking out at the fields.

"Do you feel caught up in it, like there's no turning back

now?" she said.

"Yes."

"So do I, and I don't know what to make of it," she said, bringing the jar to her lips, sipping at the whiskey, speaking in a flat voice. "It's like being caught in a storm."

He stared down the long road, tracing a finger around the top of the jar. He took a swallow and waited as it burned deep into his chest. He felt like someone trying to catch moonbeams; everything was escaping him in confusion. He didn't know what to make of the executions and for the first time he began to wonder if both sides hadn't crossed some unholy line that even in a time of war God could not sanction. Nora shivered and quickly took some more whiskey.

"Here," Johnny said, taking off his jacket. Afraid of touching her, he laid it on her shoulders and pulled away, leaning back awkwardly in case she turned on him. She did indeed, but slowly and without fury. It felt like he was truly seeing her for the first time. Her dark eyes were sardonic, full of melancholy and intelligence. Her lips were fuller and mouth wider than he'd thought, her well-defined cheeks set higher. Summer's leftover tan brought a dark strength to her face despite the veil of moonlight. The deep set of her eyes gave her an almost masculine appearance, yet she was unmistakably feminine, undeniably beautiful.

What would she have him say or do? The quieter they became the more self-conscious he felt. Her dark eyebrows arched slightly revealing horizons struck by the quarter moon, as though the sliver of light had been etched in them. He couldn't tell if she could see him and he moved slightly to the side as if to look behind them. Her head tilted and the light slipped across her face and disappeared. The challenge of a moment ago was gone, replaced by a searching gaze.

"I'm not a whore."

It took him so off-guard he didn't know what to say.

"Back there in the glen, the bastard called me a whore," she said. "I just wanted you to know I'm not."

"I never gave it a thought. I know better."

She went on as his voice trailed off. "It's true I pretended to be that night at the hotel. That's what lured Gaggins. We knew, well, I knew from a friend of my father's who worked in the Castle, that he had an eye for women of the street. So, I went to the bar and waited until he came in." She paused and smiled. "The Tans were guarding him, and if I'd had ten good men I couldn't have gotten through them, but a smile, a nod and a shake of my hair that's all it took, and the toughest scum merchants in the British Army introduced me to their savior and left us alone. What does that tell you?"

"It tells me you're brave as hell."

"It should also tell you I'm notorious now, a target."

"So are we all."

"But hardly with the same distinguishing features," she said.

"Thank God for that."

They sipped at their whiskeys and let the conversation sink into the silence. After a few moments of playing at the rim of her glass with her lips she looked up at him. "We'd better go in."

He felt the moment slipping away and knew he was about to do something strictly forbidden. The harder his heart beat the less he cared, however. Quickly he set his whiskey down on the wall, did the same with hers as she watched puzzled, and then gently taking her by the arms kissed her, softly, pausing with his lips barely against hers, trying to sense what she was feeling. Guardedly he backed off, opening his eyes. Had her eyes been closed, he wondered. They were open now and unflinching. The old defiance was back and he tensed, not knowing what she was about to do. But behind her stare lay something kinder, a suggestion to him that although he had not been invited, she had not taken offense. He faltered and this time her hands reached out and steadied him, smiling.

"Easy," she said.

He felt himself sway forward and she pressed a hand against his chest as if thinking he was trying to kiss her again and breathed, "No."

That stilled him. More than that it immobilized him, but as the paralysis waned his courage grew and he grabbed her shoulders roughly and brought her to him, sealing his lips against hers. She tried to twist away but he held her firmly. The heels of her hands pressed into his chest and for a moment he thought she was about to kick him in the groin but her hands withdrew and she kissed back. When the kiss ended he was gasping and then realized he'd been holding his breath the entire time. Even in the pale light her face looked flushed but still defiant as if she stood before him proud of what she had done. His heart was racing and he had a sudden urge to apologize but he didn't give in. Placing his hands on his hips he braced as she brushed past him.

She turned and touched her face as if to check its warmth. "Goodnight," she said, briskly moving away.

Chapter Twenty-five

The Essex Regiment, the down and dirty British officers from the Continent whose behavior had grown too disgusting even for the British, stepped up their raids on the villages and increased their brutality with each bloody assault. Their tactics consisted of stocking lorries full of troops and firing at will as they sped through the villages. Moments later they would round back to jump out of the lorries and beat many of the survivors to the ground with pistol butts. No one was spared, neither women nor the elderly. Though the men were stripped before their beatings, the children were made to watch and were prevented from covering their eyes or closing them, even if the victim was their father. The tots were warned that if they cried, their mother would not only be beaten but stripped as well and a pike rammed up her bare arse. Death exercised no discretion. Those who died, died without any regret on behalf of the Essex. The survivors struggled home with the help of family and friends to bolt their doors and maintain watch through barely open shutters.

While this was going on, the attacks on the Volunteers, eleven dead within a fortnight, were beginning to take their toll on the brigade and its sections. These deaths and the savagery in the towns soon had Johnny withdrawing any sense of leniency. Seething at the stories of the Essex atrocities, he often thought of Durbin and his call for the enemies' limbs to be hacked off and scattered in the streets as the only way to deal with the Brits. Viciousness was all they understood.

On Saturday, in the woods away from the O'Brien's, as though hatred had found contagion, Sean Buckley called the sections together. His face was taut. "We'll be living in the woods for now, using the house for the wounded attended by the women of the Cumann. We'll be returning here to gather only after our raids," he announced. "Supplies will still be kept in the coal bin, but all arms, ammunition, and personal gear must be removed this night and brought in your haversacks. The reason is this: it is time we took it upon ourselves to change the course of this war. We can no longer pretend that being brave on the defensive and bearing up under British inhumanity is gaining us an edge. We must assert ourselves."

He stopped, as if to let the anticipation build but there was no need. It had crested and now the word was relief that things had taken such a turn. Johnny smiled and clenched his fists. All eyes remained on Buckley.

"Tomorrow we will converge on Bandon, the Essex stronghold. We'll attack over the Bandon Bridge just after curfew when the Tans are thick at a pub by the Freemason Lodge. As Satan would have it, the hellhole is called Angel's. The Regiment gathers there after curfew to celebrate the day's killings. They are left unprotected because those in the Regiment regard themselves as superior to the rest, in need of nothing but their own taste of blood. Tonight they will get their fill. When they rise to boast their tally, we'll be there to stand them a last tankard.

"There will be no mercy shown. We'll take no prisoners. Each of you is to tuck all the ammunition you can carry into your tunics, a pocketful for your Enfields and the same for your Colts. Sarosa, how fast can you run?"

"No man has ever caught me," she answered. Chuckles cracked the tension. "Why do you ask?"

At last Buckley smiled. "I'll explain when we set up for the advance."

When they had drawn within a quarter mile of the town, the moon was so bright it seemed like late afternoon. The storefront windows were gilded with the reflections turning the damp cobblestones into streets laced with gold. Other than in an occasional alleyway or behind a pile of debris there was no place to hide. Buckley reminded them that although the locals were decidedly on their side, it only took one curled lip and the Tans could be on them in an instant.

He led both sections into a nook behind a fabric store whose walls had been hollowed out by artillery fire. Using the hole which the Tans had blown in the walls, the section hurried through a store with bird cages that reminded Johnny of the contraption over Connolly's leg and a meat shop with the rodent debauched carcass of a horse still hanging by the throat from a rafter. Beyond these the tunnel narrowed like that in Johnny's travels and without realizing it, his hands reached for its imagined walls.

He felt Buckley eying him and dropped his arms. "Feeling the pressure?"

Johnny swallowed and looked away.

"It's all right," Buckley said, "I feel it, too, like a cave closing in on you." As the section squeezed out of the tunnel and encircled him, his eyes returned to Johnny. "I'm sure Michael Collins would have me lynched if he ever found out I asked a section leader to go on point, but that's how important this mission is. Ordinarily, I would send a speedster like Liam over there to mark the enemy's position and come scampering back so an officer could set the timing, but the town center is open and dangerous to a fault. The success of our mission may come down to seconds. Thus, I must send an officer who can put the advance and the final attack into effect at will. Johnny, will you stand the task?"

"Commander, you know the answer."

"I'll take that as a hearty yes. Very well, render your best judgment as to our advance and when done, signal your backup, Sarosa. She will follow you at thirty paces. Signal her with a pump of your fist, precisely like that of the executioners at Kilmainham. In turn she will beat a path into our view and give the same." Buckley turned to Nora who was pumping her fist excitedly.

"Sarosa, you will let your hair down and remove your tunic, replacing it with a tattered citizen's coat Hap has packed for you. While you will hardly pass for a local, it should give any doubters a moment's pause. Every hesitation is to our advantage. It appears you are willing."

"Indeed, I am."

Buckley spread out a map on the cobblestones. As everyone leaned in, Johnny tried his best to stay focused. His heart was racing as he watched Nora replace her tunic with the shabby overcoat. She raised her arms and hopped up and down on the balls of her feet to encourage the coat to settle around her. Fleetingly a vision of Pearse bounding out into Stonebreaker's Yard came to Johnny and he found himself wondering if the hidden irony of death was its attraction.

The streets on the map were convoluted, resembling more a loose spool of yarn than a town. Buckley inched his finger through a netting and pointed to a thread so thin and dark it resembled a shrimp's vein. "Best I can tell, this is where we are, but this damn map..." Squinting, he followed his finger as it curved to a short but slightly thicker line. "With any luck here is the bridge and just beyond it, this smudge must be the center. Johnny, if intelligence has it right and God your witness, you should be able to get a solid look at the pub from there. Are we all clear, lads?"

Enthusiastic whispers passed around the section as everyone clasped one another's shoulders. Buckley folded the map around the route and handed it to Johnny.

As he started out, he glanced at Nora expecting to catch a gleam of even more anticipation and pride in her eyes, if not a broad smile, but she was staring down the street, her face rigid as if she too were peering into the tunnel. He wanted to ask if that were the case but there was no time, so he broke away without looking back and quickly picked up his pace, weaving around the few locals who dared to be out on the streets as the ten o'clock curfew drew near.

He tried to scan the stragglers for anything suspicious, a hateful glance, a weapon of any sort, even a short military haircut but he found only smiles and nods. A few even reached out to him, as if he alone was the one they had been waiting for. For a moment he felt suddenly set apart, released from his fears. He thought of Cuchulain and the raven rising from atop the livery and imagined himself soaring above the earth with all of Ireland's enemies his prey. It lasted but a few seconds, until Nora's image managed to obscure his vision. She was present as surely as the locals, still possessing that faraway look, veiling any sense of tenderness as she sliced through the reflections of moonlight, pistol in hand.

The screeching honk of a lorry brought him abruptly to earth. Another shrill bark followed in its wake and yet another, three lorries altogether, the number necessary to carry the thirty-man Essex Regiment.

The street curved but it he thought little of it for it had curved on the map as well. He jammed the map into his tunic and hurried around the bend fully expecting to see the bridge just ahead, but to his alarm a heap of stone and wood blocked the street. Beams jutted out of the pile like nettles. A street merchant's push cart was pierced by one, a pram for twins, fortunately empty, by another. An aura of what appeared to be gas light lay unevenly across the rubble like sunset on a bombed hill. The bridge was nowhere in sight.

The lorries were grinding louder. The noise reverberated through his body like a bad chill. And then, seemingly on the crest of the rubble, the silhouette of a lorry surfaced, closely followed by two others. They lumbered along the shortened horizon like a toy train. As they approached the end of the heap they appeared to sink slowly into the debris. Their clatter faded into silence. The air stilled. Gradually a series of gas lamps flared high above the debris as though the vehicles were being welcomed home. Johnny then realized what had happened. The Tans had crossed the Bandon Bridge, which ran on the far side of the junk pile and were now descending into the town center.

He was trying his best to figure where he had taken the wrong turn wrong when a man, bald long before his years, came hobbling toward him on handmade crutches, pounding the stalks onto the cobbles and swinging his legs like a hand puppet.

Johnny jerked a pistol from his coat and the man halted, quickly lowering his armpits onto the crutches and raising his hands as high as he could.

"Put it away, lad! I'm on your side," he gasped.

"What side would that be?" Johnny said, watching the man's hands carefully.

The man looked down at his legs. "Look at them, bashed to chafe by the Tans a year ago. It's all I can do to lock me hips and stand, and you ask what side would that be." With that he grimaced and clutched at his chest.

Johnny was tempted to rush to him but as he himself had experienced, many a Tan had feigned injury or sickness only to dive into his cloak for a pistol. "Straighten up, mister." His voice came out softer than he'd intended.

The man slowly raised his head. A bright redness drained from his boney cheeks and he gradually regained control of his breathing. "God keeps trying to take me, but I've a fairy in me heart, and the little bitch outsmarts Him every time." He paused to take a deep breath and his smile disappeared. "I'm part of your intelligence, a gatherer of the Essex stupidity as they say. Who'd ever suspect a cripple like me? Buckley's plan of attack was relayed through our boys in Kinsale. Three of us were sent from Malloy as silent lookouts. We were shocked. Bandon's been turned into a maze but we didn't have time to get the word back. It's no wonder you missed the bridge, lad."

"I thought the street went straight there."

"Before the plunder it did. Now you have to skirt the

wreckage. There's an alley just before the curve. It's full of rats and rubble but you can get through. It'll empty you at the foot of the bridge. Cross over and the pub you're looking for will be dead center between the Lodge and the Bank. Remember, lad, they are beasts. May the fairies steady your aim and that of your comrades."

The man pivoted on one crutch, planted the other and headed toward the ruins.

"Where are you going?" Johnny called out.

"To bear witness!"

Johnny stood for a moment, wondering if sympathy had ambushed him or if he, too, was in the hands of the fairies. Regardless, he had no choice but to do as the man had suggested and dash for the alley. Just as he cleared the bend he found the clogged passageway, and then as if a forgotten prayer had been suddenly brought to mind, Nora's silhouette appeared a block away. Hands on hips, she stood looking back, waiting for the section. Afraid of shouting, he began to sprint toward her. His eyes blurred, creating twin images of her that reminded him of what Connolly had said of Lillie, that when she stood in front of a mirror it was like seeing two beautiful, dark angels. Unable to contain himself any longer, he shouted, "Sarosa!"

In one motion she jumped in surprise and began to run toward him. They grabbed each other to keep from colliding. Their eyes froze.

"I thought the worst had happened," she panted.

"I got thrown off. The street's blocked by a mountain of trash. But one of our spies, at least that's what he claimed to be, showed me the way." He pointed to the opening. "Through there. The bridge is just on the other side."

"And you believed him?"

"I had no choice. *We* have no choice. Signal the section."

Nora spun and took off down the street. She had almost reached the end when the section came into view. She began pumping her fist. Buckley thrust his arm into the air and they started running toward her. Johnny wanted to cheer. He pumped his fist as much in celebration as a signal for them to follow and headed into the alley. Stumbling through the trash and loose brick, he held his breath at the stench of rotting vermin, but when he made it out, the sight of the bridge let him breathe.

The section entered a minute or so later and slogged through. When they exited virtually everyone was coughing. Pale and gasping like the rest, Nora bent over and clasped her knees.

Buckley came to her side. "You can outrun a bad wind, and that's what most of us men are," he joked, patting her on the back and then looking at the bridge. "Johnny Flynn, you stood us proud, mate."

"Thanks to this bald fellow on crutches who routed me, claiming to be one of ours. I only hope he wasn't playing me for a fool. "

"On crutches? Bald? That would have been Marley O'Donald, as good a lookout as there is. The bastards broke his thighs in the bog by Timoleague and left him for dead but somehow he crawled two miles home and lived to tell about."

As the backup section came into view at the far end of the alley, Buckley held up his hands to keep them at a second attack distance.

"Three lorries crossed over ten minutes ago," Johnny said.

"Just enough time for the animals to get into their pints. Hap, stay behind until we've crossed over. We'll signal you when we're in position. Then bring the second section through. Let's go, mates. Johnny, take the lead. Sarosa, you're staying with us now."

At the bridge they hunched below the barrier and crept single-file behind Johnny into the center. With no cover save the clouds, Johnny hurried them into position. He halted them within twenty yards of the pub, just beyond the trail of candlelight that spilled out of the wide front window setting the word *Angel's* aglow. The place was packed with Tans bunched together and draped in bloody orange shadows.

Johnny ordered them to hold their fire until the second column made it over the bridge. He watched Hap pump his fist to bring them over and then suddenly the silence was broken by the clatter of Tans rushing out of the pub. Before Johnny could tell if the section had been spotted, a shot rang out from the bridge and one of the Tommies fell. Instantly a barrage followed from both sections and all of the enemy went down. Then all hell broke loose.

The Brits fled from Angel's to be met with gunfire so loud Johnny couldn't hear himself think. He shot with a vengeance but couldn't tell if he hit anybody. Tans poured out of the door like proverbial lambs to the slaughter. A succession of steely thuds racketed across the cobbles and Johnny knew someone had thrown a Mills bomb. Instinctively he counted to five and the windows of the pub blasted inward. Flying glass shards gleamed like pieces of frozen light. The exodus stopped as did the gunfire. Twenty or more Essex were down in the street. No one moved except those who were moaning and struggling to stay alive. *The ambush was over at last,* Johnny thought.

But straightaway the lumbering of armored cars shook the stones and the sounds of shots could be heard coming from the barracks.

"Go back! Back to the bridge!" Johnny shouted, but it was too late. The vehicles were upon them.

He began to run toward Hap as a car skidded to a stop between them and opened fire. Bullets caromed off the stones in fiery sparks. Realizing he was cut off from the others, he wheeled to catch a glimpse of Liam and Nora running toward a narrow lane next to the Lodge. She was looking back over her shoulder and he followed, looking over his to watch the sections hastily come together and make for the bridge. The armored cars stayed in place firing crazily into the buildings and cobbles. They seemed to be shooting at their own men, for the sections stood at the bridge, watching as if the Brits were gladiators in a pit. They were safe for now, Johnny told himself, but a mad dash to cut across the center to try and rejoin them would be suicide. He had to catch up with Nora and Liam and take the long way back separate from the rest.

At the corner of the lane he passed a milliner's where people had gathered inside and were looking out the window like spectators. Someone yelled for him to squeeze in but he could see Nora and Liam's shadows ahead of him and kept running. At the next corner they were waiting for him.

"Did the others get out?" Nora asked.

"It seems so," he labored. "They were at the bridge, watching the gunfire. It was as though the Tans weren't even aware of them. They were just shooting up the center."

"Dumber than the snakes what hatched them," Liam said.

"Let's get out of here," Johnny said but just as Liam started running he fell face forward, making no effort to break his fall.

Johnny glanced down the narrow way but saw no one. "Go! Stay to the side and keep going!" he shouted at Nora as he stooped over Liam. The bullet had struck their mate in the back of his neck. Johnny knew by the way fell that he was dead but slipped a hand inside Liam's jacket to feel his heart. It was still. He pressed his fingers against Liam's bloody neck searching for a pulse, but here was none, only a hole where the bullet had shattered the bones. Johnny looked up to see Nora trembling behind him. "He's gone, Nora. Let's get out of here!" He scrambled to his feet, shoving her along the sidewalk.

They ducked into an open hardware store where an elderly man was sitting in a chair holding a rifle in his lap. Motionless, he seemed to stare into the space between them. Johnny thought maybe he was feeble or deaf, but then the man's wrinkled face broke into a grin.

"Run from Death as long as you can," he said, "but sooner or later it will catch up with you."

Johnny put his hands up. "Can you hear me? Do you understand me?"

"What's there to understand?" the man said. "You two have brought the troubles to my doorstep, but I forgive you. It's what people do when they're young."

"Listen to me," Johnny said, bending over until he was looking directly into the man's eyes. "We mean no harm. We just need to pass through your store here."

The man looked puzzled. "The back way?"

"Yes," Johnny said. A large crashing sound, barely discernable from that of a Mills bomb rattled the building.

The old man let go of the rifle and clinched his face with both hands. He held the grimace for a moment and grabbed his rifle again. "Go before I kill you!" he yelled. "Just go!"

Grabbing Nora, Johnny pushed her toward the back of the store, staying behind her. If the old man fired he'd be hit but she'd be out of danger. The loudest noise wasn't that from the man's rifle but a withering, screeching collision. Johnny couldn't tell if it came from deep in the street or from the center itself. It was following by the endless whine of metal scraping stone.

At the end of the hall Nora flung the door open and they jumped off the loading dock into a courtyard. Through an opening in the wall they made their way into a long alley between two rows of small houses where the screeching seemed to lodge in the air.

Dodging laundry on lines and garbage cans scattered on the steep slope, it felt as if they were running up a never ending obstacle course, struggling with the passage of time, their lives shortening with each gasp as if they'd gotten far behind it somehow. When they reached the top of the hill, the terrible noise had ebbed and the town center had been reduced to a vague and shimmering stillness. The three armored cars were one dark triangle, bunched together as if seeking refuge. The dead had not been carried off. Thankfully, the bridge was clear.

Chapter Twenty-six

They had to skirt the town to get back to the O'Brien's, a distance of twelve miles or so. Johnny was convinced the sections had gotten away unharmed but worried that the house would be destroyed and the men hunted down on the way back. He and Nora said little to one another. Liam's death was bearing down on both of them. The journey back was going to be all the more fatiguing because the Bandon and Cork Roads would be much too risky. It meant they would have to crisscross through and around the endless stretch of hedgerows, constantly climbing over the stone walls designed to protect what few cattle remained.

They twisted and turned through the hedgerows for what seemed like a mile, then cut through a pasture and made for the hills. The pastures became mud-filled bogs and the walls harder to climb. Nora fell twice and Johnny once, slipping as he tried to catch her, but they kept on until they cleared the last wall and stood on the top of a hill afraid but feeling strangely victorious. It seemed they had been climbing forever and at last had reached the top of Carrantoohil.

"My God, look," Nora exclaimed.

Johnny couldn't believe a manor house would be just below the summit. It sat in the stillness like something out of a fairytale. The stone structure was dark but the clouds had thinned enough for him to make out the condition of the place. The front door was unhinged. Several shutters were flapping free in the wind. The windows they exposed were filled with the deep blackness that comes when glass is missing. It reminded him of the openings at Kilmainham.

"It belonged to traitors," Nora said.

Johnny brushed the sweat from his eyes. "Some landowners were on our side, you know."

"Not according to my father," she said, looking at him embarrassed, having caught herself talking as if her father were still alive.

"Come on," he urged, reaching for her hand. She did not return the clasp but let her hand lay limp in his as if to say she still stood on her own two feet.

They moved cautiously toward the side of the house. Pieces of the stone walls were scattered in the main yard and part of a widow's walk lay like the remains of a pirate's plank in the bushes by the portico. A large part of what appeared to have been a game room was open to the elements. The faint smell of gelignite lingered.

"These weren't traitors," he said.

She removed her hand. "Let's go."

They left the house in silence and headed toward a group of small outbuildings a hundred yards away. At the doors to the coach house Nora looked at Johnny. "I'm exhausted," she said.

"Why don't we rest here for a while? It will be light soon and make the way easier."

She nodded and he lifted the post that kept the doors shut. They drifted open, letting out the aroma of oats and hay. Inside, Johnny looked around. There were stalls for four horses, though all were empty. Saddles and harnesses still hung in place. A wood ladder led up to the loft where moonlight pressed through in a haze of pale light.

"We'll be safer up there," he said, nodding to the ladder. He took a few steps and stopped, wondering if the floor would hold, but she nudged him in encouragement and he went up the ladder. She was right behind him as he cleared the top rung and crawled toward the back wall testing the floor ahead of him. "It's solid," he said and started raking up a bed of hay. "Here. You rest and I'll stand guard."

She rose up from the ladder like a being from another world – her beautiful face adrift in moonlight. The light showed off every nuance and as she knelt her eyes seemed to say something to Johnny about what she was feeling inside.

She took in his mesmerized look. "What do you see?" she said.

He tried to answer but his mouth had gone dry. She was shedding her jacket but he could not take his eyes off her face. She removed her gun belt without breaking her own stare. Letting it drop quietly to the floor, she shook her head violently until her hair came undone and fell to her shoulders. With a little tremor she brought his hand to her lips, kissing it, then leading it slowly across her cheeks to her neck. She slipped her hand away as his fingers felt the nape of her neck and traced a line back to her mouth.

They stood for a moment, mutually transfixed. He was dazed, looking but not seeing what he knew she wanted him to see, her desire. She seemed so removed, yet so close; so close, yet so small, standing there, her body on the edge of the shadows, her face glowing, fumbling with the buttons of her shirt as if extending an invitation for him to help out.

At last, smiling, she whispered. "We are in the midst of a war, aren't we?"

Johnny was trembling so he was afraid to move his hand, but he leaned into the warmth between them, touching her cheek with his, feeling her warm skin and letting its own special scent drift through him. He kissed her cheek and tasted a slight saltiness while an unlikely fragrance of lilac came from her hair. Her hand caressed his cheek and slowly her lips sought his, and his hers, dry as they met. With a flick of her tongue she moistened his lips and their mouths slid together. When he hesitated to kiss her deeply, her tongue encouraged him and he grabbed her roughly, forcing her mouth wide and scraping his teeth against hers.

Out of breath they broke off the kiss. She knelt down and stretched out on the hay. Deftly now, she undid the buttons and pulled off her shirt. Then cupping her breasts she tantalized him, giving a little nod. But he still hesitated. With a slight frown that was part of a smile, she said, "Here. Come here."

Johnny stood still for a few seconds and then could stand no more. He sank to his knees beside her. As she brought his head down to her breasts, he felt himself losing all control. Not only their softness, but also the softness of her entire being closing around him. He kissed her breasts until her nipples rose fully, and then he slowly moved up her neck until his mouth was on hers again. As his eyes closed he felt he was drowning in her. He could feel her hands unbuckling her britches and her hips raised so she could slip them down. He straightened up then, looking down into her eyes, tore off his shirt and shinnied out of his pants. As she swayed into his embrace he slipped between her legs and entered her.

Fingers intertwined and with her breasts tight against him they ground against each other until his pubic bone burned. There was a savage fierceness in her eyes and she rolled her head back and forth. She lifted her head and bit his lip and in one motion he reached back around her legs and raised them toward her shoulders. With each long stroke she moaned in pleasure and he was driven to penetrate even deeper. It seemed like every nerve in his body poured through his manhood into her and at last he cried out, slumping over, shuddering uncontrollably as he lost contact with the world around him.

She had shuddered and gasped somewhere along the way and it was all he remembered. Whether he blacked out for a moment or was so submerged in exhaustion that he slept, he couldn't tell. When his eyes opened, she was lying in his arms. Her hair was tangled and shadowing her eyes. Through it her eyes were open, staring at the roof. Her breasts were rising and falling in a cadence with her fingers, which were twitching beside her, palm-up in a tunnel of light. Almost shyly he rolled onto his side facing her, waiting for her to move or speak.

They lay like this for a long time. He began to stroke her arm and moved to her breasts. Her breath became uneven again. And before he knew it she was on top of him, this time alone, it seemed to him, grinding her pelvis against his already raw flesh until he winced and bit his lip. Her eyes were closed and her head high as she grabbed his hair and brought his mouth against her breasts. He sucked like a child, kneading her back with his fingers and moving down slowly to squeeze her buttocks. She moved faster. By her breathing he could tell she was about to surrender and pulled away from her breasts to watch. Her face was distorted in pleasure and as her legs opened wider and she mashed down in one last excruciating grind, he knew she was lost.

He tried to catch up, not caring if she waked the dead. He seized her by the hips and bucked, trying to shove high into her.

"Jaysus!" she moaned, jerking uncontrollably before slumping against him and burying her face between his neck and shoulder. Although she nuzzled him lovingly, he lay there brought back to earth and oddly frightened, staring up at the ceiling, having no idea why but thinking they were inviting a tragedy darker than any he could imagine. He felt her fingers on his lips and tasted her.

"Johnny Flynn," she whispered.

He shivered and tried to smile and for a moment her eyes smiled back, but he felt his face start to sag.

She noticed instantly. "Is anything wrong?"

He could barely breathe. "You are beautiful," he said, touching her cheek with his hand.

Shaking her head as she turned toward him, she smiled broadly but her eyes suggested she hadn't been taken in. "For itself beauty has little value," she said.

The spell was broken.

"But what about love?" he said.

"What good is love if there is no freedom? If we put ourselves first now, we sacrifice a chance of wider love," she said, rubbing her brow. "Did you ever hear your mother or father say they loved one another?"

Johnny didn't have to think about it. "No, not in so many words."

"Nor I," she said. "Love was there, I'm sure of it, if nowhere else than in their eyes and in the way they treated each other. It was certainly there for Ireland, as if She was his true love."

Johnny was disappointed she'd routed the conversation away from the two of them but at the same time he'd heard her voice, honest and sincere and below the surface wondered if he had actually heard what he'd wanted to hear, only spoken in code. He decided to rest on the hopes that he had. "My father was like that, too. When he sang it was always about Ireland," he said. "He'd rage, you know, claiming he hated her but that was the lie. He couldn't bear not to be part of her."

"Maybe it's the hating, too, maybe that's love in a way. Like this war we're in."

She had spelled it out clearly, though he still felt at a loss. Kneeling behind her now, he held her shirt so she could slip her arms into the sleeves. "No matter the killing?" he said.

She tossed her hair over her collar and began buttoning the shirt. Reaching for her jacket, she glanced over her shoulder. "Without it, we die, not England. Tyranny is the enemy here."

"So, there's no room for sharing the rule with England?"

She turned so swiftly he flinched, wishing to hell he'd kept quiet.

"You mean Home Rule? I'd sooner die first."

"I'd sooner die first." As they lay there for the better part of an hour the words rang in his ears. He could not sleep but was content to simply listen to her soft breathing and watch as her chest barely rose and fell. The worries over his section alternated with those about her and in an effort to restrain both he thought about the war and what he had signed on for – if ever he could recall what it had been. Revenge, though seemingly justified?

Forgiveness? For what he had done in Kilmainham, for the boy with a bullet through his eye, the woman murdered at Trinity College, Nora's father? The good of Ireland at any cost? He stewed until the sun began to blush the loft. Then he gently awakened her and felt the weight of his despair fade when she smiled.

Chapter Twenty-seven

They dressed and made their way toward the O'Brien's. The dirt roads crossed were unmarked paths into the wilderness, but at last they found an old, narrow section of Cork Road that appeared abandoned. The deep ditch beside it gave them coverage. About an hour later they had to duck out of sight as several armored cars rolled slowly past, shaking dirt and pebbles into the ditch. Barely down the road, the cars ground to a halt to fire a dozen rounds into the morning, the arcing trails brighter than the rising sun. Afterwards, when they rumbled away, Johnny and Nora wiped off the rubble and ran bent over like cripples until the awkwardness forced them to straighten. As they began to recognize the land, they ran harder. At last the O'Brien's came into view and they jumped out of the ditch in unison and sprinted across the meadow to the house.

Three mates, Jonas Halas, Tommy Rule and Hap were standing guard in the woods beside the house, and when they recognized Johnny's flailing arms they emerged waving their rifles and shouting as they ran towards them. The lads grabbed Johnny and Nora and lifted them off the ground. They yelled for the rest who joined them in the merriment, tossing Nora and Johnny like ragdolls and even kissing them. Refusing to let them down, they carried them laughing into the house.

When Johnny informed them of Liam's fate, the celebration quieted momentarily. There were prayers and praise for Liam, but given the number of lives that could have been lost, the return of Johnny and Nora and the rousing success of the ambush overcame the sadness. The number of the Essex dead was tallied in an outrageous auction with bodies for the bid. A dozen, no fifteen, no twenty, yes! Twenty bodies left motionless in the center! A roar went up when the count reached an estimate of at least another twenty trapped in Angel's, a total that far outdistanced any the Brits had ever experienced. They would deny the count, of course, and the English papers would side with them, but there would be no mistaking the devastating effects the truth would have.

When Johnny asked about the deafening noise that had flooded the lane during their escape, the fellows almost competed for a chance to tell the story. Cass won the honor.

"The fairies were at play, I tell you. Two of the eejits' cars slammed into one another, leaving the third to back the throttle and spin like a child's carriage while the driver tried to decide whether to keep firing at the buildings and his mates or halt the shelling and stop the damn thing from turning – if he could. It was a fool's choice! We stood there laughing so hard we didn't know which of the three outcomes to place a chit on. It was foolish of us. I mean we could have been ambushed if more Tans had fled the barracks but I suppose it's a case of who's the greater fool! By God, the Essex won that distinction by a landslide! We saw them hanging out the barracks' windows watching, same as we. But I'll tell you now, it wasn't a minute after we left the bridge that the dread overtook us: not knowing what had happened to you two. Welcome back, mates!"

Their homecoming became a festival. Everyone took to the woods to drink whiskey and smoke and laugh at the constant upgrading of the story. The lads even bid the auction again, this time running the totals to thirty dead in the center, having forgotten, as they admitted, the five member crew in each of the two lorries and those barely alive on the street who no doubt had eventually perished.

"No way out for those buggers except through Hell's gates!" Hap weighed in.

Nora sat by Buckley on a log across from Johnny. She seemed thrilled with the camaraderie. *It was as if her father was watching,* Johnny thought. She joined the fray, raising her tankard and cheering at the slightest reason to do so. Whenever she looked at him, there was a smile in her eyes. He hoped it was an acknowledgement that their relationship had changed forever. She had allowed him inside her very being. But if that was clearly in her eyes, there were also her unforgettable words of caution, "I'd sooner die first," a warning that levels were layered within souls and some had preference over others, like those that lay between her and her father.

As evening approached, everyone headed off for a good night's rest. Nora and Johnny waited until they had said their goodnights and were alone before turning to kiss him. The touch of her lips made him realize he had never felt so close to another person. Though she had not really acknowledged her love for him, her eyes revealed she wasn't far from it. He waited, his hand tracing the contours of her face.

"No doubt the Brits are craving revenge," she said.

He let his disappointment drain into the silence. "That's not what I was hoping you'd say."

"I know that, but we're at war, Johnny. What happens if one of us is killed, or maimed?"

"All for the glory of Ireland," he said.

"You're being sarcastic."

"But you've said as much yourself."

Her eyes were unflinching. "It's true." She paused. "But it is also true I love you."

Stunned, his head whirled with elation. He wanted to shout but instead spun around in the fallen leaves and tried to dance with her.

"Stop it," she protested. "You'll wake the entire section."

"Worse than that, we'll wake the Tans," he said. He stopped moving, held her in his arms, and kissed her again.

She pulled away gently. "I've said it, Johnny, but it doesn't change things. It only makes them worse, I'm afraid."

As they walked to the front door, he held her hand. "Then we'll fight apart," he said. "You can go into Dole's section. That way, if something does happen…" His voice trailed off.

"We won't witness it," she finished for him.

Chapter Twenty-eight

The attack on Angel's had been the greatest success of the war, but there was to be no rest. Intelligence from Ballyhandle reported a large scale build-up of British forces in west Cork. Nora had gotten it exactly right. The enemy was gathering en mass, Tans, Auxies and the R.I.C. to surround the Volunteers and revenge their embarrassment at being caught so flatfooted in Bandon. They had learned the Volunteers' positions from three outlooks who were caught and throttled in Upton. Of the three, two were broken and revealed the locations. The third revealed nothing and was hanged for it.

To prepare for what was coming, Volunteers were hurrying to enlist every available man in the area's small towns. They now totaled a hundred and four men – and one woman, yet the number paled in comparison to the estimates of over a thousand British troops preparing to tighten the noose.

Johnny listened dutifully but given the counts he wondered if the small flying columns, though a bit larger with the additional recruits, could be effective against such odds. The number of sections had increased to seven from five and the number of members within a section to fourteen from eleven. Thus, on the grand scale they were outnumbered about ten to one.

As if Buckley had a window to his thoughts, he smiled. "The odds have been narrowed considerably by the addition of a piper, Florence Kerry. They call him the Pied Piper of the Rebel Fields. He's such a boon to our fellows the Brits have more than a hundred shillings on his life."

"It must be the fairies what's protecting him," Hap replied.

Chuckles came and Hap put up his hand. "I'm not joshing you. I seen them stand between a man and death before. 'Twas before I joined up. In the bogs of Fermoy just after we'd fed a section of Volunteers and put them up for the night. The Tans raided the town the next day, taking hostages and demanding we tell them what we knew. When nobody spoke up they forced us out to the bogs where the fairies swarmed down from the trees. A nest of them formed a shield around us. The bastards emptied their guns at them but the little angels just laughed. That's when the Tans broke and ran. I seen it and I swear to it."

No one laughed. No one spoke. They just stared at Hap.

"They were in Kilmichael as well," Nora said. "When I cleaned the face of poor Jimmy Teague. I didn't know it at the time but, but now I do. We were in their presence."

"And perhaps with Piper Kerry with us they still are," Buckley said. "The Brits are making a crucial mistake in their effort to surround us. Intelligence has spotted about three hundred on their way from Kinsale, but in their stupidly rigid way of waging a fight, a column of one hundred has been ordered ahead of the rest by two kilometers. That leaves an even larger than normal gap between the advance section and the backup. So, we are now their equal in size and much their superiors in morale. Had they drawn the noose evenly all around, it would have been suicide to engage them, but as it is, they're going to meet their Maker. This is what we have been hoping for, a huge mistake in our favor."

Buckley looked at them and his eyes settled inward, as if he'd just realized that his enthusiasm had betrayed him. The silence was broken when he appeared to regroup.

"We will intercept them at Crossbarry this very night and strike with Kerry piping." He had lowered his tone but his voice was firm. "Have no doubt, he will lead us to victory. We will join him and the other sections as we approach Ballyhandle. We have but forty cartridges a person, so make sure your aim is certain. Take as much ammo and as many weapons from the dead as you can carry. Any questions? If not, Johnny, may I see you for a minute?"

Johnny followed Sean behind a stone wall out of earshot of the others. "Remember Marley O'Donald, our spy in Bandon?"

"I'll never forget him."

"Then, remember him as you do. Marley was one of the three Volunteers the Tans caught and thrashed. Two of the lads spilled their guts out, but Marley was not one of them. He kept his mouth shut to the bitter end when he was hanged from a tree. It is dreadful but I thought you should know."

On the way back to his section, Johnny could not shake the vision of O'Donald hanging from a tree, crutches on the ground and his battered legs swinging in the breeze. He felt terrible for initially doubting the poor man, especially knowing now that O'Donald had saved his life and that of his mates and if that weren't enough, he'd ultimately provided the path to the Bandon victory. To beat and hang Marley, no matter his role in the Volunteers, was as cruel and unforgiving as the killing of Nora's father.

All bets were off at last. Leniency, pity, sorrow and guilt were no longer stakes on the table. At last the confusion had cleared, the back and forth, the sympathy and guilt. His conscience was clear as purpose had narrowed to the incorrigible purity of revenge. *Forgiveness had no place in this war, and perhaps nowhere else*, he told himself.

He hustled back to get his ammunition. Taking more than his share, he caught Nora staring at him askance, as if to remind him that with any extra bullets he was denying someone else an equal chance to protect himself. So, he emptied his pockets in front of her, making sure to count out no more than forty rounds, loaded his weapons and tucked what remained into his pockets. He would make sure every shot hit its mark and then help himself to the spoils.

He replaced Nora in his section with Jordon Lucy. With that she'd turned away quickly and had not looked back. As evening approached he tried to find her and explain how he just could not keep his mind on his mission if she were close to him on the battlefield, but with the newly added sections the column was much larger, so along with the other section leaders he set off across the valley and the hills beyond, trying his damnedest to stay on purpose.

Just short of Ballyhandle, Buckley stopped the advance and Johnny took the lead section to the western entrance of a double crossroads and positioned them in the ditch on the far side of the road. The second and third sections stacked stones waist high beside the road as a barricade to the Tans' gunfire. Johnny assigned two men the duty of tossing Mills bombs as the lorries passed by. To the east a farmstead was visible, said to contain a handful of elderly Volunteers, who were too old to man the ditches but with rifles resting on the windowsills could help create the illusion of an even stronger force. Farther down the road the added sections were setting up. Anxiously fingering the trigger lock on his pistol, he found himself wondering if Nora was thinking of him.

The distant sound of lorries came first as a low but persistent hum. The sections waited in total silence until the noise became a rumble. Everyone unlocked his weapons. As the vehicles crept into view Johnny thought he'd never seen as many as a dozen bunched together, not even in Dublin. They filled the road for as far as he could see, but just as he was beginning to worry that the Brits had changed their battle plan and closed ranks with the rearguard, the expected break in the line appeared. Though the gap was not as great as he expected, even so the enemy had made a colossal mistake.

The first few lorries lumbered past and he clenched his jaw to kept from giving the order to fire, but when six vehicles had passed, placing the lead within a toss of the Mills bombs he stood and shouted, "Fire!" The sections rose as though tied to one overarching leash and opened fire.

Immediately Kerry seemed to come from nowhere and started playing the pipes. The two lead lorries were blown apart by the bombs. Instantly the others stopped. In a panic the Tans started jumping out of the vehicles, yelling, and pointing in every direction. Bullets whistled through the air, overcome only by the screams of those who were hit. It went on for only a few minutes but to Johnny's shock the British then broke and ran, leaving their dead scattered over the road. Like panicked field mice they scrambled through the ditch on the opposite far side of the road and made off into the fields.

Some of the men in Johnny's section started to give chase. He shouted for them to come back but Casey Nelson and Deft Martin fell as more shots rang out. Before he could get to them the Tans rearguard was closing much faster than Buckley had figured.

The counterattack was not much to begin with because the lorries from the rear stopped short and the Tans had to run toward the lagging sections, making them easy targets. But the attacking weapons were now machine guns and helped erase the difference in time. Had the Tans actually outsmarted them?

Johnny hit the ground and fired until he ran out of bullets. He crawled over to Nelson's body and stripped him of his rifle and ammo, then fired through the dry grass until the belt was empty. Fifteen yards away Martin was lying face-down on the ground. Without thinking Johnny scrambled to his feet and ran to him. Kneeling over him he fired into a curtain of smoke that was descending on the road. He stood again, not caring if he lived or died. He kept on firing, calling out repeatedly, "You fecking bastards!"

The armored cars opened up and he felt the vibrations of shells bursting. From their chilling whistle overhead and the shaking of the ground when they hit, he knew he was directly in the line of fire. Suddenly he realized the piper was silent. It had all turned for the Tans so fast. It was only a matter of faith that Nora had found a way out.

And then the noise of heavy gunfire passed like a barge bell on the Liffey, slowly and steadily fading southward. The lorries that had not been destroyed were starting up again. Through the smoke he could see them beginning to inch away, slowly backing off the road to turn toward whence they had come. Johnny was stunned. Just when they appeared to be gaining the upper hand, they shockingly turned and ran. Pawth had been right.

Rifle in one hand, pistol in the other, he made his way to the road. The whole scene reeked of gunpowder and scorched earth. Johnny began trudging toward Nora's section. He stepped over bodies from both sides. His eyes skipped over everything, afraid of finding her dark hair. The lads had set a couple of the lorries on fire, burning them with the Brits' own fuel. Cordite from the smoke caused his eyes to burn so much that they began to tear, blurring his vision. The mist on the road glistened, making it even harder for him to see. He called out for Nora, using Sarosa, but his voice seemed to drown in the victorious shouts of the men as he passed by. He felt their joy and wanted to return it in kind but now he was certain she'd been killed.

He heard a soldier's voice off in the field calling for help. He started to leave but the voice became a cry of pain, then a faint scream. What if it were a Brit? He continued along the road to distance himself but he couldn't keep the cries out.

At last he slowed. "Shut up, damn you! Shut up! Shut up!" he called but move towards the voice. He'd hardly gotten into the field when he came upon the young Tan. Next to him lay his rifle. The man's scorched face told Johnny he, too, was surely dying but his eyes still pleaded for help. The fellow broke into a strange, shocking smile and his fingers danced on the breast pocket of his uniform.

"In here," he rasped, fumbling at the button on his breast pocket. "Take it to the post, will you mate?"

Johnny reached out to help and the man grabbed his wrist and squeezed. Johnny tried to draw back but the soldier clung to him, pulling him closer. "It's a letter to my father."

"Yes. All right," Johnny said. As he attempted with his free hand to unbutton the pocket, the soldier stiffened and fell back dead. Johnny tried to offer up a prayer but the words stopped deep in his throat. Puffing his cheeks and sighing, he reached for the envelope. There was no name, just an address he could barely make out, somewhere in Liverpool. He turned it over but there was no return address. He slipped it into his pocket, telling himself it certainly wouldn't be treason to send it.

When he stood up he was lightheaded. His mind returned to Nora and he looked around again. The mist had risen and he was amazed to discover he was almost a mile from his section, but before he had a chance to fully orient himself he saw a soldier standing in the distance. He was thin with a mat of uncombed hair and for a moment he wondered if it could be Nora and then as he watched the soldier gather arms from the British dead, he knew his mind was playing tricks on him. He was battle-fatigued.

As Johnny approached, he saw that the soldier was limping under the load of a half-dozen rifles slung across his back, a new British machine gun and several fully loaded pans of ammo. Then, he saw a discarded bagpipe lying riddled by the side of the road and recognized the man as Piper Kerry.

"Hey, there!" Johnny called again, waving as he broke into a trot.

Kerry's eyes were glazed and he appeared stunned at the sight of another human. Staggering, he tried to steady himself and Johnny saw a leaking gash on the broad face. The piper had tried to cover the wound with a bandana but blood still seeped from his beard and ran down his neck and shoulder.

"You're in no shape to be doing that," Johnny said. "Let me help you."

Kerry grabbed for one of the rifles but it tangled in the others and the whole mess spun him around so he had his back to Johnny. Then, he whirled as if he was afraid of being attacked to face Johnny again. "I'm a Volunteer," Johnny said. "Here, sit down. The Brits are gone. That wound needs tending."

Kerry gaped at him. "But we need guns."

"Aye," Johnny said, "that we do, but we need men even more, and taking care of yourself is the most important thing now."

At that Kerry's mouth moved and he swayed. Everything on his back clanked and shifted, staggering him. His feet tried to keep up with his body but gave out and he fell, clanging to the ground. Johnny ran over to him. Pain was written all over Kerry's face. A portion of his beard had been ripped out. The exposed shin was a mass of thickened blood.

"We beat the bastards, but they took a measure of us," he said, squinting at the sky. "The ammunition here is for the boys. Would you bring me pipes over, lad?"

Johnny retrieved the broken pipes and handed them to Kerry. "Bless you. We loved your playing," Johnny said.

A natural gap appeared in the beard. Johnny thought it was a hidden smile. "The sound of the pipes," Kerry said, "is the lullaby of God."

Johnny knelt beside him. Feeling as guilty as a believer who has cursed Christ, he leaned over. "By chance did you happen to see the woman amongst us?"

Kerry's eyes widened. "Aye. A princess among men," he said. "No one fought harder or braver."

"Did she...is she all right?"

Kerry stared at the sky and did not answer.

Johnny tried again. "The woman, do you think she's all right?" No sooner were the words out than Kerry's chest went still. Johnny shook him gently, then more harshly as anger at the man's dying welled up inside him. "Damn you! Is she alive?" he shouted.

He grabbed the bagpipe and started to jerk it out of Kerry's arms but stopped, realizing this was the behavior of an Essex. Now overcome with exhaustion, he got to his feet and looked down at Kerry. He could have taken a couple of the rifles or maybe a pan or two of ammunition. For God's sake, he could have buried the man, but none of that made much sense now. So, he simply reached down and closed Kerry's eyes.

The smoke was lifting but the fields still held a deep layer of thick mist. The air was so still Johnny felt that if he called out his voice would carry to Kinsale Bay and Nora would hear him no matter where she was. He did call out to her, several times, yet his voice seemed to travel only to the edge of the field and die there. Wading into the fog he glanced back to the fallen piper and moved in the direction of his section.

His thoughts were filled with the shadowy images of faces that had haunted him before. Only now there were more. He saw the features of a hundred dead strewn on a panoply of months. There were the faces of Billy O'Neill and Liam Casey, Jimmy Teague and countless others he didn't know. There were faces of the enemy, the startled faces of the men who had jumped out of the lorry only to find the Volunteers already firing at them. There was the farmer holding his lifeless dog, assured the animal would return to life and that of Marley O'Donald hanging from the branch of a tree. There was Nurse Shannon who treated him, the face of the boy in Dublin and the strange unseen face of Judge Gaggin just before he was shot. His father was there, too, in this weird hell of the dead, accompanied by Pearse, sarcastically admiring Kilmainham's murals, mocking heaven, and James Connolly sitting before him, his voice oddly still. And drifting between and among them all, Nora's stunning face, looking at him, moving toward him.

Tears came to fruition this time; at long last they flowed. He stood until they slowed, licking at the salty brine as if it were an elixir of sorts. As the tears slowed he wiped his eyes, licked his fingers and headed toward the last of the column thinking of her all the time, but the farther he walked the more alone he felt.

He was well past the farmhouse before anyone spotted him. Had not Nora come running out with two Volunteers on her heels, he most likely would have passed it by or gone there only as a last resort. His heart leapt. Everything that had been plaguing him vanished and he ran toward her. The pursuing Volunteers stopped at twenty yards and watched as they collided.

He kissed her hard on the mouth as she clung to him and then buried his face in her hair. "You're safe," he whispered, thinking how small she felt in his arms. She pulled away slightly, wiped her eyes, and looked at him. He had never seen her smile so enthusiastically and believed it to be the most incredible smile he had ever seen on anyone, man or woman. It narrowed her lips but only added to their sensuality. Her eyes beamed and her face glowed while narrowing into a trustful joy.

"We won!" she said, ebulliently. "The British ran! The cowards ran!"

Her eyes danced in the expectation he would be overjoyed but the elation he'd felt at finding her began to slip away. "I didn't know you had been sent to the farmhouse."

"We were on road firing in the midst of the pipes when an elder was shot. I was sent to help."

"All I could think of was you..."

"And I you," she said evenly, rescuing the moment.

Chapter Twenty-nine

At the second victory celebration within a fortnight, the cooks served potatoes, eggs and a double rasher of bacon in beer broth. They brought wine to wash the whiskey down and as Buckley gave an inspired account of the battle, they let their spirits soar. They drank and drank some more. Johnny was soon downing his wine with a determination that no one get ahead of him. He laughed at the jokes and watched Nora as the men became raunchy. She did not turn away once or even blush but laughed into the shock of the humor. Soon a young soldier by the name of Seamus stood up and after removing his cap began to sing.

His voice was sure. The words of *Carrickfergus* came drifting out on the rise of an eerie tenor and swept among them like a warm cloak. Johnny could feel the lilt of the young man's voice caressing his mind and calming him. He made his way to Nora and put his arm around her shoulder as she, too, began to sing, softly at first. He watched her lips barely move and wanted to kiss them ever so lightly but didn't dare in front of everyone. She was leaning into him only to rock slightly so that his arm slipped from her shoulders. She stood like a man, both feet planted, and began to sing louder until her voice blended with that of the young soldier's. Soon the others stopped to listen as the two of them faced each other and sang. A pang of jealousy hit Johnny and he almost tried to join in, but caught himself and remained quiet. At last they finished and after a silent moment a soldier began to clap and then others until everyone was cheering and calling for more. Nora blushed and glanced away as if she was concealing something. As she slowly raised her head, he saw tears pouring from her large brown eyes.

"That was beautiful," he said with sincerity, though it sounded slightly insincere to his ears. She took it demurely, bowing her head, then surprisingly took his arm and whispered,

"I want you," she said, "now."

His heart raced. "But we can't. Not here."

"But we can. Out back. There's a little wooded area past where the prisoners are being kept. I'll meet you there in five minutes." She raised a finger to her smiling lips and moved past to a second chorus of cheers, brushing him as she passed by.

Watching her go, Johnny pictured her naked body and his ardor was instantaneous. He struggled to wait a few minutes so their leaving wouldn't be so obvious. He started to sip at his drink but was afraid he'd already had too much to perform. He felt the pressure in his groin and sat back to hide his growing member when a cook named Lon came out of nowhere and slapped him on the back.

"We're glad you're back. How was it out there?"

"A bout with Satan's brood, lad...but see here, my bladder's killing me. All the whiskey..."

"You go and hurry back. I want to hear all about it."

As Johnny made his way to the rear of the house he heard voices coming from what appeared to be a tool shed. He assumed they belonged to the prisoners and wondered what would happen to them but the thought was fleeting as he headed down a path covered with freshly trampled ivy. He went cautiously until he heard Nora laugh and then he stopped, having no idea what direction it came from. She laughed again, quieter this time.

"Up here," she said, "straight up the hill."

He couldn't see a thing. "Where are you?" he called softly.

"On top, of course," she laughed.

The hill crested in short order and he stopped, hoping his eyes would adjust to the dark. In a small clearing five feet away he saw her, courtesy of the moon, completely nude except for a pair of dark stockings that rose to the middle her thighs. Reflexively, he looked away and then caught himself, realizing he'd never seen her full body before, at least not from a distance that allowed him to take in all of her. Her breasts were generous but firm and her small waist flared into sensual hips that set off the deep and wide triangle between her legs. He stared between her legs without meaning to, and then grabbed at his belt like a crab digging sand, shoving his pants down onto his boots. Trapped in embarrassment he hopped to the nearest tree. Standing first on one foot and then the other he snatched at the laces, tore his boots off and yanked his feet from his trousers. Overcome with desire, he rushed toward her.

In a flurry of motion his hands were all over her, from her shoulders to her back. Cupping her buttocks he drew her up and onto him. In one rough move he backed her into a tree. She gasped. He felt her legs go around him and she took control. She had gained leverage and in turn the advantage and rode teasingly up his shaft to the tip as he rose up on his feet and virtually clawed at the tree to shove deeper into her. But try as he might she had too much leverage and the taunting smile on her face told him she loved it. Without warning she sank down until he was buried to the hilt. Just as he was preparing to lose it all, she slipped up and off.

"Damn you," he moaned and she bit his ear, rimming it with her tongue and whispering.

"Lie down on the ground," she said, letting her legs slip from his waist.

He backed away, feeling behind him as he lowered himself into the ivy, watching her stalk him. Staring at his groin she came to him and straddled him, kneading her breasts. She squatted slowly and he closed his eyes waiting for her. To his surprise she took him into her mouth, forcing him between her barely opened teeth so that they scraped roughly over the tip. As the pain shot though him he stifled a cry, almost whimpering as she raised her head and straddled him on her knees.

"I want you to last," she said, briefly taking his cock in her hand and positioning it at her damp opening. She slid it back and forth a few times as the pain diminished and then she slowly impaled herself. At first, though he was still rigid, his penis was numb from her teeth, but as she pulled his head to her breasts, the feeling returned and he wondered how long he could last. He held on by sheer willpower, looking over her hunched shoulders at the moon and trees, trying not to think about what was happening. It worked but only briefly. Things started to give way. She must have sensed it, too, for she began to move faster, rising and plunging furiously. At the last moment when she must have sensed he was going to cry out she jerked his mouth away from a nipple and clamped her lips over his so that the sound stayed within them, a long breathless moan that seemed to echo through them both, lodging so deep within him he heard it in his chest and gut.

At last she released him and let him lie back in the ivy, but she was not done. Once was not enough for her. Like in the coach house, she did not wait but quickly slipped him inside and spread her knees. He was numb at first and thought surely he would be of no use to her whatsoever, but to his amazement, as she moved her hips against his pelvis, he hardened again. She bore down, splaying her legs so that she mashed herself flat against his pelvis and then began to move in small circular motions. He thought she would never stop and pushed down into the ivy to relieve the pain but she did not ease off. Finally, he took her by the hips and tried to raise her slightly to gain relief but she grabbed his wrists with the force of a man, pinning them to the ground as she fought to stifle her cry.

It came from deep in her throat and then she slumped over him, chest heaving. Her hair fell over his face and she lightly kissed his throat. Her body twitched as she nuzzled against him. Gradually she let her weight bear on him as she straightened her legs, slipping him out of her. After a few minutes her breathing had slowed so much he thought she'd gone to sleep and lay there stroking her back.

"I've never felt anything like that," she said, sounding

faraway, as if in a daze. "I didn't know where I was." Lifting her head, she looked at him. "I thought I was dying."

He brushed the hair from her eyes. "I love you," he blurted out, feeling the last vestiges of this particular secrecy leave him and with them a loss and lightness, the way he'd felt in confession as a child, shame with pride, nakedness and embarrassment. He waited, hoping she would say she loved him, too.

Tears glazed her eyes and she continued to smile, but she said only this: "Love between two people, strange that." Her eyes raised as if she was watching the words spin around in her mind.

"What's strange about it?" he said.

"Hearing it, for one." She glanced at him. "Hearing someone say he loves you...it sort of shocked me."

Johnny chuckled. "It shocked me, too."

She kissed his hand and whispered, "If it weren't for the war, I would let myself be so in love with you, the rest be damned."

It was a big admission for her, he knew, and so he did not press her to define it further. It was the most he could hope for and he was delighted. He pulled her jacket up over her. "When the war's over, I'm going to hold you to it," he said. "I'll remind you of tonight."

"Remind me?" she said, dreamily. "You won't have to remind me. I'll never forget."

"You sound like I'm never going to see you again."

She hesitated. "It's not that so much as..."

"What?"

"I don't know exactly," she said, putting her hands on his chest and resting her chin on them. "It's just the way I felt...like you'd pierced my soul..." She paused. "Like the day my father died. They wouldn't let us go there." Her eyes widened as if Johnny had asked her a question. "Yes, I would have gone. It would have been unbearable but I would have. Not being there was worse, but I heard the firing squad as clearly as if I had been, and I know it was no mistake, a quarter to four, one volley..."

Johnny was almost holding his breath, remembering how Connelly braced himself in the chair and called out. "And then what?" he said.

But Nora showed no indication she suspected anything. "The final act of murder," she said, "the coup de grace, for lack of a better term, that single shot fired into my father's brain." She backed away from him. "I heard that, too, all the way over the walls of Kilmainham, and that's when I looked at my watch. 'Twas a quarter of four."

Johnny tried to draw her to him, but she stayed her place, her moonstruck eyes searching over his shoulder into the darkness. "It's past," he said, hoping to assuage her and at the same time seeking to change the conversation, but her eyes were fastened on the darkness and she shuddered.

"He called out before they shot him," she said, glancing at Johnny.

He froze, thankful for the darkness, knowing she couldn't see him blanche. He felt the blood seeping into the pit of his stomach, leaving him cold and speechless. He told himself she was fantasizing, that she'd heard nothing. Of course, she hadn't. Her family's flat had been miles away, but his body wasn't convinced. His hands felt numb. As he dragged them over her back he couldn't feel her skin. He tried to tell her again that it was all in the past but he couldn't speak as her father's voice descended, commanding him.

"Shoot straight, Johnny Flynn!"

Hesitant words escaped his lips. "You couldn't know that."

She stared at him for a long time and he froze.

"I overheard it from the soldiers who accosted me." She glanced at him. "You're shivering."

Johnny tried to look at her. "What did they say?"

Nora drew her bottom lip under her front teeth and shook her head slowly. The words seemed stuck in her throat. "They said...they said he begged forgiveness, which he would never have done. They said he cursed Ireland." She paused, moving away and picking up her clothes. Her voice broke. "They said he asked for me."

Johnny tried to hold her again but she refused, putting on her clothes instead. "That was damned cruel of the bastards."

"I wanted to kill them, but I couldn't move. It was like someone had knocked the breath out of me. I knew it wasn't true. To this day I know that, but even now it gets to me. I loved my father more than anything in the world, and I would give anything to know what he really said. Anything."

"Maybe there's nothing," he said softly. "Maybe it was all a lie."

Buttoning her jacket, she glanced up at him. "As surely as words just came from your lips, they came from his at that very moment. There's no doubt about that. He called out. He did. No doubt 'twas for Ireland."

Johnny tried to keep the memories of that day at bay, but it was impossible. The ambulance drove into his mind as surely as if he were seeing it for the first time, and in no perfect order he heard the rustling of the men's feet when the lieutenant gave them the order to kneel, felt the weight of the rifle and sighting along the barrel watched Connelly brace and his huge brown eyes open wide as he shouted.

"Shoot straight, Johnny Flynn!"

"I want to see the prisoners," Nora said.

He had trouble distinguishing her voice from her father's but he knew she had spoken. "I'm sorry. I didn't hear you," he said as they emerged from the woods onto the field.

"The Ashbourne section took three prisoners at Crossbarry and I'd like to see them," she said.

"It's after midnight."

"You go on then," she said, heading toward the shed.

"What for?" he called.

"Maybe one of them is the sonofabitch who put me up against

231

that wall."

"You can't be serious?"

"You think I'm joking?"

"No, no. Of course not, but there's not a chance in a million."
Her eyes scanned his face. "I said, you go on, turn in."

"What the hell," he said. "I'll go with you. Somebody's got to
protect them."

"Very funny," she said, leading the way.

He followed her down to the small shed, a lean-to built into
the rise of the hill, lit by lanterns from inside, causing the slats to
glow in ribbons of fire and filling the corner of the field with a
glow. There were no windows and no chimney and as he got
closer the light seemed to singe the air around it. Gavin Duffy
and another volunteer Johnny didn't recognize were standing
guard at the entrance. They smelled of whiskey and tobacco.
"Johnny and the missus," Duffy said, slurring his words and
faking a bow.

"Watch your mouth," Johnny snapped. "We want to see the
prisoners."

"See 'em?" Duffy said. "Nothing to see. Pasty white bastards.
We're going to run 'em naked in the fields tomorrow and bring
'em down like crows. See 'em? Hell, yes, you can see 'em!" He
started to cackle and the other fellow joined in.

Duffy lifted the bar and pushed the door open, bowing again
and waving them inside. "You can see 'em all right, every last
inch of them."

When they stepped into the room the bright glow of two gas
lanterns made Johnny blink. Squinting, he reached for the
lanterns and turned them down. Nora gasped at the sight of three
naked men groping to cover themselves with handfuls of straw.
Johnny looked up at the patches of soot on the ceiling and slowly
lowered his eyes to the beaten, nude bodies before him. As he did
so, he reached out to turn Nora away but she shrugged him off.

For a moment the men were motionless, then one scrambled

into a corner and shouted for them to get out. Another scraped straw over his lap and sat there flushed like an embarrassed child. The third, still lying on the floor, was slow to move. Johnny could see he'd had the worst of it. There was a bullet hole in his shoulder and the thin bandage was matted with blood. His ear was covered with wrap and a piece of shrapnel had ripped a hole in his side. At least someone had had the compassion to pour iodine on the wounds. He lay on his good side, legs bent double and his face hidden from sight. Slowly he rolled on his back, groaning when the wounded shoulder came down on the straw. His face was battered, his eyes almost swollen shut but his voice carried the same gentleness as it had when they'd been shipmates from England.

"You went over, Johnny, back to Ireland."

Johnny's overturned mind was reeling in fear and confusion. He looked at Nora, wanting to shield her from this but knowing it was too late. But she stared straight ahead, resolved, as if a great mystery were unraveling in front of her. "We came together to Ireland – Dahl and I," Johnny managed, incapable of anything more.

She glanced at him, her eyes remote. He could not read the expression on her face but it did not seem to be one of anger or suspicion. He wanted her to say something but she remained silent, as if acknowledging this was his to resolve, not hers.

Johnny knelt beside Dahl and felt his burning forehead. "I'm glad for you," Dahl said. "I should have followed ye, but I just wanted out of it. It was only twelve months more. I didn't have the courage."

"Shut up, you fucking coward," said the Brit in the corner. He glared at Dahl. "A turncoat and a coward, bedfellows queer, if you ask me."

Johnny sprang to his feet and grabbed the man by the throat. "You've got exactly one chance to live and that's me. Another word out of you and you won't have that."

The other soldier spoke to his comrade. "Be still, damn you."

Through a forced and cocky grin the man sneered at Dahl. "You'll go down with us."

Johnny tightened his grip on the man's throat. "Duffy, take these two and run them. Now!"

"In the dark?"

"Yes."

"Does Sean know?"

"He does. These are regulars, not Tans. Send them off with a bullet, if they give you trouble. Otherwise, let them go," he said, releasing the soldier.

Duffy grinned. "We'll let 'em off on Cork Road. It'll give 'em half a chance. That's more than they'll have in the morning. Let's go," he said, taking his gun out and motioning toward the door.

Nora pulled her jacket tight around her shoulders. She spoke distinctly and slowly in a voice heavy with understanding. "It was the only way to save your friend."

It seemed like the first time he'd ever heard her sound this way – forgiving. And it had happened here, now, in this very awkward moment.

He looked at her. The strong features of her face calmed him. "Would you wake Sean and tell him what I've done?" he said. "If I haven't proven my loyalty by now, I never will. And something else. Kindly send us out some whiskey?"

She smiled back at him. "You've proven more than loyalty." She quietly closed the door after her.

Johnny accepted the idea he would never hear those words said with such genuineness. They bought him peace and he smiled. He turned the lamp to a flicker and lay down on the straw next to Dahl, putting his arm over his friend to keep him warm. As Dahl shivered, the heat of his fever waned and Johnny felt great tenderness toward him. Closing his eyes he smelled the straw and thought of his mother who had protected him just so in childhood. He thought of winter and mufflers and cardigans, comforters and yes, the futbol. He thought of fires and embers on the hearth, even the warmth of the pubs and the scratchy tweed of his father's long coat. He wanted to reach out and embrace it all, every memory, as if to keep them alive, and in so doing he held fast to Dahl in the fear that his mate's life might slip through his hands. As he clung to him he thought of all he'd done in the last year and asked forgiveness, hoping that somehow it would pass to help his friend.

The weak voice came to him from faraway, across time. It perplexed him at first and he heard himself mumble in reply.

"Who is it?"

"Dahl."

"Dahl?" Johnny said, trying to clear his head.

"Johnny, was that Nora Connolly?"

Johnny awoke with a start and moved back, allowing Dahl to roll up on his good shoulder. For a moment he was shocked to hear Nora's name but then remembered Dahl had seen her in the Castle.

"Yes," he answered. "Keep your voice down."

"What's she doing here?" Dahl whispered.

"She joined the Volunteers, just like I did. The rebel county drew us both."

Dahl tried to smile. "You finally found her."

"I guess I did."

"I can see her as a soldier," Dahl said, coughing so hard he jack-knifed upward. Johnny helped him back down. "She's got her dad in her. He was a fine man, Johnny. I don't ever think I told you – you left so soon after his execution – he asked me about you."

"Easy there. We'll talk some more in the morning. You need rest."

"I'm going to die anyway. I don't have time to rest," he said. "You know, her Da asked about you. Said he was sure in his heart you'd lay down your life for Ireland before it was done." Dahl's voice was as gentle as ever and concerned. It was as if his life reached out and never in.

Johnny smiled. "He was a wise man," he said, tucking Nora's jacket under Dahl's chin. Dahl had always been pale but now his face seemed strangely transparent, like onion skin. The veins of his temple pulsed in a knot and his eyelids fluttered.

"Nora Connolly, may the Lord have mercy..." Dahl said, barely audible. He coughed again and Johnny wiped phlegm from his lips. Then Dahl barked like a seal and grimaced in pain. "Cigarette?" he rasped.

"Now that would kill you sooner than you'd like," Johnny said. "No, I'm out, but when they send out the whiskey I'll get you one."

"Could you get me body back to Inishmore, Johnny? What's left of it, that is."

"Don't dwell on that. I've seen much worse make it."

"If I'm alive in the morning, they'll shoot me."

"We aren't British, Dahl. I'll speak up for you. You'll be fine. Count on it, and Nora and I'll nurse you back to health. Then you can walk to Inishmore, if you like."

Dahl smiled weakly. "That'll be the day." He paused as the door opened.

A soldier Johnny didn't recognize leaned in with a pint of whiskey and handed it to him, staring at Dahl. "Would you be drowning him in it, Sir?"

"Drowning myself first," Johnny said. "Lad, you wouldn't be having a couple of fags?"

"Sure," the soldier said, reaching into his jacket pocket and pulling out a pack of cigarettes. "Take 'em," he said tossing the pack to Johnny. "This detail can't be a lot of fun."

"I've stood guard before. This one's as good as a friend. Leave the bolt off when you go."

"But it's supposed to be down at all times."

"Not when there's a section leader inside. Never know when

we'll be needed, you see."

The soldier thought about that for a moment. "I do see," he said, at last, and closed the door without dropping the bolt.

Johnny twisted the cork out of the bottle and raised it cautiously to Dahl's lips, letting it trickle over them. Dahl licked at the brown liquid and coughed quietly. Johnny lit a cigarette and held it for him. Dahl sighed as it stuck to his lips and he inhaled, letting his eyes follow as the smoke drifted toward the ceiling. "God, that's good."

"Hell, you're easy," Johnny said. "Enough whiskey and tobacco and you'll be fighting for Ireland in no time."

"In no time I'll be fighting meself out of the fires below…" Dahl started to laugh but the coughing became too severe and the cigarette flew from his mouth onto the floor.

Johnny quickly mashed it out with his boot and waited as Dahl blinked several times.

"Johnny?"

"I'm here."

"I can't see, Johnny," Dahl said, voice rising.

Johnny was up on his knees. Dahl's eyes were blazing wide in panic. "It's all right," Johnny said, turning up the lantern.

Dahl sank back, sweating and lips trembling. He looked squarely at Johnny. "Dying's no fun, paddy," he said. A flicker of a smile played on his lips. "I see you better now. You're in a haze, but better."

Johnny mopped Dahl's brow with the sleeve of his jacket. "This fever is trying to break, that's all. You hang on."

Dahl's smile widened, but he coughed vehemently and when the spell eased he closed his eyes and stammered. "Johnny, what are you doing here? Help me understand the real reason. It ain't just about winning a war, is it? Tell me the truth, please."

Johnny did not want to answer but felt he should. He found himself nodding. "There was this feeling I had and still do, I suppose, that I needed to earn forgiveness fora all the all wrong

I did in Dublin and all I just stood by and witnessed." He hesitated and blew out a long breath. His eyes followed as if it were smoke.

Dahl looked both concerned and perplexed. "So you deserted your mates to earn forgiveness or something akin to it? I'm hard at trying to make sense of that, Johnny."

The word *deserted* stung but Johnny kept it to himself.

Dahl stared at the ceiling. "Well, maybe so. Considering the shape I'm in, I reckon I didn't earn no forgiveness for staying a Brit. Is that the doorstep I'm lying on? Is that what my dying is, the truth?"

"No," Johnny said, sadly. "It isn't. I know that now, though your blood can be stirred into believing anything when you see the horrors of it."

"Now that...that there has the ring of truth," Dahl said, struggling. "So, what'll you do, just finish it out just to see who's left standing?"

Johnny thought of Nora. "Somehow," he said and his voice trailed off. "I don't know. There's Nora, you see, and she's different than I am. The war's so personal for her, and she was brought up to give her life for Ireland."

"That's a bad father who would teach that."

"I'm not sure of that. It's just in the blood somehow, I think."

Dahl nodded. "But what about her? If Ireland wins, what will she do?"

"Dunno. If Home Rule is what we get, she'll not settle for that. I don't know if it will ever end for her."

"Then what about the two of you?"

Johnny took another drink of whiskey and looked at the floor. "I'm in love with her and I think she's in love with me. That's all I know. I can't think beyond that."

Dahl's hands were shaking as he took the bottle and brought it to his lips. "Does she know, lad?" He coughed.

"Know?" Johnny said, realizing full well what Dahl was

asking. He gulped at the drink and shuddered as it went down.

Dahl looked at him in disbelief. "About your being on the firing squad."

A draft swept over Johnny and he turned to stare into Nora's shocked and bewildered eyes. With a motion it seemed like she was going to collapse. She clutched at the door.

Johnny jumped up in alarm, unable to speak. Nora glanced at Dahl. She covered her face with her hands, looking at Johnny. "What did he say?"

Dahl tried to sit up. "Nothing, missus. I was just commenting..."

"I'm not talking to you." Nora's eyes were wild in confusion. "Answer me!"

Johnny stood trapped in his own deceit, which over the months hadn't seemed like deceit at all, but more like a story he'd been told. Now the weight of it struck him with a force that stunned him. He stared aghast at Nora's horrified face, knowing that his only option was to throttle Dahl for telling such a treacherous lie and then his voice overcame the moment and time collapsed around all logic.

"They sent for me when you and your mother left the Castle that night," he said. "He knew, your father knew. He didn't tell me in so many words, but he knew..."

Nora seemed to shrink as he spoke, drawing back inside herself and putting her hands over her face again.

"No!" she shouted, reaching out and waving her hand frantically.

"He wanted to die, Nora," Johnny pleaded. "He said so, for Ireland...his death meant..."

Fire shone in her eyes and she came at him, stopping an arm's length away. "Don't dare tell me what his death meant! You don't know that any more than what his *life* meant..." Her voice dropped. "I don't want...this."

"I didn't have a choice," he said. "I was ordered..."

"Don't lie! We always have a choice!"

"Your father didn't!" he countered. "He was determined to die. He wouldn't have gotten out of it if he could have."

"So, you think you were justified serving on his firing squad?"

"It didn't matter to him."

"But it should have mattered to you. And to think you let me fall in love with you. How could you? How twisted is your mind? What would have happened if we'd gone further? Would you have lived with it forever without ever telling me, and when you just couldn't live with it any longer and confessed, what do you think I would have done? Nothing? Just let you admit you were one of the men who killed him and dismiss it just like that? How goddamn cruel are you?"

Johnny tried to find something that would tell him what to say, but nothing came except the idea that James Connolly knew he had to die. That entire night Johnny had felt that Connolly had been pleased he was chosen to serve on the firing squad. But now as he stood frozen his mind seemed to shut down.

"Say something!" she screamed, tears streaming down her face.

The fear of losing her ran through him again. He had to keep himself still to prevent reaching out and grabbing her, holding on until she collapsed against him. He wanted desperately to tell her he loved her. He fought with the will to tell her again what her father wanted and yet knew it was the wrong thing to say. Nora's breath was coming fast and her eyes bored into him as she waited for more. There was nothing he could do but finish what he'd started.

"'Shoot straight, Johnny Flynn.' That's what he said, what he called out, and he meant it."

Johnny breathed in deeply, slowly, so his fear would not show. He let his arms fall to his sides not daring to speak or move. He felt like one of the condemned. Nora seemed no longer on the verge of rage and for this he was grateful. The silence lasted for a long time but gradually a message came to her eyes that said there was something he had to understand because everything else depended on it. It was a truth, perhaps the truth Dahl had asked about, he thought, a feeling beyond her emotions. She could say the words that applied, but at the same time he knew he had to figure it out without her saying a thing.

The quiet went dangerously on as she backed toward the door. He raised a hand to stop her but just before his fingers touched her, he felt the piercing sting of her hand against his face. It jarred him and he faltered, shaking his head as he caught himself. His cheek burned. He felt the imprint of her hand on his skin and fought the urge to rub it. A tear broke from the cusp of his eye and trailed down beside his nose and over his upper lip, one tear, that's all.

The fierceness in her eyes faded as she watched the tear curiously, like a great mystery unfolding. In the midst of his shame he felt a sense of relief. "I'm sorry," he said.

She glanced at him and then fixed on the wall. He could see the bitterness of the moments before returning. Her lips quivered. "I never want to see you again," she said. "If you are not gone from here by morning, I'll tell Buckley and you can deal with the Brigade."

"They'll think I'm a spy. Is that what you want?"

"It's not a matter of what I want. You've put an end to that. It's a matter of what is. You are one of the men who killed my father. That's what is and it can't be undone. I'm offering you life. That's more than you offered him."

"I would have freed him, if the choice had been mine. But it wasn't."

"The choice to shoot him was."

Johnny was frantic now. "But he was determined to die! You must believe that. I did what he wanted!"

Her hands clenched at her sides and she held her stare as her eyes brimmed with tears. "You…" she said in a whisper and then tried again, but her voice failed. "You..."

"He wanted to set Ireland free," Johnny interrupted. "I was an Irishman, helping to set Ireland free!"

Her mouth twitched. "You've got until sunup," she said, biting off the words. Then she was gone.

He held his eyes painfully closed, then opened and knelt to take his friend's hand in his. It was thin and delicate and warm as though blood was still coursing through his body, and holding it, Johnny bent and placed his head on Dahl's chest. There was no sound of life except that of his own heart echoing through his mate's ribs, mimicking life. For a moment it was enough and Johnny spoke to him as if he were still alive. "What can I do, lad? What in God's name can I do?"

The door opened, utterly soundless, as if Dahl's soul had that moment chosen to leave the room. Johnny raised his head and placed the lad's hand back in his lap. Outside, there were signs of false dawn and he reckoned he had an hour or so before the sun rose. At the sound of a twig snapping underfoot, he looked around. He recognized the silhouette of Duffy's huge body before he stepped into the struggling light.

"You still here?" Duffy said.

"For now," Johnny said. He was about to say more but turned back to look through the doorway at Dahl. Duffy glanced over his shoulder.

"Figured him for gone when I left. Hope he didn't give you any trouble. He was a strange one, not manly. Seemed like he belonged with the nurses, if you know what I mean. Sure didn't have the makings of a soldier."

"What would that be, Duffy? Tell me, just what is your so-called 'makings of a soldier?'" Johnny said, voice rising.

"The courage to do the right thing," Duffy fired back. "Nobody says it. You just know it. It's in your heart." He stopped, looking curiously at Johnny. "What's going on with you?"

Johnny was walking away, wondering the same thing, when

Duffy called out. "We took care of them."

He stopped. What are you talking about?"

"The prisoners." Duffy started laughing. "You should have seen them, naked as newborns, hopping and jumping down Cork Road. I thought they was going to make it, but the dancing finally wore them down. We left them there for the Brits to find, or the crows. All the same in the end. We'll dump this one out there, too. Soon as I get some coffee."

"No, you don't. You make him a coffin and put it on a lorry."

"Now, wait a minute. That's a good waste of wood."

In an instant Johnny had seized Duffy by the jacket and slammed him up against the front of the house. He was breathing so hard he could barely get the words out. "You build him a coffin or so help me God, I'll kill you."

In the total silence Johnny was sure Duffy was going to hit him but the blow never came. For a moment the big man's glare flamed but then he dropped his stare. "I'll see to it," he said, "as soon as I get some coffee."

Johnny tightened his grip. "You don't have time for coffee. It has to be done by dawn. Seal it with pitch and remember, a horse-drawn lorry." He paused. "And there's a pint of whiskey in it, if you keep your mouth shut and meet me at the fork."

Duffy managed a smile. "I could always use a spare pint and so could Lester McCord."

"Then get help, but I'm warning you, say nothing to anyone else."

"Sir?" Duffy said as Johnny stepped into the shadows.

"What?" He turned in exasperation.

"What'll you be doing with the body, anyhow?"

"I'll be giving it back to Ireland."

Duffy seemed puzzled. "Back to Ireland?" he said to himself and his eyes widened. "You're setting a trap for the Brits? That dead one in there's the bait?"

"Aye," Johnny said, nodding. "And for it to work we have to

keep it squarely amongst ourselves. The rest of the lads can't know. Now, get on with it."

"You can count on me," he called out as Johnny moved into the darkness.

He looked at the farmhouse where lights were beginning to come on and wondered if Nora really wanted him to leave. Maybe he should try once again to set things right before he left, but it was way too soon to approach her. She wasn't in any frame of mind to listen. He stepped outside and skirted by the house, hoping to catch a glimpse of her but the curtains and blinds had been drawn making the shadows indistinguishable.

He wanted to stop and go inside but knew he couldn't. He wanted to call out for her but knew he mustn't. He could only continue into the darkness where death waited.

Chapter Thirty

Out on Cork Road a mist gathered while he sat on the stone wall waiting for Duffy. The mist swirled and thickened and for a moment he felt naked and debased and did not know what had made him think he and Nora could have ever made it together. Yet what he'd rationalized had been true and still was: Connolly had blessed his own death and Johnny's role in it. That was true but now the truth seemed absurd. The truth had become a lie, as much as the mist on Cork Road had become a disguise.

In the distance he could hear hammering and knew it had to be Duffy making the coffin. He made a sound in his throat that was a cross between a moan and cry. Dahl had no business dying; he'd never hurt a soul. And what would his family think when the body just showed up out of nowhere? Maybe he would write a note at the station and explain, tell them Dahl's last request had been to be buried on Inishmore soil and how he'd died. Bravely, of course, courageously. But for which side? Would his family know Dahl had joined the British Army? Christ, Almighty! Then, Johnny remembered. Dahl was naked. There was no uniform, no identification whatsoever. He didn't have to say which side he'd been on; just let them draw their own conclusions.

The shadow of a farmer came walking through the mist and Johnny watched as the man, head-down, passed him by without a glance. He did not worry that the fellow was a Brit on patrol or sent to collect intelligence. He didn't know; he didn't care. Johnny jumped off the wall and started to pace. He kept walking up and down the road imagining Nora confronting him, demanding that he say it wasn't true, that she'd misheard, that Dahl had been lying. He could have turned on Dahl, called him a liar and she would have believed him, very likely – but it had never crossed his mind. He felt the emptiness of believing he would never see her again.

Just before dawn Duffy approached with a horse-drawn lorry carrying an ominous black casket. Struggling to pull the cart, the horse snorted as it stopped.

"There was wood behind the shed. I took the pint away from the Brit here. God knows he'd have a time getting it down now," Duffy said. "You don't owe me nothing. This horse's just a nag, but she'll get you into town, if that's where you're headed."

"I'm taking him to Skibbereen, his home," Johnny lied. "I knew him as a boy."

"He's a traitor, then?"

"He just got caught up in things. He never raised a gun against Ireland," Johnny said. He climbed up on the flatbed wagon and took the reins.

"What'll I tell Sean?"

"That I've gone to bury a friend and will be back in a day or so."

"He won't like it, your taking off like this, and suppose you're not back when you say. We won't know what's become of you."

Johnny glanced at Duffy. "I'll be back."

"And the lady?"

There was no answer to be had.

He climbed up onto the buckboard and seated himself on the bench. He didn't look at Duffy as he left, snapping the reins over the horse's rump. He bumped along trying to avoid the worst ruts, afraid he might bounce the coffin off. He had taken heart from telling Duffy he would be back. It gave him confidence to think time might work in his favor with Nora.

His confidence carried to the outskirts of Kinsale. The rising sun spiked over the hills to the slate rooftops glistening from a passing shower. It lit the bell tower above the train station. A wheel dropped into a deep rut and jarred him so hard his head whipsawed, wrenching his neck. Rubbing it, he glanced back to make sure the coffin was still aboard. It had turned at an angle, wedging itself between a side and the driver's bench. It looked huge, as if Dahl had been seven feet tall, and shined with pitch oozing through the slats. Johnny wondered if Duffy really had put Dahl's body inside and was tempted to stop and check but didn't think he could go through with it.

"Haww-there! Haww-there!" He snapped the reins again. The animal started, jerking the lorry out of the rut. The road swept down to Kinsale on a narrow curve and he could see the sea. A childlike sense of joy came as he remembered the day he and his father went fishing and searching the horizon he considered how it would be to cross an entire ocean. He thought of excited voices and someone crying out, "New York!" and with it a blessed end to all this madness. And then he thought of Nora and wondered if love could span an ocean and if so, would it bind him to a life spent in memory.

Gray dawn had settled on Kinsale when he entered the west end of High Street. A few buildings were shuttered but others had windows boarded up as if they had been vacated. He felt alone again, he and his dead friend creeping slowing into a mostly abandoned town. He saw a sign for the train station and as he followed its point he was greeted by a bracing sea wind. The station was at the end of the block where he heard the sigh of a steam locomotive coming to rest. He saw it before he saw the station. The huge iron chassis dwarfed the tiny building and as he stepped down off the lorry and looked up, the engine seemed larger still. The engineer was not visible. It was as if the train had shown up all by itself, stopping on this very spot to meet just him and Dahl.

"You'll be sending it on?" The question seemed to come from afar.

An elderly, shriveled man wearing a stationmaster's cap and suspenders over a wrinkled shirt was staring at him from the entrance to the station.

"Yes," Johnny said, startled and then collecting himself. "To

Inishmore."

"Inishmore? A godforsaken place, if I've ever been to one," the stationmaster said. "A man has to be plenty strange to live there. Goats and rocks, wind and fairies. A harder life I can't imagine, but it's no doubt they'll know who this poor lad belongs to. Not more than twenty families live there, I suppose. He'll have to change trains a couple of times," the man said, delving into his jacket for a large yellow tag. He handed it to Johnny. "Fill it out, if you will."

"I don't know the exact address," Johnny said, glancing at the tag. "I'll just mark him to his family name and that only a last one. Could you wire ahead for someone to call them?"

The porter rubbed his chin. "You're sure the name's right? Nobody wants a spare body on his hands. No offense." The man looked at Johnny. "You're a member of the family?"

"A friend," said Johnny.

The porter paused and came closer, whispering. "Was the deceased Irish? The man looked toward the far end of the station. "Truly Irish, if you know what I mean?"

"Aye," Johnny said, "Irish, through and through."

The man drew even closer. "If you don't mind, can I ask how he died?"

Johnny hesitated. "In battle," he said.

"The last battle I got word of was Crossbarry," the man said. "Could that be it?"

"Aye," Johnny said, remembering being lost in the mist there. "Crossbarry."

"Fill it out, then," the man said, seemingly relieved. "Let's get him on the train. Some of the I.R.A. boys are in the waiting room keeping warm and having coffee. They're a rough bunch. I just didn't want any trouble. We're told to let the boys know when a body's being sent. The Brits have been known to ship guns in coffins. Our boys want to check. That's all. But this lad here, dying for Ireland, there's no problem whatsoever."

The man took the tag from Johnny and wrote on the back, then took a small hammer from his coat and nailed the tag to the coffin. "That'll be ten shillings."

Johnny paid the man five. "It's all I have."

The man considered it and nodded. "That's all right. The rest you've paid in loyalty. If you'll bring him down to the baggage car we'll find a comfortable place for him."

Johnny led the horse onto the platform and followed the stationmaster alongside the train. As they approached the baggage car, two men came out of a small door at the end of the station and looked at him. Three others followed. Johnny knew from their dress they were Volunteers and he felt safe knowing they were there. One of the men, a man with long black hair and strong cut jaw raised his hand as if to wave and then put a finger up and called out. "A minute there."

The group came over slowly. The sergeant's eyes were fixed on the coffin. Despite what the stationmaster had said, something in the sergeant's cold face told Johnny to be on guard. In the steady stare of the man's eyes, Johnny suspected the fellow could have easily passed for an Auxie. The men gathered around the coffin while their spokesman examined the tag.

"Inishmore?" the sergeant said to the stationmaster.

"Aye, homeward bound, poor lad. He died…"

The sergeant's eyes narrowed, cutting the stationmaster off. He glanced at Johnny. "Who are you?"

"Johnny Flynn, a friend of this man. We served together."

The sergeant lowered his head and slipped his hands into his jacket pocket. Johnny knew he was feeling for his pistol. "Where'd you serve?"

"Third Brigade, Bandon, under Sean Buckley."

The sergeant looked at the others. "Do you have identification?"

"No. None, but you can send up to Bandon…"

"You're a long way from Bandon. What're you doing down

here?"

Johnny thought quickly. One slip now and this was going to go on and on. He glanced sharply at their faces. They were poised for him to make a mistake, but it was only right they should be alert. Trust had to be proven. "I was given leave to bring my friend here, where I could find a train without worrying about the Brits. Cork was too busy a place, too dangerous."

The sergeant's expression changed. He took his hands from his pockets and smiled a smile Johnny didn't completely believe.

"You won't mind if we have a look inside that coffin?" he said. He wasn't asking, but telling Johnny what he intended to do. But there was no reason to oppose him. He would just find Dahl's battered naked body. Now he regretted not checking the coffin back on Cork Road. What if he'd been set up? What if Duffy had filled it with rocks or worse yet, thrown in a rifle or two to make it look like Johnny was trying something? But then he steadied himself. What reason would Duffy have to do something like that? It didn't make sense.

"Go ahead," Johnny said as evenly as he could.

The sergeant turned to the stationmaster. "Mr. Casey, could you find us a crowbar, please?"

"Sure, but I can vouch for this man. I know you can trust him," Casey said.

The sergeant glanced at Johnny. "I'm sure I can, too, but we can't take any chances. It's not personal, mind you. I'm sure Sean Buckley runs things the same way."

As Johnny watched Casey hurry off, one of the other men said. "I'm having a hard time placing your accent, Flynn. Just where are you from?"

"Cork, born there," Johnny said.

"You haven't lived there all your life, now have you?"

There was a brief silence, filled only by thoughts rushing through Johnny's mind. He had to chance the truth. "My family took me to Birmingham years ago. We lived there until they died.

Then I came back, to fight."

In another silence the men glanced at each other and then stared at him with eyes of stone that were questioning still, but Johnny knew there was nothing he could ask that he didn't now control. The danger had been in his admission but the truth had left them with nowhere to turn, except to the coffin and he was confident Dahl was there, alone in death.

"Move your arse, old man. It's cold out here," the sergeant called out to the stationmaster, now shuffling down the platform with a crowbar and hammer.

He handed the tools to the men in the lorry. They used them to scrape away the pitch along the edge of the top and then eased the claws under the lid and began to pry. Cursing, and with the nails screeching as they came out of the wood, the men raised the lid all around the coffin. Then they laid down the tools and gathered around, bending over to grasp firmly a section of the lid.

"One, two, three!" the sergeant called out and they jerked it off.

"Sarge, you better get up here," one of the men said in alarm.

The man scrambled up into the lorry, took one look into the coffin, grabbed for his gun and straightened, holding it on Johnny. "Stay right where you are," he demanded, jumping down.

Johnny pushed by the sergeant and scrambled up into the lorry. Two of the men grabbed him by the arms but he was able to see Dahl's purple face and the torn British uniform Duffy had dressed him in. At once, Johnny realized Duffy hadn't meant to trap him but had only done what he'd thought right, to dress Johnny's friend so if anyone opened the coffin they would not be disgraced.

"Pull the bastard out of there and check for guns," the sergeant shouted.

"What is it?" said the station master. "What's wrong?"

"It's a dead Brit. This here Flynn's been lying to us."

"I'm not lying. He was an Irishman, as true as any of you," Johnny protested.

Quickly they surrounded him. "You're coming with us. Stationmaster, nail up the coffin and have the body burned," the sergeant said, stepping forward.

"No! You can't do that," Johnny shouted, lunging at the sergeant as the men grabbed him by the arms. "All he wanted was to be buried at home. He was an Irishman, I tell you! You've got it wrong, all wrong!"

He was held steadfast and before he could finish speaking a blindfold was over his eyes. He struggled and for that his arms were twisted behind his back and his wrists tied. For a split second a thundering noise roared in his ears. For several moments after the gun's blast he couldn't hear a thing, and in this confusion they hustled him off. He was forced to step up on iron steps and did so only as they shoved him. He tripped on a step and fell face forward. A moment later a door slammed and an engine started and as he fought to sit up he realized he was in the back of a British lorry – like the day they shuffled him and the others in the firing squad to Kilmainham – in a cylinder of steel, the remains of boilers welded together for secure transport. There were benches down both sides and he managed to crawl up on one and sit, his back curved against a tube. The others must have taken Dahl away.

Chapter Thirty-one

He was pulled roughly from the vehicle and scurried inside a house and down the steps into its cellar. From the smell of earth and furnace coal there was no doubt about it, another farmhouse commandeered for the Irish cause. He relaxed as they slid a chair against his legs and sat him down. They removed his blindfold and he opened his eyes to an array of Volunteer faces, only one of whom he recognized – the sergeant from the train station. Someone brought a lantern and hung it from the rafters just in front of him. For a moment it shrieked into his eyes and he closed them. He felt someone tugging at his wrists and then his hands were free. His arms hurt as he stretched them out and rubbed his wrists, squinting into the light. His eyes became fixed on a soldier's face tilted slightly upward, the lips so thin they were almost nonexistent and the eyes anxious, worried, as if the soldier had been given a particularly distasteful mission to perform. Johnny noticed a heavy pistol sagging from the man's belt.

"Search him."

"It's as good as done, Commander Doherty," one of the men said, spinning Johnny around.

Johnny knew what that meant and struggled as they brought him out of the chair and stripped him. They bent him over the back of the chair headfirst until his forehead was pressing against the seat and shoved a nightstick up his rectum. Then, it was swiftly withdrawn.

"Nothing in there," a voice said and he heard the nightstick hit the floor.

"No brain neither?" another said as they raised him to a standing position.

One of the men was emptying his pockets. Johnny saw him take out the letter the dying Brit had made him promise to take to the post.

"What do we have here?"

"A letter to a soldier's family," Johnny said. "A British regular gave it to me after the battle of Crossbarry. I promised him I'd send it to his family."

Doherty reached for the letter and began to read it. "Says 'the fight is going well, but the battles are becoming more dangerous as the Irish are more brutal and less honorable now. I am being a good soldier, something you and Ma never thought I'd be, but I can't shake the feeling death is all around me, stalking me as I have my morning coffee and prepare to ambush Irish troops at a godforsaken place called Crossbarry. This very day I might die and if so I want you to know I love you. I don't have time to write Margaret and Timothy, but kindly tell them my last thoughts, if I am given a moment to have them. It will be as they were the day I left them standing by the fence waving and hiding their tears. Tell them gently, Father, as gently as you can. Make it seem I have died for something, though I'm not altogether sure about that, but I will have died bravely, yes, with them escorting me off to heaven. Make it seemed like dream, a journey of the mind, one that if they really concentrate on they can enter and accompany me, for I will always be with them. Your loving son, Richard.'"

Doherty folded the letter and handed it back to the soldier who had taken it from Johnny's pocket.

"So, you foretold your own death, Richard?" He glanced at the envelope as he handed it back.

"That's not me. I didn't write that letter," Johnny protested.

Doherty bent down. "You're a bad liar, Richard, and a worse Irishman," he said and in a single motion stood and brought the back of his fist across Johnny's face. Johnny could taste his own blood and spit it out, fighting to bring his head up.

"Send for Sean Buckley," he slurred.

Doherty eyed him sharply, then glanced up over Johnny's shoulder and gave a brief nod. It felt like a brick hit his shoulder as someone struck him from behind with a nightstick or a gun butt. He yelled and grabbed at his shoulder, falling out of the chair. He felt tears rushing to his eyes as they picked him up and sat him in the chair again.

"Sean Buckley is it? Why not Michael Collins or de Valera himself? They're known to everyone in Ireland!"

Johnny tried to reach for his shoulder but the pain stopped him. "It's no use lying, lad," another voice said. "We'll get it out of you in the end. You don't want to meet your Maker with every bone in your body broken. How then would you stand and face Him?"

Johnny faced them blankly. How could he make them believe him? He had no proof of anything. All the evidence was in their hands and was all against him. He tried to clear the blood in his mouth but his tongue was numb and he spat like a drunk who'd bitten off the end. The blood simply drooled down his chin onto his chest. It hung there in a dark red spool. He pushed at it with his tongue but the strand would not break. There was laughter and he stopped, letting it hang there, wondering what was coming. He knew the way the Volunteers did things. They might run him; they might put a bullet in his brain in a few hours but they would not kill him immediately; they would check out his story, no matter how bizarre it sounded.

Someone hit him hard in the side. His breath escaped in a hiss of blood and he grabbed onto the seat of the chair and held on with all he was worth as the pain reverberated in his head. A blow came into his ribs from the other side and he knew he would not be able to hold on much longer. He gritted his teeth as Doherty jerked him back by his hair.

"I see it this way; if you're a Brit, you're the enemy and you're up to something we haven't figured out. If you're an Irishman, you're a traitor. Either way we have no need for the likes of you. Which is it?"

A glob of blood caught in his throat and Johnny began to

choke. Doherty jumped back, letting go and the mass came tumbling out. "I'm Irish, but not a traitor. Get Buckley!" he managed with all the strength left in him. He saw one of the men rise into the light and he cringed, expecting another blow. His head felt like it was on a swivel as he dizzily raised it. He fought to keep from blacking out, hearing himself moan like a wounded animal. He hoped it wasn't a cry and as he coughed out another bolus of blood and heard the awful noise it made, he hoped he wasn't sobbing.

Dimly, he was aware of the soldiers gathering in a huddle and heard their voices. They seemed to take turns looking his way, gazing at him. It was more than mockery he felt in their eyes. Their attitude toward him wasn't about hate; it was about conviction – certain that they had in their hands a symbol of all the wrongs wrought on Ireland by the English – a turncoat. Now Johnny realized they weren't planning to call Sean Buckley or even make the lamest enquiry on his behalf. They were going to kill him and use his death to justify everything dishonorable and horrible they had done until now and everything still to come.

He tried to raise an arm. *One more word with you*, he thought as his hand fell back to his knee. *Once more word, mind you, and it's this*: "Shoot straight, Johnny Flynn!" he called out and fell out of the chair onto the floor. As they gathered around him, laughing, he could see even less now. The men were looming over him, their shadows wavering like dark angels on the ceiling. He suspected he was dying. He remembered Dahl asking about truth and wondered when it would come to him. His mind went dark.

When he awoke he was in a cramped space that smelled of must and dampness. In the dark, unable to straighten his legs, he thought for a second they had put him in a coffin, but when he glanced around he saw light under the door and realized he was in a small closet. He had laid on his side so long that when he tried to move he found his legs were numb. He turned and groaned, then moved his legs slowly as he crawled up on his knees. Hit with a sharp pain in his side, he rolled over in agony. For several minutes he lay there with his head and side throbbing, then came to his knees again. In short slow stretches he managed to turn over, sitting on the floor and leaning his back against a wall. Again and again he let his legs out and brought them back to his chest. Strangely, he wasn't afraid, and yet he knew in one way or another it would be over; in time they would either beat him to death or shoot him.

His eyes adjusted and he could see clothes hanging above him. Around him shoes and boots were scattered. He felt for a weapon of some sort, anything sharp, but there was nothing. He came to his knees and rummaged through the clothes for something sharp – a penknife, even a pen itself – but the pockets were all empty. Suddenly the door opened and he was struck with a burst of light. The silhouette of a huge man filled the doorway and leaned in. A hand seized Johnny's arm, fingers digging into his elbow. Pain shot up his arm into his neck and he tried to pull away but the man's grip only tightened and jerked him out of the closet.

In the light the man's ruddy face became blotchy and he dropped his hand. "They're waiting for us downstairs," he said. Johnny looked around and tried to see over him but he was too tall and his shoulders too broad. The man watched him. "You looking for a latrine, you'll have to go outside," he said.

Johnny shook his head.

"Then you walk ahead of me down those stairs, and remember, if you make one wrong move it will be your last. Do we understand each other?"

"Where are we going?"

"To the Devil's whipping post. Strip down, all the way."

"I'm not going…" Before Johnny had a chance to get the words out the man had landed a blow against his temple, knocking him to the floor.

"Take 'em off or I'll do it for you."

"Tom, you need help?" A voice came from downstairs.

The man named Tom glared at Johnny. "Do I need help or not? You be the judge of that."

"You'll need all you can get!" Johnny yelled, jumping to his feet dizzily and swinging wildly as he lunged at the man. Tom laughed as he ducked and Johnny sailed toward the other side of the room. He turned to see the man standing there, hands on hips smiling.

"You Brits are a bunch of women," Tom said. "Come on. Give it another try."

"Tom, sounds like trouble?" someone called out.

"No trouble, lad. Sport 'tis all," he bellowed.

At that Johnny waded into the middle of the room with his fists up. He realized what he was doing was insane but he didn't care. He swung at the man's face but Tom seized his arm in midair and in one motion swung him around, twisting his arm up behind him and cinching his forearm up under Johnny's chin. The man leaned back lifting Johnny off the floor by his neck. "I'll bite your bloody ear off or choke you to death. It don't matter to me."

Johnny reached back and clawed at the man's head, trying to get his fingers into his hair. He felt his arm drop free but it was almost numb and useless. Then the man cradled his head between his big hands and twisted his neck at the same time. Johnny's windpipe was completely blocked. He began to suck at the air. Darkness closed in from the corners of his eyes. The man laughed as he blacked out.

Moments later he barely realized he was being dragged by his feet. He tried to focus his eyes but it like he was still asleep. He felt his head sliding over the wooden floor. His head and shoulders dropped out from under him and banged on the steps. He grabbed the back of his head to save himself but his knuckles were pounded so hard it felt like they were breaking and he let go. He shut his eyes, hoping he'd black out again but he still felt it, banging, banging, banging until he thought his head would split open. Then, it stopped and the man let go of his feet. His heels struck the floor with a thud and he felt a bolt of pain shoot up his right leg. Still stunned, Johnny tried to feel his head for cuts and gashes but his hands would not obey. His left slapped against his bare chest and for the first time he realized he was naked.

He was too weak to care and wondered what he was supposed to do now. Just lie there and be shot, he suspected. Surely they would at least drag him outside. The man named Tom was straddling him and before Johnny could close his eyes a bucket of water was hitting him in the face. Someone came up from behind and drenched him with another pail and he gasped. Coughing and spitting out water, he rose on his haunches and shook his head.

"A sorry day for us all."

Sean Buckley's voice was unmistakable and Johnny's head snapped up, but it was Nora's eyes he stared into. She bit down on a quivering lip but simply looked away toward the darkened windows as Johnny squirmed to cover himself.

His ears were ringing and his head hurt so badly he was forced to close his eyes again. "My clothes," he said, barely opening them, and when no one moved he pleaded. "Sean, tell them who I am."

"Put him in a chair," Buckley said curtly.

Two men stepped forward and jerked Johnny to his feet and then, like the night before, they sat him harshly down in a straight-backed chair. His buttocks struck the wood seat with force, sending a dull pain into his groin. He heard a gasp he thought was Nora's and struggled to open his eyes. She was looking straight ahead now, across the room, and he strained to make contact with her but her eyes refused to meet his. Again he became aware of his total nakedness and covered his crotch as best he could.

"Nora," he said, quietly. She glanced at him quickly and Buckley looked at her, puzzled.

"Nora? Nora, who? He's out of his head," Buckley said, more to Doherty than anyone. Then Buckley moved toward Johnny, his face thoughtful and concerned. He knelt in front of him and reached out, cupping Johnny's face in his hand and with his thumbs lifted his eyelids and looked into his eyes as if he could see behind them. "You've deceived us, Richard. What's your last name?"

Johnny couldn't believe his ears. "I'm Johnny Flynn," he said. "You know that."

Buckley dropped his hand. "Not according to this," he said, leaning back and pulling the letter out of his breast pocket.

"A British soldier gave it to me on the battlefield at Crossbarry," Johnny protested. He glanced at Nora and for a brief moment she took notice. In one way or another she was here for him, he told himself and went on with a sense of hope. "I was separated from the section, lost. He was beside the road, dying. This is a letter to his father," he said in a strengthening voice.

"And the body of the prisoner?"

Johnny tried to straighten up, staring down on Buckley's black curly hair. Buckley raised his head. His face was a picture of forced calm. It brought to Johnny a frightening unreality, as if he'd realized for the first time since seeing Buckley he was in real trouble. His voice was rushed. "He was by the road and died there, before I left. He wanted me to take the letter to the post. I said I would."

"I mean the body you brought to Kinsale?" Buckley snapped.

Nora turned and looked at him. Johnny searched her eyes. They were wet and filled with confusion, but even so he felt warmth in the darkness, a co-presence that mattered more than anything. And then she made a little movement of her head, looking at Buckley, searching as if she was waiting for him to tell her what to do.

"What about it?" Buckley demanded, breaking Johnny's stare.

"He was our prisoner, an Irishman, and he was dying. He asked me to see that his body got sent home to Inishmore. I brought him here because I thought Cork would be swarming with Brits."

"But it wasn't the British you should have been concerned with. They were on your side," Doherty said.

"Strange that in two questionable instances a dying Brit asked you to carry out his last request. It makes your lies so transparent...I'm disappointed in you, Richard," Buckley said.

"Ask her, ask...Sarosa. She was with me in the prisoner's shed. And Duffy. Did you bring him with you? He was there, too," Johnny said.

Buckley looked at Nora. "Well?"

"I heard nothing of the kind, but then I wasn't there the entire time. I went for whiskey. Johnny, or whatever his name is, wanted me to."

"He deceived you, too," Buckley said, lowering his voice and scouring Johnny with his eyes. "You stopped at nothing, did you? For what? Intelligence? That's what it had to be, and how many of our maneuvers did you get to the Brits? Crossbarry? Was their attempt at an ambush your doing?"

Johnny drew back as Buckley advanced to within inches of his face but he could not keep it inside. "I was almost killed at Crossbarry!"

"Plenty were," Buckley snarled. "You should have been. You say you were cut off from us, but in light of this I judge it a lie! A damnable lie!"

Buckley looked over his shoulder at Nora. The frustration in his voice was overwhelming. "You, you ... must not have known this man at all."

"I did not," she said, her eyes now on fire as if the collective sense of Johnny's betrayal had lit a blaze in her.

The words were barely audible but they silenced him. He

tried to tell himself that she could not possibly sanction this…he tried, he tried, but then thought of her father and knew that all this simply magnified what she considered to be his betrayal of him.

Doherty stepped into the silence, addressing Buckley. "What would you have us do, Commander?"

"Most likely he's killed more Irishmen than any Brit in the County. You know what to do," Buckley said, slowly standing. Doherty took out his pistol, but Buckley grabbed his hand. "Not here, not you. I bought his story. I'm responsible for those who died."

"No. I am," Nora said, stepping between them. "This is for me to do. I owe it to my father. My name is Nora, Nora Connolly. My father was James Connolly. He gave me the nickname, Sarosa."

"James Connolly," Buckley said, aghast.

She looked at Johnny. "And this man, I just discovered, was on his firing squad. If anyone has been deceived, it has been me, and if ever anyone deserves to take this man's life, she stands here before you."

"But the men said the two of you…" Buckley started.

"All lies. This man trained me, taught me. I spent a lot of time with him, but never other than soldier's time. They can think what they like." She looked at Johnny with intense earnestness, as if she wanted to halt and change her story, but denial of that possibility came with swift ferocity. "I want him dead," she said.

Johnny started to protest, but knew he would only end up harming her and gaining no credibility in the doing. He could have asked her questions, could have exposed almost everything she'd said as a lie, but for what? There was nothing he could do to help himself short of exposing her – he was a dead man.

He felt more lost than ever. He had done the right thing for Dahl, his trusted friend, and yet it all seemed to betray him. Nora was someone he no longer knew. He could never have married her, should never have loved her. It had been his mistake to pretend about her father. Now, it seemed like another woman altogether stood in front of him, an image of everything he'd lost, the possibilities, the freedoms, the unbound journeys. And then something clutched at his heart. Was he lying to himself? Truth be told at last, had all of this been bound up in her, every thought, every possibility, every chance for redemption?

"Run him," Doherty said, smiling at the thought of it. "My men'll cut him down at a hundred paces."

Buckley cut the smile with a glance and turned to Nora. "Are you sure you want to go through with this?"

The silence was unendurable. A minute passed and just when Johnny thought she was going to break down, she threw her head back, pulled out her revolver and spun the chamber, checking it for bullets. Then she put it back into the holster. "I saw some woods behind the house on the way in. Take him there."

Buckley turned to the men. "You heard her. Now get to it."

"I only need a couple of men," she said.

"You two," Buckley said, motioning to the men closest to him. "I don't want to see him again. Get him out of here." Johnny watched as Buckley walked over to a window and opened the dark blinds so that daylight filled the room.

They dressed him and bound his hands behind his back. Then they led him down the porch stairs and on down a stone walk to a bridle path. Searching for Nora he looked into the eyes of the two soldiers guarding him. They stared ahead solemnly, then grabbed him by his arms and flung him onto a horse. Slowly, the four of them made their way down the path. Johnny looked around but there was no sight of Buckley. He felt the eyes of the other men trained on him and his body braced in the cool air. They went into the woods slowly, the trees deepening and darkening as they made their way to a glen on the far side of a hill. Johnny saw a small cemetery and beyond, at the edge of the clearing, an obelisk made of an old tree trunk, its bark long ago stripped away. They moved to its right and the curious object stayed in view, visible from anywhere in the glen. Nora turned her horse toward it. As they got nearer, its size seemed to overpower the field.

She dismounted and walked up the stone path leading to it. "Here," she called back. "Bring him over here." They held Johnny's arms as he dismounted and took him to where she was staring at the column. There the words *"Remember the Rising!"* were inscribed.

Nora placed her fingers on the letters and traced them to the end. She leaned her forehead against the column and was silent.

"Nora?" Johnny said.

One of the men stepped in front of him. "You, shut up! Can't you see she's praying?"

"Alone, as you wrote," she said to no one, stepping back out of the prayer or whatever it was. "Is that right?" she asked, turning and looking up at the sky as though something had been etched there too. "Alone. Why didn't anyone tell me?" She ran her fingers through her hair.

"Missus, you go on back now and we'll finish this up," the soldier said. "'Tis not for the likes of you."

Johnny tried to dodge the soldier and run to her but the man easily shoved him to the ground. Hands still behind his back, he rolled over on his knees and started to crawl awkwardly toward her. The other soldier planted a foot in the middle of his back and mashed him to the ground. He kept the pressure on as Johnny dug his knees into the dry grass and tried to inch himself free.

"Tie him here," she said, indicating the column, "and blindfold him. This is mine to do and no other's."

After they had tied him to the column one of the soldiers approached with a bandana. Johnny closed his eyes as the man tied it. He thought of Pearse, and for a moment wondered if this was what he'd meant by redemption, the way fairness recycles itself and rewards the mistreated. Maybe there was no such thing as forgiveness or if so, maybe it was as his father had said: forgiveness was reserved for the damned.

"Leave us," Nora's voice broke into his thoughts and he turned his head as if he could still see.

"We'll wait for you across the glen," one of them said.

"No," she said, "I want your word you'll neither wait nor watch. I can find my way back. But I want no witnesses other than my father and my God."

"But it isn't safe."

"And your being here doesn't make it so. What difference does it make if we are one or three?" Her voice was soft, the tone one of supplication. "Go now."

"How long will you be?"

"I'll be back in the morning."

"In the morning?"

"My father died at dawn."

There was no more said. Johnny heard them mount and ride off. "They'll wait for you," he said, sensing her presence.

"No," she said quietly. "I'm a section leader now. Sean gave me your command. They will do as I ordered."

"It must be dark by now. Would you at least take off the blindfold?"

"No," she said, and that was all.

"Will you talk to me?"

"There's nothing to say."

"Nora, what I did was wrong, but it's in the past and I can't change it. It's gone."

"It's passed, but not gone," she said.

"I love you," he said, but this time she did not reply. He heard her walk across some leaves and stop. She was still within the sound of his voice and so he said it louder this time. "I love you."

He heard the leaves again and in his mind's eye he could see her start to run with her hands over her ears, and he shouted, "I love you!" There was silence, a deep and protracted stillness, made all the more by the abrupt absence of his voice. "Nora?"

Her name faded and the silence thickened. He shivered as the emptiness settled around him. Time dragged on for what seemed like an hour. He tried again and again to reach her, but she never answered. Once she coughed from afar and that was the only way he knew she was still there. He worried that she might sneak up on him and put a bullet through his brain without his knowing a thing, without any chance of seeing her again. And he pleaded with her not to do it that way, but still she said nothing. As the minutes drifted slowly by he became aware of the ache in his shoulders and his head began to throb. Soon he was drenched in sweat. Yet when he tried to wet his lips with his tongue it was dry. The tense effort required to stay on his feet drained him. He couldn't hold out any longer and started to sink to his knees. Then he heard her sob. It percolated through the darkness as softly as the cry of an infant.

"Nora?"

He felt her hands at the bandana. When it fell around his neck he blinked and strained to see her. She was right in front of him, holding the pistol at her side. He let his breath out slowly, hoping to still the sensations fluttering in his chest. She was breathing so hard she was panting. She put the gun to his head. The darkness around him breathed and he was in the midst of it, deep in his core, between the beats of his pounding heart, wanting to live, wanting to rest. What was this after all? Had he really done wrong? Had he been a fool to love her? It was his last moment, Dahl's eternal moment, and he searched for something, anything to say or think as she cocked the trigger. Then in a reprieve of what seemed like eternity, she stepped back, counting.

"One, two, three, four, five..." And on until she had stepped off ten paces.

He tried to search her eyes but she was too far away. The fading moonlight barely shone in them; she was a creature of the night, of the forest eternal and he told himself he had no right to live, that he had joined in the killing of her father. There was no one to argue otherwise, not Nora nor any voice from his past, only Dahl's labored memory asking about truth. Johnny saw the pistol rise into the apron of light. Secure in both of her hands its trembling barrel stared him in the eye and fired. Fear seized every muscle in his body as the ropes cut into his wrists. The gun remained in the air for a second and then dropped to her side.

She fired into the ground. "The coup de grace," she said. "You are as dead as my father."

In that moment he felt but one life and that one life was more than a memory or surrender, more than a dream or a feeling of joy or suffering. It was more than history, more than a father's vision, more than a lover's hush, more than love itself. It was hope and in a strange way it was redemption, convoluted and veiled but all the same, redemption. Now he knew. At last he knew. It was what he had come for, all he had, all he'd ever had, really.

Nora went to him, avoiding his stare. With a penknife she cut the leather straps and his hands fell from the tree. He rubbed his raw wrists as she walked away from him. Blind impulses rose up in him and he couldn't sort them through. He moved his fingers to get the blood circulating and touched his trembling lips. He could not speak. Bitterly he wished that things could be different, that somehow he could turn back time and meet her long ago, in a village where everyone was poor and knew nothing but stories of the fairies and were not touched by war. Tears rolled down his cheeks and the taste of salt wet his lips at last.

"Wait," he said, looking at the pistol as if seeing it for the first time.

She quickly slipped it under her waistcoat. "I couldn't do it." She looked off across the glen. "I'm so ashamed, but I just couldn't. I heard what your friend Dahl said but then saw my father looking at you, seeing the good in you, the Irish in you, and knowing you'd come home."

When he put his hands on her shoulders, she immediately shrugged them off, stepping back. "Don't," she said.

"Leave with me," he pleaded. "We don't have to stay here. We don't have to be a part of this, this war, this horror, this…"

"This cause," she said, looking in his eyes for the first time. "This noble cause. Our fathers…"

"And theirs before them and on and on. And from here…to our children and theirs…" Johnny stopped, realizing what he'd said and searched to see if it had struck her the same way.

Her mouth was barely open but the surprise lit her eyes and for a moment her face was younger than he'd seen it in weeks. She looked like a startled little girl. "Children," she said. "Who has children anymore? I don't remember ever being a child."

"That's what I mean. It has to end someday."

She kept scanning his eyes, as if she wanted to know something for herself, something she trusted him to tell her. "You really believe that? Then how was it you took turns fighting for both sides? It was *fighting* you did, not peacemaking."

"I admit it, but now I know better. One side's no better than the other. It all depends on where you were born. That's a poor excuse for all the killing and not a place to turn to for forgiveness." He paused and when she did not speak but stood immobile, gazing into his eyes, he said, "How come you told them who you were?"

"It was the only way they'd trust me to bring you out," she replied in a rush. "I wasn't sure what I was going to do when we got here, not until the last minute, but I had to keep my choices open. I meant to kill you, I think, until I raised the gun…"

Johnny stood there, trying to hold himself together. He watched her hand rub against her waistcoat and wondered what she would do next. The moon played on her face the way it had so many times before, placing her in and out of the shadows. "Why?"

She shook her head and her hair loosened from its bun and fell over her ghostly shoulders and landed alive on them where the moonlight touched it. She seemed much smaller and oddly shy. He could not take his eyes off her. She shook her head again and for a moment he thought she intended the gesture to pass for an answer. Her fingers left the coat and brushed away something in the air – a gnat? a thought intruding? – and came to rest on her breast. "Why did I change my mind?" she said. "Did I change my mind? I don't know. Maybe I came here wanting to free you all along."

"But you just said…"

She shook her head. "I know what I said, but I'm trying to answer your question truthfully. And the truth is, I'm not sure. I only know when it happened, when I was sure what I was going to do. When I had you in my gun sight, it was you, specifically you, and what we had together. It made me unsure of myself, in a way." The words lingered, but he was afraid she wasn't going to continue.

"I'm not sure what you mean," he encouraged.

She remained silent, turning again toward the glen, which now seemed like a wide lake, a black chasm that threatened to bring his words back to him. She stared back over her shoulder at him. Her eyes were full of anguish and had great weakness in them.

"I'd never been in love before," she said. "I was determined not to be with you. I fought it, told myself it was a sign of weakness." She turned abruptly to him. "Was it? Was it?" She shook her head as if the answer was unfathomable. She took two steps toward him and planted her feet determinedly. She held her hands up straight as spears, framing something in the darkness, which only she could see. "It was like a disease. It ate at me until I couldn't think straight, until I almost forgot what I was doing here." She looked up, holding her hands wider as if to let him see inside. "And then this, you, you…Mother of God, death would be a sweet substitute for what I now know you did."

Johnny's mind was racing to find the connections she was making. He didn't understand it all but took it to mean there was still time, still a chance to win her back, and so he ran to her, seizing her by the arms. She stiffened at first, looking up as if to say how dare he and then her face softened. He took it as permission to kiss her. Softly at first, trying to gauge if he'd misread her and when she did not resist he pulled her to him, fighting the urge to press her mouth into submission. She whispered "no," but did not pull away and he tightened his grip on her arms and brought her firmly to him, feeling her body rise and lean into him. She was trembling and biting at him hungrily. His arms went around her and their tongues met and he felt her cool tears touch his cheeks and inhaled the clean pure fragrance of her hair and skin. His arms went around her waist and he picked her up, breaking off the kiss and whirled her around in the cool salt air.

"I love you!" he shouted. "Let's leave this place, this war! We can go away…to America!" He set her down and smiling broadly said, "Marry me. Marry me!"

The moonlight torched her tears. They shined like drops of mercury, bringing a sharp reflection to her eyes and setting off her face like a piece of fine crystal. But he knew something was wrong when she pressed his shoulders lightly to be let down. Her fingers stole down his shoulders to his arms and lingered there for a long moment. Then, she removed them, looking away, her eyes almost disoriented. At first her voice caught in her throat and it came clearly, firmly. "It's over between us, Johnny." She hesitated. "I have to go back now."

"No," he said adamantly, grabbing for her, his fingers catching the loose folds of her jacket. He tried to pull her to him again, but she swiped his hand away.

"Let me be. Please, while it's still there," she pleaded. "While I can never forget you."

Blundering, stumbling he tried desperately to reassure her, to tell her how love once found should never be surrendered, how it could overcome all obstacles, how she didn't have to keep fighting, that any obstacles could be overcome by love. Besides, hundreds of years had attested to war's futility. Without a pause he began to speak wildly of America, as if he was a native and knew its riches, its freedoms and bounty, and then clutching at straws he told her they could be married in a Catholic Church, if she wished.

She looked at him in astonishment, shook her head slowly and for an instant the tears came again, glazing over the disappointment in her eyes. Johnny thought she had recanted at last and with an awkward, faltering movement, he reached out to wipe the tears away. His fingers slid gently along her cheeks and just when he thought she might take them in her hands and kiss them, clearing the past forever, she flinched and stepped back. She stood motionless but for the narrowing of her eyes. They bore into his as her whole face changed into something unrelenting and urgent.

"To forgive, one must forget, and I will do neither, though it may be that oddly you have earned it," she said.

Though pliant the finality in her voice was unmistakable and in its silence she turned and ran for her horse. She mounted, slapped the reins to its side and set off down the hill at a gallop.

An overwhelming need to stop her struck Johnny. He ran to the edge of the slope and cried out. "Nora! Nora!" But all that came back was the eerie echo of her name carried on the sound of fading hoof beats.

Devastated, he stood there lost in sadness, wanting her back, wanting to call out again, to beg once more for her to return. But he could bring himself to do nothing more. As clouds crossed the moon a cold wind stirred. Thoughts struggled to form but there was no coherence, only the pounding of his heart drowning out any attempt to reason, to make sense of anything. He forced himself along the crest of the hill, looking back again and again, praying that he would see her riding toward him with a fierceness that screamed out she had overthrown her decision. Each time he glanced the field was empty, the woods still, the moonlight immobile, seemingly forever trapped in the trees.

For a while he felt he wasn't moving at all, and as the crest of the hill gave way to the cliffs of the Bay, he looked back once more, and this time saw her, if only in his hopes. She, they, lying on the matted edge of woods, she above him, moonlight framing her, forgiveness and love inseparable from the expression of bliss on her face.

From the Bay the dull horn of a ship destroyed his reverie, bringing with it a damning loneliness that seemed to turn upon itself and sweep down on him in an unseen avalanche. For moments, maybe minutes, until, as if conjured by the wind, a spirit with a small and indwelling voice spoke to him. Nora was gone, it said, and he was alone, but there was more, it said, more – if he would only *choose* to listen.

"But I love her..."

Quiet, damn you. Quiet!

He swept at the wind in anger, and the Bay was still. He fought to make himself listen to the voice, his, hers, the fairies. He would listen. It did not matter now.

It whispered.

The love they had would carry for as long as he *chose* to keep it alive. It would not give up on him; he would have to give up on it. It *would* cross the seas. That was the way love worked.

The horn sounded again. What appeared to be a large coffin ship lay at anchor, and from a mast high on its stern there was the faint glow of a lantern. Seeing it, Johnny saw her face in the dim light of the prisoner's shed the night Dahl died – her curious smile as she opened the door and whispered, "I love you."

Those blissful words. One's past was tied to them. They would last forever. They would make his journey possible. Johnny knelt to tie a loose bootlace and felt the dampness of the morning against his knee. *Here, the dampness could be blood,* he thought. In America, it would be dew and only that, the gentle wetness of untrammeled land. He gathered himself, and started to run toward the ship. And now running, his tears were brushed away by the wind.

Bibliography

Barry, Tom. *Guerilla Days in Ireland*, Mercier Press, 2013

Boran, Pat. *A Short History of Dublin*, Mercier Press, 2000

Breen, Dan. *My Fight for Irish Freedom*, Anvil Books, 1981

Cahill, Thomas. *How the Irish Saved Civilization*, Anchor Books, 1995

Caufield, Max. *The Easter Rebellion Dublin 1916*, Roberts Reinhart 1963, 1995

Connolly, James. *The Lost Writings*, edited by Aindrias O'Cathasaigh, Pluto Press, 1997

Coogan, Tim Pat. *1916: The Easter Rising*, The Orion Publishing Company, 2001

Coogan, Tim Pat. *The IRA*, Palgrave, global imprint of St. Martin's Press, 2002

Cottrell, Peter. *The Irish Civil War 1922-1923*, Osprey Publishing, 2008

Dangerfield, George. *The Damnable Question*, Barnes and Noble, 1976

De Rosa, Peter. *Rebels, The Irish Rising of 1916*, Fawcett Columbine, 1990

Foy, Michael and Barton, Brian. *The Easter Rising*, Sutton Publishing, 1999

Gleeson, James. *Bloody Sunday*, The Lyons Press, 2004

Golway, Terry. *For the Cause of Liberty*, Simon and Schuster, 2000

Hart, Peter. *Mick – The Real Michael Collins*, Penguin Books, 2007

Hart, Peter (intro). *Rebel Cork's Fighting Story 1916-1921*, Mercier Press, 2009

Liam, Cathal. *Fear Not the Storm*, St. Padriac Press, 2011

Llywelyn, Morgan. *1916: A Novel of the Irish Century*, Forge, 1998

Llywelyn, Morgan. *1921: A Novel of the Irish Century*, Forge, 2001

Macardle, Dorothy. *The Irish Republic*, Farrar, Straus and Giroux, 1965

McCourt, Frank. *Angela's Ashes*, Touchstone Press, 1996

Moran, Sean Farrell. *Patrick Pearse and the Politics of Redemption*, The Catholic University of America Press, 1994

Neeson, Eoin. *The Civil War 1922-23*, Poolbeg Press Ltd., 1989

O'Brien, Nora Connolly. *The Unbroken Tradition*, Boni and Liveright, 1918

O'Conner, Ulick. *The Troubles*, Norton and Company, 1975

O'Neill, Marie. *Grace Gifford Plunkett and Irish Freedom*, Irish Academic Press, 2000

O'Reilly, Terence. *Our Struggle for Irish Independence*, Mercier Press, 2009

Osborn-McKnight, Juilene. *I Am of Irelaunde*, A Forge Book, 2000

Pinkman, John A. *In the Legion of the Vanguard*, Mercier Press, 1998

Sassoon, Siegfried. *Memoirs of an Infantry Officer*, Faber and Faber Limited, 1965

Uris, Leon. *Trinity*, Doubleday, 1976

**TOP HAT
BOOKS**

Historical fiction that lives.

We publish fiction that captures the contrasts, the achievements, the optimism and the radicalism of ordinary and extraordinary times across the world.

We're open to all time periods and we strive to go beyond the narrow, foggy slums of Victorian London. Where are the tales of the people of fifteenth century Australasia? The stories of eighth century India? The voices from Africa, Arabia, cities and forests, deserts and towns? Our books thrill, excite, delight and inspire.

The genres will be broad but clear. Whether we're publishing romance, thrillers, crime, or something else entirely, the unifying themes are timescale and enthusiasm. These books will be a celebration of the chaotic power of the human spirit in difficult times. The reader, when they finish, will snap the book closed with a satisfied smile.